A MOST DIFFICULT DINNER

Never had Sarah anticipated a social occasion with more dismay—and never had her worst fears been better founded.

On one side of her at the elegantly set dinner table was Darcy Ashton, the man whom she so thoroughly detested and who now was her lawfully wedded lord and master.

On the other side was Sir Nicholas Ashton, the lord whom she had so adored from afar and who now was so temptingly near.

Darcy was fuming with jealous rage. Nicholas was smiling with mocking amusement. And Sarah was faced with the choice of keeping the marriage vows she had taken against her will—or losing all she had sacrificed so much to save. . . .

The Kidnapped Bride

SIGNET Regency Romances You'll Enjoy

The Kidnapped Bride

by
Amanda Scott

A SIGNET BOOK
NEW AMERICAN LIBRARY
TIMES MIRROR

NAL BOOKS ARE AVAILABLE AT QUANTITY DISCOUNTS WHEN USED
TO PROMOTE PRODUCTS OR SERVICES. FOR INFORMATION PLEASE
WRITE TO PREMIUM MARKETING DIVISION, THE NEW AMERICAN
LIBRARY, INC., 1633 BROADWAY, NEW YORK, NEW YORK 10019.

 SIGNET TRADEMARK REG. U.S. PAT. OFF. AND FOREIGN COUNTRIES
REGISTERED TRADEMARK—MARCA REGISTRADA
HECHO EN CHICAGO, U.S.A.

SIGNET, SIGNET CLASSICS, MENTOR, PLUME, MERIDIAN AND NAL BOOKS
are published by The New American Library, Inc.,
1633 Broadway, New York, New York 10019

First Printing, April, 1983

1   2   3   4   5   6   7   8   9

PRINTED IN THE UNITED STATES OF AMERICA

To
Ellen, with Love
Wynne, with Gratitude
and
Sarah, with a Smile

I

The coach jolted wickedly from chuckhole to chuckhole across Finchley Common. The road wasn't much of a road, nor the coach much of a coach. For that matter, the horses were mere hired cattle, little deserving to be called a team, and the driver was not a coachman but a valet, inexperienced in the delicate art of tooling unmatched nags across rough ground.

The occupants of the coach did not complain, however. The gentleman was having all he could do to keep his seat; and the lady, bundled up as she was on the floor beneath his feet, with her hands tied and her mouth gagged, could not have complained whether she wished to do so or not.

Actually, there were a good many things the lady would have liked to say to the gentleman, but she was not even allowed the luxury of a glare, since he had dropped a heavy and very dusty blanket over her at the outset of their journey. She could only lie there helplessly while her body was bruised by the erratic bouncing of the coach.

He had spoken to her only once, as they approached a turnpike, lifting the blanket from her face to do so. The gesture had brought with it a rush of welcome fresh air, but the menace in his voice when he warned her to keep silent so astonished her that she nearly failed to take advantage of it. He did not bother to spell out the consequences should she dare to disobey him; his tone of voice had been enough. They had passed through the turnpike and two others like it without incident and, less than a quarter hour after passing the last one, had turned onto this track. The lady did not know where they were, but she did know that they had left the highroad, for although it had been by no means a perfectly smooth road, it had been smoother than this.

Until he had spoken to her so sharply, she had thought the

1

whole thing to be nothing more than a rather stupid jest, and she still had no thought of being in any real danger. She was much more concerned about what sort of figure she would present when she should finally be released.

When she had left her uncle's large house in Berkeley Square that morning, her clothes had been immaculate and her hair its usual shining glory, for Lizzie, her maid, took particular pride in seeing to it that she was turned out in style. Was she not the elegant Miss Sarah Lennox-Matthews, popular belle of fashionable London and heiress to a vast fortune besides? Of course, Sarah thought now, if one had to be perfectly truthful, and thanks to Grandpapa's very peculiar Last Will and Testament, she was not an heiress at all in the ordinary sense of the word. But fashionable London was not the least bit interested in technical dithering, and a fortune the size of the Lennox-Matthews fortune was not to be sneezed at. Therefore, Miss Lennox-Matthews was labeled *heiress* by Society and accorded all the very flattering attention merited by such a label, despite the fact that she would very likely never possess one farthing of her grandfather's fortune—unless, of course, a small portion should be left her as a widow's jointure to see her through her old age. And that likelihood depended upon the generosity of her future husband as well as the necessity of his predeceasing her, since it was to that future husband that Sir Malcolm Lennox-Matthews had left his entire personal fortune.

With bitter hope that her grandfather's current host had to have his hats and trousers altered to accommodate horns and a tail, Sarah reflected ruefully that she was, thanks to his misogynous predilections, prodigiously uncomfortable and no longer immaculate, and—most galling thought of all—that she should have listened when her aunt and uncle, Lord and Lady Hartley, warned her not to encourage the amiable attentions of Darcy Ashton, fourth Earl of Moreland.

The coach lurched into a pothole and out again, bringing Sarah's head into painful contact with the wooden coach door. Directing a mental curse at his lordship, she recalled uncomfortably that one of his own relatives had also warned her against flirting with him. Of course, Sir Nicholas Ashton, at the ripe age of eight and twenty, more than ten years older than Sarah herself, was quite arrogant—besides being ancient—and habitually offered one advice that one did not wish to hear, so nobody could wonder that she had not listened to him.

Had he not, from their very first meeting at Lady Holland's ball, made a point of correcting or rebuking the slightest impropriety or impertinence? It was as though he meant to depress any pretensions caused by her London reception, to point out her every fault rather than to follow the fashion for praising the elegant Miss Lennox-Matthews to the skies. But Miss Lennox-Matthews had a good deal of spirit, and she was not in the habit of meekly allowing herself to be ordered about by anyone.

By nature, Sarah was a friendly, even-tempered young lady who had most fortunately been granted more than her share of beauty and charm. She was, as a result, blessed with a great many friends—indeed, as many amongst the Season's debutantes as amongst the swains rivaling for their favors. But she was intelligent enough to realize that a vast portion of the attention accorded her was due, not to any of the above-mentioned virtues, but rather to the spell cast by the Lennox-Matthews fortune. However, if such insight brought moments of cynical resentment, they were brief, for she possessed a quick wit that enabled her to laugh at herself as easily as she might laugh at the foibles of others, and a keen, if sometimes mischievous, sense of the ridiculous as well. If she incurred censure, it was due to the latter trait, which sometimes prompted her to cross the narrowly drawn lines of proper conduct just for the fun of seeing what would happen. It was perhaps a sad commentary on Society's principles that these escapades usually brought no more than indulgent smiles or, at most, a shaking of heads, but behavior that would have been swiftly condemned in most young girls was generally forgiven the rich Miss Lennox-Matthews. Her aunt might scold her privately, but it was only Sir Nicholas who did so publicly.

That he was one of the handsomest, most dashing of men himself only made matters worse. His strictures might make the sparks fly between them, but his eyes had a disarming tendency to twinkle when she least expected them to, and Sarah was honest enough to admit to herself that she was more taken by Sir Nicholas's charms than anyone hearing her frequent condemnations of his character might have believed. She was not in love with him. She had told herself so more than once, quite firmly. It was merely that she found his lack of romantic interest a challenge to her resources.

Having decided to teach Sir Nicholas a lesson, Sarah had

chosen his own relative to help provide it, making what looked
to everyone like a dead set at Lord Moreland. She had meant
only to demonstrate that she preferred men who appreciated
her charms and did not harp on her faults, but even Aunt
Aurelia had said that his lordship would be the better catch.
Of course, that was on account of the Title, and it was also
before Lord Hartley discovered that Darcy had a reputation
for deep play, the habits of a confirmed rake, estates that
were mortgaged to the gateposts, and no known source of
income. Once discovered, however, these defects were promptly
pointed out, and Sarah was encouraged instead to cultivate Sir
Nicholas who, as a war hero with reputedly well-lined pockets, was certainly *un bon parti*. And, truth to tell, by that
time she had tired of Darcy's airs and affectations and would
have preferred to cultivate Sir Nicholas, despite his annoying
habits. But two days after the Regent's daughter, Princess
Charlotte, had walked down the aisle to meet her Prince
Leopold, Sir Nicholas had most inconveniently and unexpect-
edly left Town.

With no proper audience, her show of interest in Darcy
Ashton would have died a natural death had it not suddenly
occurred to Sarah that if she began to ignore Darcy and so
much as smiled at anyone else, she would be thought fickle,
and if she looked to be dancing from one partner to the next,
Sir Nicholas would scarcely be taught anything useful. He
would be more likely to condemn her flightiness or, worse, to
laugh at her, and that would never do. Therefore, assuring
herself that Sir Nicholas would soon return to Town, she had
continued to display a friendly attachment to Darcy Ashton.

Her aunt discouraged the association, and having been well-
taught from childhood to avoid Lady Hartley's displeasure,
Sarah did not precisely flaunt her continuing flirtation, but
the business began, for that same reason, to take on a rather
secretive, romantic flavor. She imagined herself to be like the
Princess Charlotte, who had proven at last, after her irascible
father had tried to foist one after another distasteful match
upon her, that she could manage her own affairs quite satis-
factorily. Certainly, Sarah considered herself as capable in
such matters as Charlotte! It never occurred to her that the
game might prove a dangerous one.

Thus it was that she did not demur when Darcy suggested
by means of a thrilling *billet doux*, delivered surreptitiously
into her hand while she promenaded one afternoon in Rotten

Row, that she meet him the following morning outside her favorite Bond Street shop. To be sure, she was a little taken aback at sight of the shabby coach, but reassured by his charming smile, she quickly accepted the notion that she could not stand chatting from the flagway and agreed to get in for what he assured her would be a brief ride. To ride alone with a gentleman in a closed carriage was extremely improper, and Sarah knew better, but it felt deliciously daring to defy such a venerable precept. So, casting a quick glance up the street to assure herself that Lizzie was not already returning from the complicated errand upon which she had been sent and, incidentally, to ascertain that no one of her aunt's or her own acquaintance was nearby, Sarah had put her hand trustfully in his and allowed him to help her into the carriage.

Suspecting nothing until the coach had turned from Bond Street into Conduit Street and immediately again into George Street, Sarah had begun to realize then that they were rapidly moving away from the shop and not, as he had promised, simply making a quick circuit. But, by the time she managed to point out this fact to his lordship, they were in Hanover Square. He blandly suggested that she admire the view of St. George's.

"Don't be absurd, my lord!" she had retorted. "Lizzie must be wondering what has become of me!"

"Then she must continue to wonder." He lounged back against the squabs with a curious little smile of satisfaction.

"Darcy! That is . . . my lord, you must be sensible. She will be frantic. My aunt will be furious. She and my uncle have already taken you into dislike, unfairly I agree, but there it is. And such a prank as this could ruin both our reputations." The coach turned into Oxford Street.

"No prank, m' dear," he said earnestly. "Sorry. Assure you. 'Fraid such a course is necessary, though. Your uncle refused my offer."

Sarah had stared at him in amazement. "Do you mean to tell me that you have offered for my hand?" she demanded.

He nodded, smiling as though he expected her to approve. "Hartley said I'm irresponsible and entirely unsuitable. Must agree with him. But you are most suitable for me, m' dear. Didn't think *you'd* be displeased."

"Oh dear." Sarah felt as though the wind had been knocked out of her, for she had never expected her schemes to lead to such an end. But she composed herself quickly in an attempt to bring him to understand his error. "I must apologize, my lord, if ever I led you to believe that I should anticipate with pleasure such an offer from yourself. You do me great honor, of course, but to tell the truth, I never even suspected that you were particularly interested in forming such a connection."

"Saw that I'm not much in the petticoat line, eh?"

"Well, yes. Indeed." It was true and one of the reasons that flirting with him had seemed so safe. Though he had always responded easily to her overtures, his attentions had seemed entirely dispassionate, sometimes even half-hearted. If she had had any complaint to make, it would be that he had not seemed ardent enough for Sir Nicholas to take him seriously as a rival. She smiled at the irony of that thought and turned the conversation back to the matter at hand. "We cannot continue this conversation now, my lord. You must take me back to Lizzie at once! I am sure she may be relied upon to say nothing of this if only we may get back to her in time. But if my aunt and uncle get wind of the fact that we have met this morning, that I have been with you in a closed carriage, there will be the devil to pay for both of us."

"But I wish them to know of it, eventually," he replied. "Thought you would be pleased. You certainly encouraged me to believe that you held at least a *tendre* for my unworthy self, and you've not seemed too terribly taken up by conventions and rules. Thought an elopement would appeal to you, would make the matter dashed romantic."

He sounded truly disappointed in her reaction, and quick words of angry denial were stifled at birth, for Sarah could certainly understand how he had come to believe such things of her. How to explain to him that she had merely reacted quite idiotically to Society's lionization of her grandfather's fortune! That she had only been playing games in a silly effort to discover just how far an accredited heiress could flout the conventions and rules he spoke of without incurring censure. She simply couldn't do it! Her pride shrank from such a confession, and nothing on earth would make her admit her foolish attempts to stir Sir Nicholas Ashton's romantic interest. But she did not want to hurt Darcy's pride either, so she attempted to reason with him.

"I can quite see, my lord," she said at last, "how my behavior might have led you to believe such things, but I must tell you that the conventions do mean something to me. I should not be happy to flout them so outrageously as you suggest now. Would it not be better for all concerned simply to let this matter rest where it lies? It is, after all, my uncle who has refused your very kind offer, not I. Perhaps, if you are still of the same mind when I come of age. . . ."

" 'Fraid I can't wait four years," he said apologetically.

She smiled at him. "Well, no, of course not, sir, but you cannot wish to force me into a marriage that I do not desire. You must take me back. This will not do!"

"On the contrary," he replied, sitting up a little straighter in his seat, the corners of his mouth creasing mulishly. "It will answer very well."

"You must be out of your senses!" she exclaimed, her displeasure now overcoming any resolution to remain tactful. "I cannot allow you to do this!"

"How can you stop me?" he inquired with simple curiosity. "Can't just leap out of a moving carriage in the middle of Oxford Street . . . ah, no," he corrected himself after a glance into the street, ". . . Portland Street. Point remains, nonetheless."

"Of course I shall do no such silly thing," Sarah retorted, finding his attitude infuriating now. "But the coachman . . . I have only to——"

"My man, I'm afraid."

"I see." She looked at him straightly. "In that case, sir, I shall put my head out and scream until someone comes to my assistance. I should not like to do that, but if you force me to, I must."

"Oh dear," he said ruefully. "Believe you would. But success of the venture depends upon no one's discovering your whereabouts for at least twenty-four hours. Uh . . you did follow my instructions, did you not? Said nothing about meeting me to your maid or to anyone else?" She shook her head, gritting her teeth in exasperation. "Good girl. Could have ruined everything. I'm supposed to be in Brighton, you see." He smiled at her, but without his usual bland insouciance. In fact, it made her a bit uncomfortable. "Sorry you won't cooperate. Came prepared though. Daresay you won't like it, but can't be helped."

He had reached for her then, and she had not been able to elude him in the close confines of the coach. He had seemed in the past to be mild-mannered, even effeminate, and his contrived, sometimes mincing, attitudes had not prepared her for such strength as he then displayed. Stifling her outraged cries

by muffling her head in the heavy blanket while he bound her
wrists behind her, he had fastened the cloth gag, pushed her
down onto the floor, and then draped the blanket over her. It
was a matter of but a few minutes' work, and by the time the
coach turned from Portland Street into the New Road, he was
resting one booted foot upon the curve of her backside as
negligently as though he rested it upon a bundle of laundry.

Passing through Kentish Town and skirting Hampstead
Heath, the coach turned onto the Great North Road at Highgate
and soon rolled through the village of East End, where the
driver gave up his last ticket at the tollgate. A quarter hour
later they turned onto the rough track leading straight across
the Common, and a few miles further on, Sarah felt the coach
slow and lurch as it left the rutted track and turned between
the high gates of Ash Park, that rather derelict seat of the
earls of Moreland and the barons Ashton before them. Some
moments later, they came to a halt, and Darcy lifted the
blanket.

Sarah was at last able to glower at him as she had been
yearning to do for some time. But he avoided her eye, pulling
her to a sitting position and assisting her to alight from the
coach. For the moment, curiosity overcame anger, and she
looked about her. The carriageway from the gate was over-
shadowed by trees and infested with weeds. Spreading lawns
that had not benefited from the application of a scythe in many
a long day had made sweeping inroads into the herbaceous
borders, and even the densely growing trees seemed shaggy
and ill-groomed. The four-story stone house seemed to have
resisted the weather and general neglect rather better than
the surrounding gardens had done, but it, too, looked gloomy
and ill-cared-for.

Darcy waved the coach on around the house and then looked
down at Sarah, his gaze traveling from curls she knew must
be disheveled down to her wrinkled skirts. She had lost her
hat in the struggle in the coach. "Sorry you got mussed," he
muttered ruefully. "It was a pretty dress. And I daresay
you've not got so much as a comb in your ridicule." Her eyes
widened and she turned sharply in the direction taken by the
coach. "Forgot it, eh? Well, remind me later and I'll send Beck
to fetch it. He's not taking the coach back until morning, so
there's plenty of time. But come along in. I sent word earlier
to Matty to expect us for dinner—country hours here, I'm
afraid. Should be ready soon. Unless she's pickled herself in

gin," he added as an afterthought, and scarcely an encouraging one.

He started up the rough stone steps, evidently expecting Sarah to follow him, but she stayed where she was, staring after him indignantly and still finding it difficult to reconcile his present behavior with that of the rather languidly amiable young gentleman she had known in London. He turned to see what was keeping her.

"Come along, Sarah." Stubbornly Sarah shook her head. Did he not realize that this escapade of his was very likely to ruin her even if she did marry him? She would certainly be refused tickets of admission to Almack's Assembly Rooms once the grand patronesses of that august establishment got wind of it, because no matter how much had been forgiven her in the past, this sort of nonsense would cause a major scandal!

He moved toward her. Late afternoon sun sliding on dust-filled rays through the trees touched off auburn highlights in his dark, windblown hair. His light brown eyes narrowed against the glare, and she scowled back at him. Darcy was a well-formed but not particularly imposing figure of a man, standing slightly less than six feet tall. He dressed with an eye to style that bordered on the foppish. Today he wore a dark brown frock coat, an orange-and-yellow-striped waistcoat, an intricately tied stock, cream pantaloons, and well-polished Hessian boots with gold tassels. Although his eyes under their narrow brows were set rather too closely together for perfection and his chin was a trifle weak, high cheekbones and a straight, well-formed nose showed his aristocratic breeding.

Of course, Sarah thought ironically, one also tended to note the effects of creeping dissipation. His lordship had been playing deep, drinking too much, getting too little sleep, and generally burning the candle at both ends for quite some time, and it was beginning to tell. Reaching out now, he laid a light hand upon her shoulder and drew her toward him.

Had she been wearing slippers instead of her dark green kid boots, the top of Sarah's head would have been no higher than the top button of his waistcoat. But she had dressed properly for her supposed shopping expedition in a light walking dress of twilled marigold sarcenet with French kid gloves to match her boots and a chip straw hat trimmed with straw flowers and green silk ribbons. The hat was gone, the dress crumpled and dusty. Her honey-bronze hair was a mass of tangles, and

her tiny face was streaked with smears of dirt as well as the
suspicion—though she would have denied it indignantly—of a
tearstain or two, but there could still be no doubt of her
beauty. Blessed with an exquisite figure, she exhibited a natural, lithe grace when she moved. Her face was heart-shaped,
and from the widow's peak of her hairline to her determined
little chin, her skin was clear strawberries and cream. Her
large, wide-set eyes were oval-shaped and hazel-green, deepening almost to emerald in a certain light or, as now, when she
was frightened or angry.

Darcy looked down into those eyes now, and his own expression was anxious. "No need to be frightened, Sarah. Daresay I'm not much of a fellow, but . . . not a cad either, dash it!
Got no wish to harm you. Assure you. Here, let me take that
thing off." He reached behind her head and unfastened the
gag. Then he turned her so that she could reach the bonds at
her wrists. A moment later she was free. She licked her lips
and rubbed her wrists. There was a red streak across her
cheeks from the gag.

"This will ruin me, my lord," she muttered through still dry
lips. "Whatever I have misguidedly led you to believe, I do
not deserve such a fate."

"Perfectly true," he agreed, urging her gently toward the
house. "But, 'fraid I found it necessary to adopt stringent
measures to recoup the Ashton fortunes. Earl of Moreland
shouldn't be penniless. Do anything to avoid it." He smiled
down at her. "Must admit though, marriage to you is more
palatable than certain other courses I've attempted."

"But I simply cannot marry you this way, my lord!"

"On the contrary, m' dear. This way, you must."

She fell silent, and a few moments later, they stood in the
front hall of his house. There was a feeling of chill dampness in
the air, giving Sarah the sudden and rather unsettling thought
that she had stepped into one of the gothic tales that she and
her governess, Miss Penistone, had been so fond of reading
and which would, had she known of their presence in her
house, have given Lady Hartley a fit of apoplexy. The hall
was large and gray and drafty with a wide, stone stairway
that swooped up one side to a railed gallery. But opposite the
stair, a set of tall double doors opened into a warmer, more
pleasant, though shabbily furnished room—the library, decided
Sarah, if book-lined walls were any indication. A fire crackling
in a fireplace between two pairs of French doors nearly dis-

pelled the gothic gloom, and a huge black dog who lay before it, nose on paws, thumping his long tail, rose lethargically to his feet, stretched, and wandered over to sniff her skirt.

"This is Erebus," Darcy said conversationally.

Sarah only glanced at the dog. Really, she thought, this was intolerable. Darcy seemed completely indifferent to her plight. Indeed, he behaved almost as though he were merely entertaining her for an afternoon, instead of having forcibly abducted her. Perhaps, if she cried . . . But the notion was quickly rejected. It would not do to show such weakness. Even the little experience she had had taught her that it was always better to play from strength. Besides, she was not by any means certain that she could simply cry at will. At the moment, she felt more like screaming.

But first things first. She turned to him with melting eyes.

"I should like to tidy myself, my lord. I must look a perfect fright. And, may I please have some water?" Her throat was parched, and her voice, usually low-pitched and melodious, sounded dry and cracked.

"Of course," he answered hastily, seeming relieved when she did not rail at him. "There is a small saloon the other side of the hall with a cheval glass. I'll have Beck bring some water."

"Your coachman?"

"My valet. I am afraid there are few servants here and no maidservants at all. It's hard enough to keep them in so isolated a spot at the best of times and with money to pay their wages, but with things the way they've been, the wenches flat won't come." He shrugged. "There's just Beck and Matty and Matty's husband, Tom, who looks after the dog and the stables. He and Matty aren't worth much, but they stay, and that's what counts with me. Come along. I'll show you the saloon. Stay, Erebus!" The big dog plopped back down, eyeing their departure with sad eyes.

Darcy took Sarah's elbow lightly and guided her across the hall to a doorway set beneath the curve of the stair. It opened into a saloon with furnishings as shabby as those in the library. No fire burned here, but the curtains had not been closed either, and golden rivers of sunlight sprawled lazily from two tall, arched windows across the faded carpet. The cheval glass stood against the stair wall where the light was not all that she might have wished, but when she tilted the glass properly, it was adequate. She stared at herself.

"Merciful heavens!"

"It was only to be expected, m' dear," he observed with a sad grimace.

"Please, don't call me that," she muttered grimly, meeting his eyes in the mirror. "After treating me so shabbily, you can scarcely expect me to believe that you truly care for me."

"As you wish." He bowed. "I'll find Beck and send him with water and a hairbrush. Can you do your own hair?"

She bit her lip. "I don't know. I have never tried."

"Well, do the best you can. Have to see about finding you a maid, I suppose." He paused as though he would say more, but then, with a shrug, he turned away and left the room.

She stared at her reflection, fighting back tears that had suddenly and against all reason decided to plague her. It would do her no good to cry. She would need her senses about her to face whatever lay ahead. What, she wondered, did he expect to accomplish by this extortionate behavior? Why, it was straight out of one of those silly novels! She had behaved quite wickedly herself, to be sure. But he! Could he really expect her to develop any of the tenderer feelings for him now, after he had treated her in such a monstrous way? Why, he had sounded much like Grandpapa—callous, unfeeling, insensitive, and perfectly selfish—as though nothing counted except his own wishes!

It was lucky, she thought suddenly, that she was not particularly missish, for if she were at all inclined to vapors, she would have been having them all over the place by now. But she was made of sterner stuff than that. She straightened her shoulders and stripped off her gloves. Darcy would simply have to learn the error of his ways. It was too bad, but there it was.

II

Her thoughts were interrupted by Beck's entrance with a pitcher and basin. He set these down upon the chest next to the mirror and handed her the towel he had draped over his arm. "Will there be anything else, Miss Lennox-Matthews?"

She was tempted to say that, yes, she would like the carriage brought round immediately for a return trip to London, but his expression deterred her. He was taller than his master, thin and wiry. He also looked a good deal more sinister than Darcy, and she realized, looking at Beck, that she ought to be frightened by all this. She wondered why the thought had not occurred to her before. But, of course, it was because she had thought of Darcy for so long as a harmless, gentle type, and he had done little, despite his determination to wed her, to alter that impression of him. Beck was another type entirely. The face below his dark, limp hair was a long oval with a great deal of chin, thin lips, a hooked nose, ears that stuck out, and gray eyes that were coldly penetrating under thick, peaked brows. But his clothing was neat, and he carried himself with an air of self-importance. Stoutly maintaining her dignity, she shook her head in answer to his question. He nodded stiffly, then turning to leave, bethought himself of something else.

"His lordship mentioned a comb, miss." He extracted one made of tortoise-shell from his waistcoat pocket. "I expect I'll find something better, but this was the best I could do on short notice."

"Thank you, Beck. I can manage now." He bowed and returned to the door. She raised her arms to attempt to deal with her hair and then lowered them again when she realized that he had paused at the door and was watching her. She

13

looked at him, and he ran his tongue over his lips, staring insolently. "I said I can manage, Beck. You may go."

"As you say, miss." He bowed again and slipped soundlessly through the door. She did not hear his footsteps retreating, and thinking he remained outside the door, she went to look. The hall was empty. For a moment she wondered if she could run out the front door without being caught. Then she sighed. Even if she could, where would she go? She didn't even know where she was precisely. Vaguely, she remembered Darcy mentioning his house near Finchley Common, and she supposed that was where she was, but it was not much help. She would certainly be worse off lost on the Common. Besides, now that she came to notice, the door to the library was open.

Well, Sarah, she thought with a sigh, you have certainly done it to yourself this time! It was a good deal worse than any other scrape she had gotten herself into, although since her parents' deaths it had often seemed to her that, one way or another, she had simply tumbled from one scrape to another. But her intentions were always good, she told herself firmly. Then, even as the thought materialized, she had to retract it. Her intentions always *seemed* good or at least understandable, but she rarely considered that there might be side effects, and this time the side effects were proving rather overwhelming!

A sudden lump rose to her throat when she thought of Sir Nicholas. Some lesson! She had only meant to teach him to respect her individuality, to cease his eternal carping and correcting, to teach him that she must be guided with gentleness, not dictated to. She was shrewd enough to realize that his attempts to rule her indicated, at the very least, a concern for her welfare, but something in her nature made her want to challenge him. And here was the result. Whatever cause she had given him for disapproval in the past, this was infinitely worse. Now, he would despise her, would think her a loose woman. Not that it would matter, she told herself with another sigh. Not if she were forced to marry Darcy!

But this would not do. Firmly, she forced the dismal thoughts aside and strode back to the mirror to do what she could about her appearance. Once she had moistened her lips and washed her face, she turned her attention to her hair. Knowing she could never recapture the style worked by Lizzie's clever fingers, she simply combed the tangles out and pushed it back behind her ears to fall in a tawny velvet cloud down her back.

It made her look more like a schoolroom miss than a young lady, but it would have to do.

Her dress was another matter. There was nothing at all to be done about the smudges and wrinkles in the skirt, but she could and did remove the spencer jacket. At least her bodice was clean. She pinched up the tiny puffed sleeves and shook out the skirt so that it fell more smoothly from the high, ribboned waist. The spencer had been cut high to her throat with a narrow lace ruff, but the bodice of the dress itself was low-scooped with a flat, pleated lace edge. The plump curves of her breasts rose softly above it, and a slender green silk ribbon encircled her throat. She shook her skirts again, gave a pat to her hair, and went back to the library, prepared to do battle.

Unfortunately for her purpose, she found the cozy scene that greeted her rather daunting. Her captor was seated in a deep armchair near the fire with his feet propped carefully on the fender, the huge dog sprawled beneath his legs. Darcy looked up, nodding at her entrance. "A vast improvement, my dear. Ah . . . forgive me, it slipped out." He got to his feet, skirting the sleepy Erebus, flicked a piece of lint from the skirt of his coat, and raised a wineglass in a toasting gesture. "Salutations. I like your hair like that. Hate it when females chop off their curls. Glad you haven't."

"Thank you, my lord." She eyed him speculatively and made the shrewd guess that his drink was not his first nor yet his second. He noted the direction of her gaze.

"May I pour you a glass?"

"If you please, sir," she replied with a smile. Perhaps if she seemed relaxed about the whole situation, it would be easier to reason with the man.

"Good stuff. Not so good as I shall be able to buy with the Lennox-Matthews fortune, but good enough." He moved to a side table and poured out another glass, taking the opportunity to replenish his own.

"Thank you, my lord," she said when he handed her her glass. She took a tiny sip. The wine was not so bad. Sarah was not particularly fond of spirits, but in a good cause. . . . She gazed at him across the top of her glass. Was it possible that he was a bit nervous? She remembered his unexpected strength in the carriage and the sudden fear she had had in Beck's presence. This was indeed a pretty predicament! She took another sip. Had someone not referred to wine as Dutch courage? She wondered briefly what the Dutch thought of such a reference. But then she took herself firmly in hand. She had come in here to do battle, had she not? Well then, Sarah, she told herself sternly. Get on with it, my girl! Darcy had clearly had several glasses of Dutch courage, yet he also seemed to be at a loss for words. So much for the Dutch. With a swish of her skirt, Sarah moved purposefully to the other chair in front of the fireplace and sat down.

Once she was seated, Darcy sat down in his own chair, slumped back, and propped his feet up again. "Tom's going to set up a table for us here. Only habitable room down here at the moment. Matty did our bedrooms but not much else, I'm afraid." Sarah perched on the edge of her seat.

"My lord," she began calmly, "we must speak of the matter at hand. There is still time to make things right, you know. My relatives will be furious, of course, there is no gainsaying that, but the rest can certainly be covered up to the point where we shall not become the latest *on dit*. I know you cannot look forward——"

"Not now, Sarah," he interrupted. "We shall talk about it after we eat. Drink your wine."

"But, sir, by then it will be too——"

"I *said* 'not now'!" he growled stubbornly.

Sarah fell silent and moments later, Beck entered, followed by a grizzled and rather untidy fellow whom she assumed to be Matty's husband, Tom. Presumably, Matty must be the housekeeper. The two men dragged a table out from the wall and began to lay covers for a *tête à tête* dinner. Her gaze drifted back to Darcy. What had possessed him? He said he had thought she cared for him. Then why had he sprung this business on her in such a way? Why had he not approached her before going to her uncle if he truly thought she would be agreeable to his suit? It occurred to her now that she had not given much thought before to what sort of man Darcy Ashton really was.

He had always seemed amiable, rather easily led, not one to take the initiative in much of anything. All she had ever had to do to attract his notice and bring him to her side in a crowd was to smile at him. But he had certainly not seemed ardent or passionate or lost to love. She knew those signs well enough, for many of the men who had continually surrounded her since her come-out displayed such flattering attitudes. But not Darcy. Not Sir Nicholas either, drat the man. He had *never* flattered her. But this was not the time to think of Sir Nicholas, she told herself sternly, forcing her thoughts back to Darcy.

He did not even follow his own lead when it came to matters of dress. He was a fop, a dandy, but not the sort who was constantly affecting outrageous styles in the hope that some fashionable quirk of his own devising would catch on and bear his name. Darcy merely followed the lead of others. When he liked a style, he took it for his own. He dressed elegantly despite his supposed lack of income, but there was nothing unique about his appearance. There had been nothing about him, in fact, to attract one's notice, except for the simple matter of his having been in some way or other related to Sir Nicholas.

Sarah did not like the direction her train of thought was taking, but she could be honest enough with herself when the occasion warranted. And if ever an occasion warranted, this one did. She had used Darcy. It was rather despicable, put that way, but there was really no other way to put it. She knew now that she would have paid him utterly no heed whatsoever had some kind soul not pointed out the pertinent relationship. She had been friendly to everyone, of course, but there had been a difference in the way she behaved with Darcy. Enough of a difference that he had been encouraged to offer for her hand in marriage. How foolish she had been!

She sighed, sipping at her drink and glancing uneasily at her companion. She did not wonder that her uncle had not mentioned the proposal. It would not have occurred to him to do so. She knew Lord Hartley received at least an offer a week, probably more than that, but he rarely mentioned them. And, having already warned Sarah to avoid Darcy's company, he would not have encouraged her attraction to the fellow by informing her of the offer. For Uncle Barnabas would assume that any offer was flattering enough to attract an impressionable young girl's notice to the gentleman making it.

The whole business would be very romantic, of course, if Sir Nicholas were to come thundering to her rescue in the tradition of all the best romances. She indulged herself in a brief vision of Sir Nicholas—tall, dashing, and handsome enough to suit anyone's notion of a hero—mounted on a white charger and swooping down upon them, sword in hand. But her imagination balked when she tried to envision him sweeping her into his arms and declaring his undying love in the manner of a proper hero. Instead, she was visited by an unsettling memory of his less appealing, though no less heroic, characteristics.

Sir Nicholas would be far more likely to assume that the whole wretched affair was her fault from beginning to end and to read her the devil of a scold into the bargain. Not that she would mind it much if only he could save her. But she had no notion where he was, and he certainly had no way of knowing where she was! Nor did anyone else. She was on her own. She would simply have to cope.

Sarah was not one to run from her problems. She preferred to attack them head on. But at the moment, and so long as Darcy persisted in his stubbornness and refused to discuss things rationally, there seemed to be nothing to attack. If she ranted at him, he would no doubt simply get up and leave or, worse, order that dreadful Beck to remove her until after he had enjoyed his dinner. Much better to remain calm. Her mind seemed to be spinning very little in the way of substantive ideas, however, so perhaps it would be best to wait patiently until after they had eaten.

Dinner came at last, but it was a mediocre affair. Matty clearly had no great turn for the culinary arts. The pigeon pie lacked salt, the rabbit stew was greasy, and the cherry fool (at least, Sarah supposed it was meant to be a fool) was watery. She assuaged the worst of her hunger pangs with bread and cheese, taking only token bites of everything else and finding the whole business rather depressing.

Tom appeared at the door soon after they began to eat and called the great dog to his dinner, but though Darcy maintained a flow of trivial small talk while they ate, it seemed a long while afterward before Beck finally came to clear the dishes and to set a decanter of port at his master's elbow. He inquired if anything else would be needed.

"Nothing. I'll ring if I want you."

Beck glanced at Sarah. "Aye, sir." She repressed a shudder and turned firmly to Darcy, as soon as the door closed behind the valet.

"I do not care for your servants, sir."

He shifted in his seat and poured himself a glass of port. "Sorry. Make any changes you like, of course, once we are married. Except Beck, that is. 'Fraid I shouldn't know how to go on without him. I know he's not very nice in his——"

"My lord, please!" she interrupted. "I do not wish to marry

you, and I wish you will put such a nonsensical notion straight out of your head once and for all."

"But I wish to marry you, Sarah," he returned simply.

"What has that to say to anything? A gentleman does not make such an important decision off his own bat, sir."

"Well, I have. Didn't realize you'd object, you know, but that don't alter the necessity for the action."

"I collect that your intention in all of this is purposely to compromise my reputation," she accused more calmly than she felt. "How can you claim to care for me on the one hand and treat me so shabbily on the other?"

He shifted again with a rueful grimace. "Well, actually . . . never claimed to care for you, you know. Only said I thought you cared for me. Don't want to hurt your feelings, of course, but did say I'm not much in the petticoat line. Must put Ash Park back to rights, however, and marrying an heiress seems a better way than most. Marrying you makes things even better, of course, since the money comes direct to me. Needn't feel I'm living on m' wife's charity. Shabby thing for a fellow, that."

Sarah stared at him, torn between exasperation and the need to choke back the sudden gurgle of laughter that threatened at his absurd reasoning. But then she realized he was perfectly serious. Though he hadn't balked at an abduction, he would think less of himself if he were thought to be living at his wife's expense!

Darcy drank off his port and refilled his glass, looking down at it as he continued. "You are perfectly safe, Sarah. Said it before, but I want to be certain you take my meaning. Won't force unwanted attentions upon you either now or afterward. Can't deny that something might have to be done later to secure the succession, but that will be only if you agree to it. Right now, I want only to insure that it shall be impossible for your uncle to marry you off to anyone but me."

"I should never have thought you capable of this, my lord." He shrugged, and Sarah bit her lip. "I wish it had been otherwise. You make me feel a fool for trusting you. How long do you mean to keep me here?"

"Overnight would do the trick," he answered, "but I daresay you'll not want to go back to London for a while. That must depend upon your uncle, of course. I had planned for you to write him an affecting little letter filled with your love for me and your despair at his refusal to countenance our marriage."

"I shall certainly do no such thing!"

"Well, I can see that you would be loathe to do so, of course," he agreed reasonably, "but do you know, I believe it is still the best course. Far easier to explain that he can avoid the scandal of a Gretna Green marriage if he will but be sensible, than to describe the sordid details of an abduction, don't you know."

"You would never succeed in forcing me all the way to Scotland," she grated, torn between fury and exasperation.

"Of course not. No wish to try. My plan will answer the purpose much better. Can't want to be barred from Society after all. Not that we would be barred for long," he added comfortably, "not with all the money I shall have. Won't be let into Almack's, of course, but I shan't repine. Never liked the place, anyway. Too stuffy, by half. Nevertheless . . . your uncle . . . you'll inform him that we desire to be married quietly in the country by special license. He may then make up whatever tale he likes to stifle the rumor-mongers."

Sarah was silent. His plan would work. It was brilliant. Her uncle cared little for her and less for her money (since he had no personal claim upon it), but he cared a great deal for his reputation. By agreeing to a scheme in which he would believe Sarah voluntarily involved, Lord Hartley would avoid a dreadful scandal. It took years, a lifetime, for a family to live down a Gretna Green marriage, but Darcy's way, any rumor arising should be little more than a nine-day wonder. That Lord and Lady Hartley would be furious with her didn't seem to weigh much with him if, indeed, he had even considered it. They would probably wash their hands of her anyway after today, but they would be certain to do so if she were to write the letter he outlined.

"I am sorry to disappoint you, my lord," she said at last with great dignity, "but I cannot write that letter."

Elbows on the table, Darcy laced his fingers together and gazed at her as earnestly as a child might. "Up to you, of course, Sarah, but I think that by morning, you know, you will have changed your mind."

She would have liked to debate the matter, but she could see nothing to be gained by such a course at the present moment. Instead, she decided to try another tack. "It was only my fortune that interested you, was it not? Perhaps it could be arranged for my uncle to pay a ransom for my release. He is quite well off himself, you know, and I am sure he would come down handsomely, sir."

"Nonsense, my dear," he said indignantly. "I am not such a low person as that! I shall do right by you, of course. I cannot deny that your grandfather's fortune is the primary factor, but that need not concern us now. You are a perfectly presentable young woman and will make quite a good little countess."

"I never liked Grandpapa very much," Sarah muttered, "but I never thought I should have cause to hate him."

"Sensible man, to my way of thinking. Tell me about him."

Sarah shrugged. There was no reason not to do so. "He despised women," she said bitterly. "That was the key to his character." She went on to explain that when she herself had been born it had not surprised Sir Malcolm that her mother had done nothing more remarkable than to produce another female to trouble the world: "Aunt Aurelia said that Grandpapa excused the error on the grounds that it was only Mama's first attempt. It took Grandmama three such, you see, before she produced my father, so he could be patient."

However, ten years later, Mrs. Lennox-Matthews still had not achieved an heir, and thus it was that Sir Malcolm greeted the news of the carriage accident which claimed the life of Sarah's parents with a shade more grief than anyone might otherwise have expected. His daughters had produced no children whatsoever and certainly seemed unlikely to do so at that late date. Although that made it a simple matter for the younger one, Aurelia, now Lady Hartley, to take charge of Sarah, it meant also that Sir Malcolm had no proper male heir.

"Grandpapa wanted to keep the money in trust until a male heir of his own flesh and blood had been produced."

"Dashed silly notion!" Darcy exclaimed, sincerely affronted. "How was it avoided?"

"It was through Mr. Smithers, Grandpapa's man of affairs," Sarah explained. "He simply pointed out that it would not be impossible for such an heir to wait a century or longer before putting in his appearance, by which time the fortune would be so enmeshed in legal quagmires as to be quite inextricable, assuming that any of it remained at all after the necessary trustees and lawyers had taken their various fees over such a period of time." She went on to explain that Sir Malcolm, with his own strong belief in the contrary nature of females in general and those of his own family in particular, had there-

fore decided that it was well nigh inevitable that a proper
male heir would be a long time coming.

Darcy frowned. "Surprised he didn't simply leave the money
with a trustee or two to look out for things until you married.
Would have been a much more normal course. Husband would
control the fortune anyway."

"That would not do for Grandpapa," Sarah replied with
bitterness. "Controlling a fortune, according to him, was not
the same thing as possessing one. My aunt once told me that
Mr. Smithers suggested just that very thing, but Grandpapa
said that if he followed such advice, I should in all likelihood
leave the money to my daughters when I died, trusting my
husband to provide for our sons. Whereas, if my husband
possessed the fortune from the outset, it would be—as, indeed, he said it should be—left to his sons. He also noted the
possibility that I might not marry, in which case I would
probably outlive my trustees." And what, Sir Malcolm had
demanded to know, would stop a court of law, in that case,
from putting control of her fortune into her own incapable
hands? Such a thing would never do. Certainly not if Sir
Malcom could prevent it.

"Must have expected fortune-hunters," Darcy observed without a trace of irony.

"Of course, but I doubt it weighed much upon his conscience." He had also expected her aunt and uncle to keep
them at bay. And Sarah realized now that they had done very
well until her own foolishness had encouraged this outrageous
start. She sighed, then looked up at Darcy again. "Is there no
way by which I can convince you to change your mind, sir?
You must realize that I shall not be a very conformable wife
for you if I am not happy in the marriage."

He adjusted his cravat. "You'll be happy enough, Sarah. I
shall make no demands, and women are always happy to make
a home. You will have whatever money you need, too. Never
ungenerous. Assure you. Ask anyone."

"Fine words, sir, since I am the source of the money! But I
promise you I shall not be happy here. I grant there is work
aplenty, since this house is a disgrace and your servants are
disgusting, but that is not sufficient. I require a great deal
more to satisfy me!"

"This discussion is pointless!" he flared suddenly. "Nothing
you say will alter my decision. It's simply impossible to take
you back! Now, I've things to attend to. You'll wish to retire."

She stood indignantly, smoothing her skirt. "As you wish, my lord. There is clearly nothing to be gained by shouting at each other."

In stubborn silence, he escorted her up the wide stone stairway and along the gallery to a second, wooden staircase that led them to the second floor. They emerged upon a dim corridor. Darcy opened the door into a bedchamber that had been swept and aired, but that was the most one might have said for it. Faded green curtains at the windows spoke of an earlier period of grandeur, but the once highly polished floor was dull and water-stained. Whatever hangings the huge bed might once have boasted were gone, and the dark wood of the posts and high frame was also dull. A gay red, yellow, and blue patchwork coverlet on the bed provided the only real splash of color in the room. A small, patterned latch-hook rug of browns and gold near the bed was the only floor covering. Other furniture consisted of a French wardrobe, a wash stand, a dressing chair and table, and a French seat near a window overlooking the front drive. A candle stand stood at the head on the near side of the high bed. Darcy indicated the bell rope hanging behind it.

"If you want anything, ring. Can't promise the response will be immediate, but someone will come eventually." With these unencouraging words he bowed and was gone.

Sarah heard the key turn in the lock and sighed, trying to resign herself to her plight. She went to the window and looked out. At least, she thought, there were no bars. The latch moved easily, and she swung it open. It was quite easily twenty-five or thirty feet to the ground, and no tree branch grew near enough to be of service. Clearly, Darcy had not feared she might escape that way. She left the window open and sat down on the French seat, curling her legs under her since there was no one near enough to reprimand her for it, then leaning back to stare out at the deepening twilight. The sun made a crimson splash on the undersides of the few scurrying clouds above, and the trees, though still showing green in the foreground, deepened their color to black farther from the house. The thick growth of trees approaching so near to the house gave one the illusion of living deep in a forest.

She watched the shadows gather, watched the brilliant colors of the fleeting clouds fade to gray and then turn silver much later with the rising moon. Once or twice she thought she heard Erebus or some other dog barking in the distance.

At first, she tried to focus her thoughts on the scenery in order not to dwell upon what was happening to her, but there was really nothing to be gained by avoiding unpleasant reflection. Her greatest worry was the future, facing her aunt and uncle, facing her friends, facing those who for reasons of jealousy or whatever, would be pleased to see her in the briars. And worst of all, facing Sir Nicholas Ashton. It would be dreadful!

But what was she thinking of? She was made of sterner stuff than to sit and wait miserably for her fate when, with a little resolution she might avoid it altogether. Though the window was clearly ineligible as a means of escape, there was still the locked door, and had there not been a similar situation in one of those forbidden books that she and Penny had enjoyed so much? She could not remember which, but that was of no matter if she could remember how the heroine's escape had been accomplished. Slowly, she got to her feet and moved back to the door, her brain working rapidly. The key! If only Darcy had left the key in the lock! She peered anxiously through the keyhole. It was comfortingly dark, so perhaps one might assume that the key was there. Now for something to probe with.

A knitting needle would be perfect, she thought wryly. Unfortunately, she did not possess one. She pondered for a moment. Then it came to her. Her stays! Sending a silent thank-you to her Aunt Aurelia, who had greeted the returning fashion with strong approval and insisted that her niece, who had no need of one, wear at least a light corset with her day dresses, Sarah quickly began to unfasten her bodice. A moment's probing produced a long, slender strip of whalebone. Sarah stared at it in triumph, remembering with a chuckle that Aunt Aurelia's approval had stopped short of another fashionable trend. Pantalettes, no matter how many ruffles they possessed, were still pants, according to that formidable dame, and therefore unsuitable for feminine attire. Sarah had actually purchased a lovely pair made of fine Brussels lace, but her aunt, shocked at such wanton behavior, had straight-away consigned them to the dustbin.

Recalling herself to the job at hand, Sarah began to insert the strip of whalebone into the keyhole before she remembered that another bit of preparation would be necessary. A quick search of the dressing table showed that the drawers had long-ago been lined with brown paper, but no piece remained that was large enough for her purpose. The drawer of the night stand produced similar results, and she stood for a moment in frustration before her eye lit upon the heavy French wardrobe. A moment later, she hurried back to the door with a longish sheet of the same brown paper that had once lined the drawers, taken from the shelf at the top of the wardrobe.

Carefully, she slid the paper under the door so that it would lie directly under the keyhole. Then, probing with her strip of whalebone, it was but a few seconds' work to dislodge the key, which fell with a heart-stopping clunk upon the piece of shelf paper. Nonetheless, even more carefully than she had pushed it out did Sarah pull the paper back into the bedchamber. Then, resting back upon her heels, her eyes sparkling with excitement, she lifted the key to her lips and kissed it.

III

A moment later, Sarah stood in the corridor outside her room. A glow from the stairwell reminded her that it was still early, that the household had not yet retired. Perhaps it would be better to wait. But no, she could not be certain of getting out of the house once it was locked up for the night. She remembered heavy bolts at the tops of the French doors in the library and assumed that similar bolts would be used on the front door. They would no doubt be too stiff for her to move easily even if she could contrive a means of reaching them. The windows, too, in this neighborhood, would no doubt have their own strong bolts. Far better to escape before such devices were in place for the night. Accordingly, she slipped down the stairs, appalled to discover that her knees were quaking. What if the library door were open?

But it was not. The hall was reassuringly empty, and repressing that weak-kneed feeling that seemed to have traveled all the way to her midsection, she tiptoed quickly to the front door. Repressing an instinct to fling it wide and run into the darkness beyond, she forced herself to work slowly and as silently as possible. Nonetheless, the door gave a squeak upon opening that seemed dreadfully loud. There was no response to it, however, and Sarah soon found herself upon the broad steps leading down to the drive. Moving quickly then, she hurried around the side of the house and into the shelter of the thick woods. Only then did she stop to consider what she had done.

She realized immediately that her action had been impulsive and foolhardy, a mere rebellion against going passively to her fate like a lamb to the slaughter. Nevertheless, she dared not attempt to flee to London on foot across Finchley Common. She would most likely get lost or be captured by highwaymen, footpads, or others of their ilk, if she did not die of exposure first. Moving further into the thick growth of trees and shrubbery until she was quite certain she could not be seen from the house, Sarah paused to give rational thought to her predicament. At the very least, she needed a horse, but she could not hope to take one until the household had gone to sleep for the night. Therefore, she decided to hide in the woods until the coast was clear.

It was chilly, but she had remembered to bring her spencer with her, and she should be warm enough for an hour or two. On this semicomforting note, she settled herself upon the springy moss, leaned back against a tree, and waited, closing her eyes, forcing herself to relax. Thus, she rested undisturbed, half dozing, until she was startled by a cold, wet nose pressed without warning into her hand.

"Erebus!" The big, shaggy dog, his black fur outlined silver in the moonlight, wagged his tail, his tongue lolling out of one side of his mouth, his eyes sparkling with delight at having found her. He woofed gently, inviting her to play. "No, Erebus. Oh, hush!" She reached out to pull him near in an attempt to stifle his exuberance, but he only danced back, woofing again, teasing her. The next moment, with a rustle of shrubbery, Beck loomed over her.

"His lordship requests your immediate presence in the library, Miss Lennox-Matthews," he said formally, but with an odd note of triumph nonetheless. "Will you be good enough to accompany me there at once?"

Sarah, raging silently at herself, surrendered with outward meekness, and it seemed less than no time before she was back in her bedchamber, the door locked, the key in Darcy's possession. He had noticed its absence and thus her own when he had passed her chamber on his way to bed, and had immediately sent Beck in search of her, but despite any inconvenience, Darcy had not been particularly angry. He had merely shaken his head at her foolishness and observed to Beck that they must be more careful in future.

She stood for a moment, staring at the locked door, but her thoughts seemed only to become dismal and disjointed, so she finally roused herself and made her way to the great bed. Tomorrow was another day. Perhaps something would occur to her then. She pulled down the coverlet and tested the sheets. Matty had aired them. There would be no dampness to complain of, and though she would have liked a warming pan or at least a hot brick, she would certainly not attempt to ring for one now.

She slipped off her dress, thinking it would look sorry enough without being slept in. Then, clad only in her shift and shivering a little in the crisp air from the open window, she climbed between the sheets under the heavy patchwork quilt where, more exhausted than she knew by the events of the day, she was barely conscious of feeling warm again before she fell asleep.

She awoke the following morning conscious of a deep sense of disorientation. Then memory returned. She sat up in bed, pushing her hair out of her eyes and feeling rather small and helpless and lonely. Drat Darcy anyway, she thought to herself. But then, she sighed aloud as honesty again compelled her to accept the fact that she had not come to her present position through Darcy's efforts alone. Drat Sir Nicholas Ashton! Drat vanity. Drat. . . .

But then she told herself firmly that such mental gyrations were silly, that there was no use repining the past or trying to diagnose the causes of her predicament. The thing now was to deal with the present. That thought, however, was not a bit more comforting than its predecessors had been, since her present situation was scarcely a cheering one. If she returned to London unmarried, she would be Ruined. Compromised beyond redemption. The fact that her virtue was still intact would mean little or nothing, for what was virtue without reputation? And her reputation, thanks to a single night passed unchaperoned under a gentleman's roof, was in shreds.

Though she had drifted into sleep the previous night clinging to a hope that some small miracle might yet occur, with the clarity of morning light, she could see the impossibility of recouping her losses. Under the strict code of behavior practiced by the Beau Monde, losing her reputation meant that she would be ostracized, that those persons hitherto counted as friends would look away when she passed by, that hostesses would delete her name from their entertainment lists. There would be no more gilt-edged invitations, no more delightful routs, no more gay meetings in Rotten Row. Darcy would be shunned too, of course, but only briefly. He was a man and would therefore be quickly forgiven. There would be a dinner party eventually where the numbers were uneven, and his name—an earl, after all—would come to mind.

Sarah gave herself a shake. This would not do! She was

allowing herself to sink into a morass of self-pity. The thought
of facing her Aunt Aurelia or anyone else in London would
cast anyone into the dismals, yet it was not even something
that must be faced immediately. Her present circumstance
was another matter entirely. That must be faced, since the
present was by its very definition a matter of undeniable
priority. Besides, wallowing in her own discomfiture was not
Sarah's way. If she was ruined, it was a fact already accomplished. The thing now was not to dwell upon it but to look to
the future, to decide upon an acceptable course of action.

The dress she had draped over the chair the previous night
caught her eye. It would be a good deal easier, she considered, to adopt an attitude of resolution if one were fully
clothed. A thin chemise, after all, added little to one's sense of
consequence. Accordingly, she scurried out of bed and across
the threadbare carpet and splintery floor, ignoring her corset
and snatching up the dress to fling it over her head, grateful
for its protection against the chilly morning air. Once decently
clad, she stepped to view herself in the dressing table glass.

"Dear me," she sighed aloud, pushing stray curls away from
her forehead again. She looked the veriest urchin! "Like something he swept up at a crossing," she muttered, pinching up
her sleeves and dragging her comb through her hair, coercing
it into a semblance of order by combing the stubborn tresses
severely away from her face and tying them back with her
ribbon. Of course, no sooner had the bow been tied than
various curls began to wisp about her brow and ears most
charmingly, but there was nothing she could do about that, so
she left well enough alone.

Gratified and likewise amazed to discover water in the cracked
porcelain ewer on the washstand, she poured some into the
basin and scrubbed her hands and face to a becomingly rosy
glow. Then, much refreshed, she plumped down upon the
French seat in the window embrasure to await events. Leaning back against comfortable cushions, she watched as noisy
birds chased one another, flitting from limb to limb, from tree
to tree, diving into the darker reaches of the encroaching
woodland. Occasionally, a gray squirrel would dart across the
drive or sit amidst the weeds nibbling at a delicacy held
between its dainty forepaws. Amusing at first, but the entertainment was limited and soon began to pall. Her thoughts
turned inward again.

There were clearly at least two possible stands she might

take. First, she might do all in her power to make Darcy sorry he had ever conceived the notion to marry her. Such a course might become a trifle wearing, however, and would certainly cut up everyone's peace, including her own. On the other hand, she might simply resign herself to the inevitable and make the best of things. Sarah sighed again. Such tame submission would no doubt be confoundedly boring, not to mention unromantic and banal. Also sensible, no doubt. That settled it. Surely, there must be a middle path, some way by which she might defy him just enough to keep him well aware of her feelings without making things entirely uncomfortable for everyone concerned—if only she could think how to manage it.

Sarah perceived that she had already resigned herself to the marriage, little though she desired it. Had her escape attempt succeeded, things would be different, but being something of a fatalist, she quite realized that, having spent the night in Darcy's house, there was nothing left now but to marry him. Besides, things might have been much worse. As a husband, he wouldn't be too bad. He was amiable and handsome enough, and she ought to be able to manage him without too much difficulty. Of course, she did not love him, and she never would. She doubted she would ever even scrape up much respect for him. He was simply not that sort of person. She thought him weak, self-centered, occasionally stubborn, even—as now—obstinate. But worse than that, he was the sort of man other people used to serve their own interests. Had she not tried to do that very thing herself?

It was not that he was particularly gullible, she mused now. It was more that he generally seemed to take the line of least resistance. Perhaps it was laziness, perhaps merely a desire on his part to avoid unpleasant confrontations with others. But whatever his particular guiding star was, something had certainly stirred him enough to accomplish her abduction. He must need money very badly indeed, she decided, staring vaguely at the gray clouds settling in above the treeline.

At this point, her rambling thoughts were interrupted by approaching footsteps. A moment later, there was a shuffling noise in the hallway, then the sound of a key in the lock. The door swung open, and Darcy entered. He was dressed in a well-fitting bottle-green coat and tan stockinette pantaloons neatly tucked into glossy, gold-tasseled Hessians, and he carried a tray. Appreciatively, Sarah noted a chubby little crockery pot and a linen-covered plate before he spoke.

"Good morning, m'dear. I've brought your chocolate and some toast. You seemed to show a slight aversion to Beck yesterday, so I decided I'd just bring it myself this morning." He set the tray down on the dressing table.

"Thank you, my lord." She had decided to be polite, but she would maintain a certain cool reserve toward him as well.

"Trust you spent a restful night."

"Yes, my lord." She rose from the French seat and moved to pour out a cup of chocolate. There were two cups. "May I pour you some, my lord?"

"Yes, of course, m'dear. Must say, you seem to be in a more tractable mood this morning." Not a word about her attempted escape, but a triumphant little smile twitched at his lips. "Hope it means you've decided to be cooperative."

Sarah set the chocolate pot back on the tray and passed him his cup before she replied. "As to that, sir, I quite see that an expeditious marriage has become a necessity."

"Indeed." He took his seat on the dressing chair, idly smoothing a wrinkle across his thigh as he watched her return to the window seat with her own cup and a piece of buttered toast. "Glad you've decided to be sensible, dear girl. Of course, your reputation has been thoroughly compromised by now, so neither you nor Lord Hartley has much choice in the matter. Beck will bring the materials for your letter."

"One moment, my lord," she interposed quickly as he drank off his chocolate and moved to rise. "I see no reason to deceive my uncle. His opinion of me must suffer enough as a result of my behavior in meeting you clandestinely. But to allow him to believe that I connived with you in an elopement is more than I can agree to do."

Darcy gave a thoughtful nod. "Quite understand your reluctance, m' dear. Nonetheless, you must realize there are certain rather unpalatable laws regarding the abduction of an heiress. Not certain you'd be so regarded under your peculiar circumstances, of course. Or that your uncle would take steps, being a gentleman so averse to scandal as he is. Still and all, no reason to take the chance. I'd look dashed silly decorating a gallows, so it's got to look as though you've acted voluntarily."

"And if I refuse?"

"In that case," he replied apologetically, " 'fraid I should have to cut my losses."

"Cut your losses!" A spark of hope leaped within her. "Do you mean that you would return me to Berkeley Square?"

"Well, yes. 'Fraid I should have to, you know. You noted yourself the absurdity of any attempt to force you to the border, and no self-respecting clergyman would marry us against your will, even if I could extort a waiver from your uncle. Most unfortunately, I don't claim acquaintance with any disreputable men of the cloth."

"Then, I think you must resign yourself to taking me home, sir," Sarah replied with dignity, "for I shall not write that letter."

"Dash it, Sarah. Thought you had a sense of pride."

"I do!"

Darcy shook his head. "Can't have considered the matter properly, then. Only think of the scandal if you return to your uncle's house after a night spent here."

"But if you say nothing about the matter and I say nothing about it, who is to know? Surely, we can still wrap things in white linen if we but put our minds to it!"

"Ah, but there's the rub, you see," he responded promptly. "Might be more than we could manage. You see, Beck's got a rather long tongue, and I shouldn't like to deny any allegations he might make about your behavior, though it would be dashed foolish to admit I took you by force. Not that people would believe that anyway if I return you to the bosom of your family with your virtue still intact." He frowned down at his thumbnail. "It would be a rather simple matter, actually, to let the world believe you had thrown yourself at my head, and that, after teaching you a small lesson, I'd decided against proceeding with an elopement. Might be thought a devilish harsh fellow, but that would be nothing to what the world would think of you, my darling Sarah."

"I am not your darling, nor am I your dear, nor anything else, sir," she muttered between clenched teeth, "and I do wish you would cease littering the place with your false endearments."

"As you like. Is that your final word on the subject?"

Sarah glared at him, but she was conscious at the same time of a heavy sinking feeling. He must know she would capitulate, for there was certainly no way she knew of by which she might counter the actions he threatened. His credibility under such circumstances as he had outlined would be far greater than hers. She was beaten, and she knew it. No longer was there any point in refusing to write her uncle, for she quite understood that marriage was the only way by which any shred of her reputation might be spared her. Nor, she realized now, had the outcome ever been in much doubt. Even had he agreed to take her back and keep mum about it, they would have been taking an enormous risk, one she was not perfectly certain even now that she would have been willing to take. She sighed deeply.

"I shall write whatever you wish, my lord."

"Good girl. Rather thought you would." He got to his feet. "Like to get to Town with time to accomplish the business today, so be quick, m'dear. I shall send Beck with paper and ink." He stepped to the door, then paused and looked back. "It won't be so bad, you know, Sarah. The money is what matters, but I shall treat you decently enough, I daresay."

She made no reply, and he went out, leaving her briefly with her own thoughts again. She finished her toast and chocolate. This was not the way she had planned courtship and marriage. Not by a long chalk! She had hoped for something more in line with the romances of her favorite heroines. Of course, she had known that she might not have a chance at such a thing, that her aunt and uncle might simply have auctioned her off to the highest bidder. Who knew what sort of brute she might have ended up with? At least, Darcy had promised not to inflict any of the more intimate marital relations upon her, she reminded herself. However, since she had rather looked forward to exploring such relations with a properly adored and adoring husband, the reminder did not serve to raise her spirits much.

Fleetingly, she indulged herself in the delicious and hitherto forbidden notion that once she was married she might participate in as many affairs of the heart as she liked. Everyone did. One married for advantage but loved wherever one found a mutual interest. It was, according to most of her friends, the accepted mode. Unfortunately, the only man she could conceive of having an affair with was Sir Nicholas.

But the very thought brought with it a shudder and a rather tremulous choke of laughter, as her ever-fertile imagination provided her with a swift vision of his probable response to any such overture from her married self. Sir Nicholas would *not* approve. Although she could not doubt that he had had vast experience with females, his own sternly voiced notions of propriety precluded any imagining that that experience had come from dalliance with respectably married ladies. And even if it had, she thought shrewdly, he would undoubtedly refuse to countenance such an illicit relationship for her with himself or, for that matter, with anyone else.

The valet entered as she formed that last rather disappointing thought, and she looked up with a nearly guilty fear that he might somehow read her mind. He was carrying a standish, which he set down upon the dressing table, having first made room for it by removing the chocolate tray. "I have brought the materials, miss, as his lordship requested. I am to remain whilst you write your letter."

His attitude was such that, in spite of her decision to cooperate, Sarah despised herself for lacking the courage to order him out of the room, to indulge herself in last-minute defiance. But she could do neither of these things. For the moment at least, Darcy had won. She must marry him. Consequently, she handed the valet her chocolate cup and stepped quickly but with her usual easy grace to sit in the dressing chair.

Beck made no attempt to hide a smirk of satisfaction as he placed the cup next to the chocolate pot and moved to set the tray outside the door. He jerked his head expressively in the general direction of the ground floor. "His lordship's waiting below for it, miss, so you'd best make it snappy. He's not wishful to be patient."

How she would have liked to give Beck to Aunt Aurelia for training! *She* would make short work of his smirks and his insolence. But Sarah gritted her teeth, swallowing the angry words she wanted to say to him, knowing instinctively that it could do her no good to make an enemy of the man. Instead, she picked up the pen, spread a sheet of writing paper on the table, and dipping her pen into the ink, began to write. The point was not as sharp as she would have liked, but she would make do rather than ask Beck to sharpen it for her.

The letter ran to Darcy's outline as nearly as she could remember it. She explained to her uncle that she had run away with the Earl of Moreland because she had feared that Lord and Lady Hartley would somehow contrive to separate them forever. Such an excellent notion, too, she thought to herself as she continued. It was a shame she had not been more obedient to their will. Reluctantly, she outlined Darcy's wish for a waiver and a special license, added that she would not return to London until Lord Hartley consented to her marriage, then made ready to sign her name; but Beck, who had been quite rudely reading over her shoulder, stopped her and suggested that she add the threat of Gretna as well as a hint that the state of her virtue had been altered. Since he put the second part of his suggestion with crude insolence, Sarah was shocked enough to protest vehemently.

"I will write no such thing! How dare you propose that!"

"His lordship wants it in, miss," Beck replied stubbornly.

Battle royal might have been joined between the two of them, had not Darcy chosen that moment to enter, wondering anxiously why it was taking Sarah so long to write a simple letter. Beck explained the matter with what Sarah could only view as righteous indignation beyond his station, but to her great relief, Darcy took her side of it.

"Don't be daft, man," he said with an oddly jollifying note in his voice. "Chit can't write that rubbish. She'd never write anything so improper off her own bat, so don't go making a mull of things by forcing her to say such stuff. Her uncle would be bound to suspect it had been written under duress. Here, Sarah," he went on in a more natural tone, "I'll tell you what to write. Let me look at what you've got." He scooped up the sheet from the table and perused it rapidly. "That's good," he said, laying it down in front of her again. "Now, you just add this bit. Put it in your own words, but tell his lordship that, matters being what they are, you are certain he will agree you cannot marry anyone but me and that you would prefer marriage by special license to an elopement to Gretna. Use that phrase, 'matters being what they are,' but put the rest any way you like. We'll let the old gentleman use his imagination. Can always hint him in the right direction if he don't look to be getting there by himself, can't I?" He paused, lifting an inquiring eyebrow at the valet while gesturing for Sarah to begin writing.

She didn't like his wording much better than Beck's, but with the two men both standing over her as they were, she simply couldn't find the courage to protest further. Beck's expression was even a trifle alarming. He had shrugged noncommittally in response to his master's glance, but when his gaze shifted to herself, she noted a glitter in his eyes that certainly didn't encourage her to trust the man. Servant or no servant, he was a villainous piece of work and no mistake. He seemed to exert some sort of influence over his master, too, and she wondered how Darcy could abide having the man around him all the time. But she certainly couldn't ask him about it now. Cheeks flushed red at the thought of how even such vague phrasing might be construed, she turned back to

her task, and having written what was wanted, she added a
brief apology for disappointing her aunt and uncle and signed
it. She did not look up again when Darcy took the letter and
patted her approvingly on the shoulder. He went out immediately, followed by Beck. Once again, the key turned in the
lock.

Relieved that they had gone at last, Sarah went back to the
window seat, and less than an hour had passed before she
heard noises from the drive. Looking out, she saw the shabby
coach draw up before the front entrance. Beck was driving.
Soon Darcy appeared, hurried down the steps, and jumped up
into the coach, slamming the door shut as Beck whipped up
the horses.

They were gone two full days, during which time Sarah
made the acquaintance of both Matty and her husband, Tom.
Matty appeared a short time after Darcy's departure bearing
Sarah's luncheon on a tray. It was the only time she saw
Matty during Darcy's absence and she was just as glad, for
the woman reeked of spirits. Her gray hair was tangled, her
dress was dirty, and her skin looked unhealthy. She looked a
perfect slattern, Sarah thought.

She saw more of Tom, for it was he who brought her other
meals, saying that Matty had declined to tramp up two flights
of stairs every time Sarah had the urge to eat. Sarah kindly
suggested that she would be happy to come downstairs to take
her meals properly in the dining parlor, but the offer was
declined, Tom explaining briefly that Beck, supposedly relaying his lordship's orders, had threatened to murder them both
if they led Sarah out of her bedchamber for any reason whatever. As though she would attempt to escape again, she thought
bitterly. Not that she wouldn't have tried, had there been any
point to it. But it would be pointless now. The sooner she was
married, the better.

Tom also took care of her other needs, too, emptying the
slops jar and bringing her, when she requested them, several
books from which to choose. Since they included *Pilgrim's
Progress* and a copy of the *Canterbury Tales*, she was well
enough pleased, although they weren't by any means among
her favorites. She would have much preferred a tale by Fanny
Burney or Mrs. Radcliffe or that author who wrote so wittily
about such ordinary people. Sarah and Miss Penistone had
greatly enjoyed both *Sense and Sensibility* and *Pride and*

Prejudice before Penny had had to leave, and Sarah herself had obtained and chuckled her way through *Mansfield Park*.

Rumor, emanating from the Prince Regent himself, had it that the author was a young gentlewoman, Miss Jane Austen. Supposedly, Prinny had had that titbit from his librarian, the Reverend J. S. Clarke, who had it from his physician, Mr. Haden, who had it from the young woman's very own brother, Henry Austen. Mr. Austen had told Mr. Haden that his sister intended to dedicate her latest work, a novel called *Emma*, to his Royal Highness. Rumor also had it that Miss Austen was not best pleased to know that her closely guarded secret had leaked out, but the Prince, having enjoyed her earlier works quite as much as Sarah had, had kindly sent his permission for the dedication, though Miss Austen had never actually solicited the favor. Sarah, as well as most of her friends, had subscribed for a copy of *Emma*, and it was no doubt sitting now in the chest under her shawls, exactly where she had left it.

It was rather annoying to think that she had scarcely had a chance to read more than the first chapter or so, since she imagined that she had quite a lot in common with the independent and fascinatingly self-willed heroine, Miss Emma Woodhouse. Of course, Sarah had not been saddled with a hypochondriac for a father, but she rather thought that she and her dearest Penny were quite a lot like Miss Woodhouse and her Miss Taylor. Certainly, Emma's father would have preferred Penny to Miss Taylor, for Penny showed no inclination toward the state of matrimony, a state vocally and most amusingly deplored by the irascible Mr. Woodhouse. On the other hand, Miss Taylor seemed likely to remain near her erstwhile charge, while Penny had dashed off two weeks to the day after her dismissal to a sister's house in faraway Cornwall. But it was no use to think of that, Sarah told herself firmly. And, however entertaining it would be to be able to finish what had begun as a completely delightful tale, she must make do with what she had. Deciding to renew her acquaintance with Christian, she tried staunchly to convince herself that his adventures were amusing and not simply dry and moralistic. When Tom brought her a light supper, she asked if Erebus might not come up to keep her company.

Shrugging, the old man allowed as how there could be little harm in it, and a half hour or so later, he reappeared to take her tray away, followed by the huge black dog. Erebus greeted her enthusiastically, and having been sternly forbidden to indulge in the habits of a lap dog, collapsed with a thud at her feet where he snoozed quite comfortably until Tom came to put him out for the night. He spent much of the following day with her as well, and Sarah enjoyed his companionship. She soon began to talk to him quite as though he were another person. His intelligent eyes would brighten at such attention, and he would cock his mammoth head with a flattering air of interest in all she chose to say to him. For Erebus, at least, the time did not pass slowly.

IV

Darcy and Beck returned Monday afternoon, and hearing the noise of their arrival, Sarah looked out to see that this time they had come in Darcy's own phaeton. He jumped down at the front, handing the reins to Beck, who then drove on around the house. She expected his lordship to come to her immediately, but he did not. Instead, after a long wait, Tom came with a small trunk.

"My lord says as 'ow yer t' dine with 'im in an hour, miss. 'E sent these." He dumped the trunk onto the floor and left, taking the dog with him. No key turned in the lock. Sarah stared after them, torn between wanting to find Darcy and hear what had happened and wanting to see what was in the trunk. The trunk won.

She opened it and sat back on her heels with a smile. It was filled with her own things. There were several gowns, a night dress, her riding habit and boots, two lace chemises, and her silver hairbrush. Right on top sat the reticule she had left in the carriage. There were also various ribbons and two pairs of sandals, some scented French soap, a string of varicolored beads, and a pair of white silk mittens. Clearly, except for the reticule, Lizzie had packed the trunk and had tried to include things her mistress might need immediately. She had not thought to send a shawl, so she had not discovered *Emma*, but one of the gowns was for evening wear. Sarah shook it out.

It was a simple dress of white muslin, the type most solidly approved by Aunt Aurelia for young ladies in their first Season. High waisted, it would be worn with a long pink sash, the colored beads, and her pink satin sandals. Maybe she could even contrive to weave a ribbon through her hair. Oh, if he had to bring her a surprise, why had Darcy not thought to bring Lizzie!

The thought had simply never crossed his mind. And, of course, it would never have occurred to her uncle that she might have need of a maidservant. At dinner, Darcy seemed actually apologetic about the oversight but explained that his plan had otherwise gone without a hitch. Lord Hartley had reacted precisely to form. "Furious, of course. Couldn't expect him to be otherwise. 'Fraid you must prepare yourself for a scold, m' dear. That is, if he ever speaks to you again," he observed amiably.

"What did he say about the wedding?" Sarah asked. A scold from her uncle was not something she need worry about. A blistering reprimand from her aunt was much more likely, though it was even more probable that neither of them would want to see her again. She gazed now across the table at Darcy. He was dressed in a coat of black superfine, and his well-starched neckcloth was intricately tied and adorned with a pearl stick pin. He might complain of poverty, but he always dressed well, and the phaeton she had seen was a well-made vehicle pulled by a team of highbred, matched bays. His voice interrupted her train of thought.

"Signed the waiver and helped me himself to arrange for the special license. S'pose it was a sense of mischief inspired me to suggest St. George's." He paused with a reminiscent gleam in his eye. " 'Fraid his lordship nearly went into strong convulsions. Turned red as a turkey cock and gobbled something about the Regent and Lady Jersey, though I had thought that affair long ended."

Sarah frowned. "You know perfectly well what he meant, sir. The Prince will be displeased as it is not to be invited to my wedding, but to be asked to lend his countenance to a ceremony with this sort of scandal attached to it—well, he wouldn't, and you know it. As for Lady Jersey, she is forever unsettling Aunt Aurelia's sensibilities with her long tongue."

He nodded. "Discovered that m'self. Suggested that your absence from Town might be hushed up or at least that an excuse might be found for it, so as to wrap things up nicely after we're safely riveted, but that don't appear possible now. Seems one of the shopkeepers noticed a pretty young lady climb into a shabby hackney coach, and your precious Lizzie burst in upon Lady Hartley bewailing your disappearance and putting forth the notion that you had been abducted by God knows what sort of wild ruffians." He paused for effect. "You'll never guess who was paying a morning call at that auspicious moment!"

"Not Lady Jersey!"

"The same," he assured her in tones of strong amusement. "Silence herself. Puts the cat among the pigeons, don't it?"

"Oh, no!" Sarah stared at him. How could he think it at all amusing that the very worst gossip in London should know of all this? All London would be talking about her by now, wondering what had happened and speculating the worst. She had not truly realized what shame she would feel until the knowledge that the tattlers were probably discussing her situation in lurid detail was so clearly brought home to her. It didn't really matter now whether they thought she had eloped or been abducted. Marriage might expiate her shame to some small degree, but it would be a good long while before she would dare show her face in Town.

Darcy watched her dismay change to resignation. "I stopped in East End on the way back, Sarah. You will no doubt be pleased to know that Mr. Stanley, the parson there, will perform the ceremony tomorrow. Tried to fob me off until Saturday, but when I explained that you are already staying in my house unchaperoned, he put forth the date with alacrity. A prior commitment that he could not break was all that prevented his coming this evening."

"So I shall not be permitted to take that first step back toward respectability until tomorrow, my lord," Sarah retorted, her suddenly trembling voice laced with scorn. "How long do you suppose it will be before time mitigates the damage you have done me?" She was astonished to feel tears rising to the surface and looked away, lest he see them. He would be sure to make some sort of apology, and such a comment at this point was likely to cast her into strong hysterics! He did begin to mutter something, but she rallied her spirits enough to glare him to sullen silence.

Their conversation was limited after that, though Darcy did mention meekly that the rest of her belongings should arrive sometime after the first of the week by freight wagon. Frigidly, Sarah excused herself when Beck brought in his master's port, but then she nearly smiled in spite of herself at Darcy's undisguised sigh of relief. She went straight upstairs to her bedchamber, not surprised that someone soon came to lock her in. Despite his airs and apologies, Darcy would not chance her escaping before the ceremony could take place.

Sarah read for a while, until the evening light faded. Then she lit every candle she could find and proceeded to put her things away. It was not a task to occupy much of her time, so it was still early when she changed to her night dress and crept between the sheets. She had put her book on the night-stand and picked it up now with a guilty glance at the numerous flickering candles. They ought to be extinguished. Eight sconces! How wasteful. Aunt Aurelia would not approve. Sarah grinned. Aunt Aurelia was not here, and if Darcy meant to have her money, the least she could do was prove to be an expensive wife. Let the blasted candles gutter! She turned back to her book and eventually dropped off to sleep.

Her dreams seemed to be filled with somewhat garish marriage ceremonies. She was always the bride, but the groom changed most oddly from moment to moment and dream to dream. First there was Darcy, of course, but he changed almost immediately to a frog who wanted to kiss her, then to a rabbit, then to a clown with a painted face. At one point, she awoke with a vague memory that a camel had been carrying the minister into a tent filled with bullrushes and acorns, but then she dropped off into another dream where the minister was a child and the groom a snake in the grass. It was all very disturbing.

Nevertheless, the next morning dawned bright with sunshine, which made a nice change after several overcast days in a row, and Darcy was in excellent spirits when he came to visit her over her morning chocolate. He was fully dressed in buff breeches, a coat of blue superfine, and a gold Florentine waistcoat. His cravat was well-starched and tied in the intricate Mathematical style that he favored, and his topboots shone like polished obsidian and sported immaculate white uppers. Sarah suddenly had the thought that, though Beck was insolent, obnoxious, and generally impossible, he did seem to know his job. The Earl of Moreland was precise to a pin. He looked at her appraisingly.

"Minister arrives about half past ten, m'dear. That gives you an hour and a half. Would you like a bath?"

Her eyes lit. "Oh, yes! But it is not enough time to wash and dry my hair."

"Never mind your hair. Looks fine, and you'll have plenty of time later to wash it. But, if you want a bath I'll have Tom and Beck bring up a tub." He left soon after that, and it was not long before Beck and Tom, carrying a huge tub between them, entered the room. Several trips later, the tub was filled with steaming water and she was alone again.

In less than a twinkling, she was soaking in the tub, lathering herself with French scented soap. It was deliciously relaxing. She stayed until the water began to turn cold and then, regretfully, stepped out and dried herself. It was but a few moments work after that to slip on a clean chemise and her white muslin evening gown. It had been washed and pressed since the evening before, and she supposed Beck must have done it. The notion struck her as being an odd one, but she could not imagine either Matty or old Tom doing an acceptable job of it. She adjusted her sash and slipped her feet into the pair of matching satin slippers before turning her attention to her hair.

She had pinned it up in a straggly knot on top of her head for her bath. Now she took out the pins and let the heavy mass fall over her shoulders and down her back. Definitely, her hair missed Lizzie's attention even more than she did herself.

Lizzie loved Sarah's hair and cared for it lovingly. At a time when most young ladies cropped and crimped at least their foremost tresses, Lizzie totally approved of her mistress's luxuriously long, thick mane. She brushed it nightly and washed it with scented water every six days without fail. Her nimble fingers coaxed it into intricate and fascinating styles that were always much admired. Miss Lennox-Matthews' lovely, honey-bronze hair was nearly her hallmark, but Miss Lennox-Matthews was confounded by the task of managing it herself. She stared now at her reflection in the mirror. Steam from her bath had left becoming little curly wisps around her face, but the rest was dull and tangled. With a sigh, she picked up her brush and dragged it through the thick tresses. It took nearly half an hour to brush it into sufficient order to please Sarah. She wished she could do something with it, however, to keep it away from her face. She was tired of continually having to confine it behind her ears with a ribbon and was still glaring at her reflection when Darcy, after a perfunctory knock, entered to inform her of the parson's arrival.

"Why such a face, m'dear? You look wonderful."

"I was wishing my fingers were as clever as Lizzie's with my hair," she admitted. "I can't do anything with it."

"Suits me to a cow's thumb," he said firmly. "Don't go messing about with it. Told you that before. Come along now. Parson's waiting." He gave her a straight look as she moved toward him, and she stopped, puzzled by the expression on his face. Not taking his eyes from hers, he placed both hands on her shoulders. "Look here, Sarah," he said evenly, "you haven't got any notions of last-minute rebellion, have you?"

She shook her head. "Have no fear, my lord," she said quietly. "I have no intention of enacting a Cheltenham tragedy for Mr. Stanley's benefit. You have quite succeeded in making this ceremony nearly as important to me as it is to yourself."

Satisfied, he offered her his arm, and they went downstairs. Half an hour afterward, Miss Sarah Lennox-Matthews had become the Countess of Moreland. Darcy insisted upon cracking a bottle to celebrate, and Mrs. Stanley, a small and dapper little white-haired gentleman, was nothing loath, having accepted a handsome recompense for his journey and eyeing with favor the bottle of champagne presented by Beck for his master's approval.

Beck, too, was invited to join in the toast as were Tom and Matty, who had also stood witness to the ceremony. Sarah could not think Matty really needed the drink and hoped she would not pass out somewhere and forget about their luncheon. Darcy also poured out a small glass for his bride. Sarah really didn't enjoy the taste of wines and spirits, but it did seem a bit surly to refuse to toast her own wedding. The two gentlemen finished off the bottle, and Darcy invited Mr. Stanley to stay to luncheon. That gentleman accepting with beaming pleasure, they adjourned to the dining parlor, and if the little minister was any the less pleased with his decision after he had partaken of the tasteless meal, he hid his feelings well. Of course, he and Darcy had imbibed a good deal of the grape by then, so Sarah thought it possible that he did not really notice that the food lacked flavor. By half past one, he weaved his way to the front door, bidding the married couple fond best wishes and farewell.

They watched his departure from the doorway, and once he was out of sight, Darcy turned to his bride with an unmistakable air of anticipation. "I shall be leaving at once, my lady, for time is short. Must present the marriage lines to your grandfather's Mr. Smithers." He wasted little time, and less than a quarter hour later, he was gone.

No longer confined to her room, Sarah thought at first that

it would be fun to explore the old house, but she soon gave it up as a lonely, dreary prospect. Upstairs, several of the rooms had beds and one or two even possessed a chest or a chair, but everything was under Holland covers, and many of the rooms were entirely devoid of furnishings. The only one besides Sarah's own that could be considered truly habitable was Darcy's.

This chamber, down the corridor from Sarah's, was furnished with a masculine flavor, and she entered quietly, feeling almost as though she were invading his privacy. But she suppressed the feeling. After all, this place was going to be her home for the rest of her life. She had a right to look it over. Besides, she meant to make changes. There was no reason that it should continue to look so uncared-for. Even though this bedchamber was furnished, it still carried the same shabby, neglected air as the other rooms she had seen. Frayed, peacock-blue velvet curtains hung at tall windows overlooking the expanse of woods on the south side of the house. Off in the distance, one could catch a view of the common, and sunshine splashed across the floor. The windows flanked a large fireplace in which, at the moment, the ashes were cold. Sarah crossed an ancient Axminster carpet in muted shades of blue, dark gold, and green, to inspect shabby bed hangings that reflected the same colors in a tapestry pattern worked long ago by undoubtedly loving fingers.

Abstractedly, she smoothed the fluffy feather comforter encased in faded blue watered silk that covered the great carved bed, and cast a disinterested eye over two worn leather armchairs, similar to the pair in the library, that faced one another across the hearthstones. A low chest stood under one window, while a large, ornate wardrobe filled the east wall, but the only article of furniture that truly caught her fancy was a dressing table with a mirror that folded down cunningly to make a writing surface. A tapestry-covered stool was drawn up before it. But once she had figured out how the dressing table worked, she glanced around again with an appraising eye. If nothing else, there was certainly scope for change here. She would have no excuse for remaining idle once Darcy arranged for the transfer of funds to his own name.

She left the bedchamber and wandered back to the gallery, where faded spaces indicated that a number of paintings had once hung. They were gone now, and she was not particularly interested in architectural details, so the once-beautiful wainscoting and frieze work in the rooms she visited made little impact. She soon returned to *Pilgrim's Progress* with near relief.

Darcy was away for several days, but Sarah scarcely had any opportunity to feel lonely, for midway through the morning after his departure, a farmer's well-worn gig rattled up to the front door, and a tall, rather lanky lady in dove-gray merino descended from the seat with as much dignity as if she were royalty descending from the state coach. Sarah, watching from her bedchamber window with Erebus curled companionably at her feet, threw up her hands with an unladylike shriek of joy, leaped up, and tore down the stairs, followed by the excited dog, to land breathlessly at the front door, throwing it open before the driver of the gig had a chance to knock.

"Penny!" Erebus loudly echoed the welcome, emphasizing his pleasure with a wildly flailing tail.

"Sarah, love, what manner of conduct is this?" the visitor inquired gently. "Remember . . . poise, posture, and propriety!"

Sarah grabbed Erebus by the scruff of his thick neck and sharply commanded his silence. "Oh, Penny, Penny, do come in!"

"One moment, love." Miss Penistone turned to the young man beside her and handed him some money. "Thank you very much for bringing me, Mr. Henderson. If you will just put my trunk on the steps there, I shall do nicely." He hastened to do her bidding, and she turned back to Sarah, eyeing her serenely from tip to toe. "Who on earth has been doing your hair, my dear?"

"No one," Sarah chuckled. "Oh, Penny, it's been awful! But do come in, do!" Tom chose that moment to shamble in through the green baize door at the rear of the hall, and entrusting the reluctant Erebus to his charge, she asked him to see to Penny's trunk and to ask Matty to prepare tea for them. "For I know you will want some refreshment after your journey, Penny," she said, drawing that lady into the little saloon under the stair, and adding apologetically once the door had shut behind them, "Not that it will amount to much, for the servants here are a disgrace. Oh, Penny, I have missed you dreadfully! How did you find me?"

"Your Lizzie told me," Miss Penistone replied placidly. "My sister was ill, you know, but she is quite well now and anxious to have her cottage to herself again, so I had planned to look about London for another position. But you know how it is when there is a gap in one's references—at least, you don't, but I assure you that it can make matters most difficult for one in my position. I went straight to Berkeley Square, however, where Lady Hartley very kindly provided what was needed. Lizzie was waiting for me in the street when I left Hartley House, and she explained things. Really, Sarah, you have not behaved at all well."

"Oh, I know, I know! But you cannot have heard the whole of it. Truly, Penny, it is not as you must have been led to believe!"

"No, I am quite certain of it." Miss Penistone removed her cloak and prim little hat and disposed them carefully over the back of a chair before taking her seat. Then, she folded her hands in her lap and bent an inquiring, birdlike gaze upon her erstwhile charge. "I am likewise certain that you will wish to explain."

"Yes, indeed," Sarah agreed. She began at the beginning and made a clean breast of the whole, feeling much as she had felt upon previous occasions when confessing some childish peccadillo to Penny, knowing now as then that she would feel much better afterward. As she had always done in such cases, Penny maintained a calm expression throughout the tale. If Sarah's behavior shocked her, there was no sign of it. She merely sat quietly, hands folded restfully in her lap, making no comment whatsoever until Sarah had quite finished speaking.

Miss Emily Penistone had been an answer to a prayer when Lady Hartley hired her to take charge of ten-year-old Sarah. With her mouse-brown hair swept severely back and confined at the nape of her neck, thus throwing rather harsh features into unnecessary prominence, and a keen sensitivity that allowed her to give the proper responses in a rather prim voice to shrewd questions about her notions of child-raising, she had played the part of strict governess to a nicety.

Quickly dubbed Penny by her charge, the quiet-spoken young woman had dutifully drummed learning and manners into Sarah, since that was the purpose for which she had been engaged, but the same sensitivity that had enabled her to give the desired responses to Lady Hartley also enabled her to guide her charge without stifling natural high spirits and to provide friendship and love as well as academic instruction. While Lord Hartley spent his days and most of his evenings occupied with important matters at one or another of his clubs and Lady Hartley kept busy with her extensive social obligations,

Penny was Sarah's own and brought order and peace into her life.

It was gentle Miss Penistone who saw to it that Sarah had dancing lessons when she was old enough for them and who notified Sarah's aunt and uncle when the time had come to let down her dresses and put up her hair. Indeed, she did such a fine job that it was rarely necessary for Lord or Lady Hartley to take any notice whatever of Sarah until it was time to present her to Society. At that time, Lady Hartley promptly dismissed Miss Penistone, since a governess was no longer required, and replaced her with Lizzie, who was much less expensive and a very accomplished lady's maid besides. But Lizzie had never become her young mistress's confidante, and Sarah had missed Penny's gentle guidance upon more than one occasion.

Even now, as she made her careful explanations, Sarah was conscious of the calming influence of Penny's presence. She felt perfectly safe again and more confident of her ability to handle the difficulties of her position. When she had concluded her tale, she gazed expectantly at the serene lady in the opposite chair, scarcely knowing what she expected her to say.

"Dear me," Miss Penistone mused sadly, "what a pity it is that your aunt dismissed me when she did, because this could all have been avoided so easily. I quite see, love, that you need me now as much as you ever did."

"Oh, yes," Sarah agreed, "though in all fairness, Penny, I am not certain that even you could have stopped me being so silly." Miss Penistone's placid smile was her only response, but it was clear that she had no doubt that wiser counsel would have prevailed. At any rate, Sarah knew better than to pursue the topic. Instead, she demanded to know if Penny meant to stay.

"Why, yes," Miss Penistone replied, "if you want me and, in the circumstances, if his lordship will permit it."

"Well, I certainly want you," Sarah declared, "and in the circumstances, as you say, Darcy will simply have to agree to it. I shall not allow him to do otherwise."

She promptly installed Penny in the room next to her own, and within a matter of a few days, that lady had made herself quite at home. Luckily for the success of their plan, Darcy returned from London in high spirits. There had been no problem about transferring the funds to his name. Mr. Smithers had been most cordial, even to the point of relaying Sir Malcolm's hope for the speedy arrival of a lusty son to inherit the fortune and many others to secure the line. Darcy laughed rather self-consciously when he told Sarah about it over dinner. Miss Penistone had dined earlier in her own chamber, having insisted that it would be wisest for Sarah to approach her husband privately first. But Sarah had been a little wary of simply plunging into the matter.

"Could scarcely tell the old gentleman of our agreement, my lady," Darcy said now. "Doubt he would understand, and I didn't much care for the notion of explaining how matters stand. Besides, perhaps one day your sentiments on the issue might alter. A proper heir would certainly be one in the eye for old Nick."

"I collect that you refer to your cousin, Sir Nicholas," observed Sarah, deciding that a change of subject was in order, though not perhaps such a drastic one as the mention of Miss Penistone's presence at Ash Park.

"Not cousin. Nick's my uncle, if you can believe it, though he's not but four years older than I am. He's also my heir at the moment and has undoubtedly damned my existence ever since he was old enough to understand what it meant to him. If you think your grandfather was a loose screw, you should have known mine." He sipped Malaga with a reminiscent gleam in his eye. "Grandmama died in 'eighty-four and he barely waited a decent year before he married a chit scarce out of the schoolroom, just seventeen, the exact same age as my father! Naturally, Papa didn't marry until a good time later, by which time she had already presented Grandfather with the Lady Honoria and dear Nick. We grew up together in this house. I am certain my father would have preferred to remove at least as far as Dower House once he married, but being a great one for having his family all under one roof, Grandfather wouldn't hear of it. At least they sent Nick and me to different schools," he added. "Would have been a bore always having to explain the relationship."

"How did he become *Sir* Nicholas?"

"Knighted because of action in the Peninsula," he responded shortly. His mood had changed again, and Sarah realized he was jealous of Sir Nicholas, but she was interested and didn't want to drop the subject.

"We missed seeing him the last week or so that I was in Town," she said now. "Where is he?"

"God knows. Lady Honoria is traveling on the Continent with Bessling—her husband, you know. They barely waited for the dust to settle after Waterloo before they were off, but they've got a brat at Harrow, so I expect Nick is keeping a weather eye peeled in that direction, wherever he is. He's damn soft on the lad. Could be in Yorkshire with his mother, I suppose."

"Oh, then she is still living?"

"Lord, yes! She's only forty-six after all! If my parents hadn't both caught the influenza, they'd still be living, wouldn't they? If yours——"

"All right, my lord, you've made your point," she said with a small sigh. Darcy shrugged apologetically and proceeded to detail his visit to Town. He had discovered that their scandal was still in high flight and had, as a result, avoided most of the fashionable meeting places, preferring to let things die down a bit first. Sarah was in whole-hearted agreement with that sentiment, but she soon realized that he had managed to entertain himself despite such abstention. Mr. Smithers having arranged for him to draw immediately and substantially upon the funds, Darcy had decided to see if his luck was in, and his conversation was full of the cards he had held and the fickleness of the bones he had tossed. He rather thought he had lost more than he had won, but nevertheless, he had come home with a good deal of money in his pocket. Sarah was astonished that he had dared bring so much across Finchley Common, where highwaymen were known to lie in wait for the unwary, but he laughed at her fears, teasing her that she should so betray her concern for his safety.

He was determined to spend money to refurbish Ash Park and had already made arrangements for three housemaids to come to them from East End village. Therefore, when Sarah told him at last of Miss Penistone's arrival, he was more pleased than she might have expected him to be.

"The place needs an army of maidservants," he admitted, "but three was the best I could do. Your Miss Penistone will be very helpful, I've no doubt. I've also got a couple of men to start on the lawn and gardens. Once we get the place cleaned up a bit we can dash up to Town and find some decent furnishings."

"With only three maidservants, my lord, that will be quite some time in the future, I'm afraid," Sarah said, shaking her head at the thought of the long-neglected rooms. The house was not gargantuan, by any means, but there were at least thirty rooms, and it would take even an army of servants weeks to do the job properly. She saw no reason to correct his notion that Penny would help with the cleaning, for of course she would help Sarah with the supervision, but with only three maidservants the job would take forever!

Darcy agreed with her, but he could see no reason to rush things. When she suggested that the house might run more smoothly if he found replacements for Tom and Matty, particularly the latter, who was not at all to be depended upon, he refused obstinately, saying only that they had remained loyal to him when his luck was out, and he would keep them on. He was full of plans and dreams, however, for improving the estate. Sarah learned that there were holdings beyond the confines of the Park itself, tenant farms, fields, and pastureland that had deteriorated over the years until they were practically nonproductive. Most of the tenant dwellings were ramshackle and uninhabited. One morning he provided Sarah with a mount and took her with him on a tour of these small farms. He was enthusiastic in his plans for rebuilding and finding new tenants, and although Sarah thought his ideas sounded rather disorganized, she enjoyed the outing.

Work on the inside of the house went as slowly as she had expected, but the lawns and gardens began shaping up well. The gardens were still pretty bare, but the weeds were soon gone, and the grass was cut back to its proper height and restricted to its original borders. The men were still working to remove the weeds from the drive, and there remained a great deal of underbrush to be cleared from the woods, but much had been accomplished.

Penny willingly took on the burden of supervising the maidservants, often working right alongside them as they slaved to make the huge house habitable again. Sarah played the lady of the manor for a short while, but then she, too, took up a broom or a rag and worked with the others. Their tasks seemed far more interesting to her than did reading or sewing while the others were physically active. The work was satisfying and served to keep her mind off her own troubles.

Darcy clearly expected Sarah to sit with him in the library each night until after evening tea had been served, but he made no demur when she invited Penny both to dine with them and to keep them company afterward. Several times, however, both Darcy and Beck disappeared directly after dinner, not to be seen again until morning, and Sarah had no idea where they went, nor was she much interested, assuming that they must have gone carousing. She took the opportunity to have a comfortable coze with Penny and to get to bed early.

About half past two in the afternoon following the third of these excursions, a man rode up the drive, was admitted to the house, and requested private speech with the master. Sarah, practically attired in a housemaid's mob cap and apron, was polishing the gallery rail when he was shown into the library. She could tell by looking at him that he was no gentleman, yet he was closeted with her husband for about an hour. Nevertheless, she would have taken little interest in him but for the fact that Beck seemed to find a number of excuses for loitering in the hall while the man was with Darcy. Once she could have sworn that the valet had been about to listen at the door before he noticed her standing at the rail above him. He had departed rather hastily then, only to return some minutes later upon another errand.

Once the visitor had gone, however, Beck went immediately into the library, closing the door behind him. Sarah, now very curious herself, decided that the hall table next to the library door needed polishing as much as the gallery rail, which was, as a matter of fact, now finished. On the thought, she gathered up her materials, descended the stair, rapidly crossed the hall, and began to spread bee's wax upon the table.

V

Sarah could hear her husband's voice upraised in anger, but his words were indistinct. Amazingly, she heard Beck's voice answer back as loudly. They were clearly arguing about something, and she wished she could hear better. The idea that Darcy, easy-going as he might appear, would allow a servant of his such a liberty astounded her.

She had been polishing the side of the table away from the door with the notion in the back of her mind that, should the door begin to open, she would have ample time to scurry across to the saloon under the stair before they could note her presence. But now, her curiosity overcame her good sense, and she crept closer to the library door.

The words were slightly clearer. She heard Beck say something about the money having naught to do with him, to which her husband responded by roundly informing him that he would, by God, remember for once who was man and who was master, and that would be the end of it. The voices lowered, and Sarah nearly had her ear against the door trying to make out what the two men were saying. She could hear nothing but the low drone of their voices, but her curiosity was well and truly piqued. The hinges on the library door, she knew, had been soaped only the day before when Darcy complained that the door squeaked abominably.

Giving no thought whatever to the impropriety of her action, she set her wax cloth upon the table and began slowly to turn the handle. So intent was she upon not making any noise herself that she did not notice when the sound of voices within the room ceased, but suddenly the latch was snatched from her grasp. Gasping with shock, she glanced up to find Beck looking sardonically down at her.

53

"Did you wish to see his lordship, my lady?" the valet asked with mock politeness.

Sarah straightened, wiping suddenly sweating palms on the once white apron she wore over her sprig muslin round gown. Her things had arrived as promised the Tuesday following the wedding, but Sarah's clothes were mostly for show and were highly impractical for housework. Her hair had nearly driven her crazy the first few days, until one of the maidservants had provided her with the mob cap. Even then, her heavy tresses kept escaping their confines. As a last resort, she had allowed Penny to braid her hair into two thick plaits with curling ends, which were easily tucked under the cap and pinned in place.

She was not thinking of her appearance at the moment, however, because at Beck's words, Darcy had risen quickly to his feet from the heavy oak chair behind the desk, his eyes wide with a mixture of consternation and astonishment. "Sarah! What on earth!"

Sarah entered reluctantly and approached the desk to face him. She was not surprised to discover that her knees were quaking, for she was appalled at herself and filled with remorse to think that she had actually been guilty of eavesdropping, something no true lady would ever lower herself to do. To be carried away by curiosity, not a pretty quality in itself, was certainly no excuse for such reprehensible behavior, and Darcy would be quite right to censure her. Perhaps, she thought with a sudden surge of anxiety, he might even beat her! Aunt Aurelia would certainly have done so, had Sarah been guilty of such an impropriety while living at Hartley House!

"Forgive me, my lord," she said in a low tone, her eyes downcast.

Darcy took his seat again and cocked his head curiously. "Do you make a habit of listening at doors, my dear? I should have thought Lady Hartley would have nipped such rag manners firmly in the bud." She flushed deeply at this uncanny echo of her own thoughts, and he went on evenly, "Don't approve of it myself, you know. Can't think of anything more likely to displease me in a servant, let alone a wife."

He paused a moment, watching her intently, but when Sarah opened her mouth to speak, to try to defend the indefensible, he silenced her with a gesture. "I am disappointed in you, Sarah. Thought you had better manners."

"I'm terribly sorry, my lord," she replied, striving to maintain what was left of her dignity. "It was an impulse, and I am truly ashamed of myself."

"Perfectly understandable, Sarah. You ought to be ashamed." But his tone was vague. Beck stood just behind her. He had said nothing, but now, Darcy seemed to look past her, sending his man a rather quizzical look, and Sarah had the odd notion that they were carrying on a sort of silent conversation. It made her uncomfortable at first, then irritated her.

"Could we not discuss this matter privately, my lord?" she asked, controlling her voice carefully. She was scarcely in a position to make demands, yet surely he must see that he ought not to scold her in front of his valet!

"It seems to me," he said now, "that Beck and I were trying to discuss a matter privately before you popped onto the scene. The man's got a right to know what you were doing there." Sarah's ears burned at the reproof, and she knew Beck was staring at her, but she would not give him the satisfaction of knowing how his presence unmanned her. She straightened her shoulders and kept her eyes firmly fixed upon her husband.

"What . . . what are you going to d-do?" she asked, annoyed by the slight stammer that betrayed her nervousness.

"Well, I shall have to consider the matter," Darcy replied, leaning back in the chair and lacing his fingers together under his chin.

"His late lordship would no doubt have punished anyone he caught listening in on a private conversation," Beck put in. "Most severely."

His tone was positively silky, Sarah thought, scarcely able to believe her ears. That Darcy could discuss such a thing with a servant! It was intolerable! Her first reaction was to protest, but the words died unspoken. It would do no good at all and would, indeed, be far more likely to set up his back, to trigger that streak of obstinacy that had made things so difficult at the outset. He would not appreciate any backchat from her, not in Beck's presence. It would be far wiser, if a great deal more difficult, to tread lightly.

She had no reason to think Darcy a particularly violent man, but she had come to realize in the past days that Beck did exert an odd sort of influence over his master. If he pressed for punishment and Sarah could not succeed in placating her husband, servant or not, Beck might well turn the trick.

"Man's quite right, you know, Sarah," Darcy observed. "M' father would have been dashed severe upon such an occasion.

But can't decide what to do without knowing exactly what you overheard." He spoke casually, but she sensed that her reply would be important to him. With the threat of possible punishment hanging over her, it was a bit difficult to collect her thoughts, but she made the effort. Perhaps, if he knew that she had heard nothing special, he would not be harsh with her.

"I heard nothing that made any sense to me, my lord," she answered, choosing her words with care, and pointedly giving her back to the valet. "There was only one point where I was able to decipher words at all. I heard Beck say something about money meaning nothing to him, and then you said he was to do as he was told. Everything else was quite muffled. I'm afraid that is why I was opening the door. I still cannot believe I was capable of doing such a thing. You are very right to be angry with me, sir, but I beg of you——"

"Talking will pay no toll," Beck interrupted harshly. "How can we trust what she says, my lord?"

"I believe her," Darcy replied, somewhat hesitantly, Sarah thought. "She's got no reason to lie, has she?"

"We can't know that, can we? Besides, even if she heard nothing today, we can't take the chance she might do such a thing again. 'Specially now that her curiosity's been aroused."

As indeed it had. Sarah still did not turn to look at Beck, but his tone made her skin crawl. She wondered what in the world the two men could have been discussing that would make them react so strenuously to her eavesdropping. Shame had quite given way to her natural inquisitiveness, and snapping an imaginary finger at the proprieties involved, she privately decided that she would seize whatever opportunity arose to discover what these two were up to. Her expression must have given her thoughts away, for Darcy's eyes narrowed, and he turned slightly in his chair.

"Perhaps Beck is right. Come round here to me, Sarah." Not knowing precisely what he had in mind, Sarah hesitated, and Darcy glanced past her at Beck. She had the sudden feeling that the valet would force her into compliance with her husband's request, and that might well have been the case had the front windows of the library not been wide open, allowing the sound of an approaching vehicle to divert them all.

A light racing curricle painted sunshine yellow, its wheels picked out in orange, its seat covered with polished leather, hove into view through the framework of trees lining the now nearly pristine drive. Sarah's breath caught in her throat at the sight of its driver, a gentleman in a many-caped driving cloak who flicked his whip back, caught the thong neatly, and slipped the handle into its lock before drawing up in front of the house with all the flair of a nonesuch.

"My God, it's Nick!" Darcy exclaimed. "What the devil is he doing here?"

Sarah stared out the window, unconsciously taking in the full scene—the brilliantly colored curricle, the team of magnificent chestnuts now pawing and champing at bits as though poised for flight instead of ending a journey, the diminutive tiger perched up behind the driver—but she was mindful only of the driver himself.

Sir Nicholas Ashton was a tall gentleman with fair, curly hair that was cropped short and worn in a cherubim style. The cloak made his shoulders look even broader than Sarah remembered them to be, and beneath it, it could be seen that he wore cream-colored pantaloons and brightly polished Hessians. As he handed the reins to his tiger and swung down from the curricle, his mouth was set in grim lines, and his deep-voiced orders to take the rig around to the stables came clearly to the threesome still frozen in place in the library.

Suddenly and most painfully aware of her untidy appearance, Sarah came to life, snatching the mob cap from her head. "Please, sir," she begged, turning pleading eyes to her husband, "may I be excused?"

He nodded. "Go to your bedchamber. We'll discuss this matter properly once I've got rid of him."

Sarah escaped thankfully, taking the stairs nearly two at a time. She looked back from the landing to see Beck watching her as though to make sure she had reached the gallery before he opened the front door. A moment later, Sir Nicholas strode into the hall, his capes swinging. There was no sign now of the grimness she had noted earlier.

"Ho, Beck, you old scoundrel!" he boomed heartily. "Where's your master?"

"Here, Nick." Darcy spoke from the library threshold, and Sarah stepped further back into the shadows, lest any of them glance up and somehow catch a glimpse of her there. She was eavesdropping again, of course, but she could no more have torn herself away than she could have flown. "What do you want here?"

Darcy's tone was barely civil, and Sir Nicholas grinned at him. "Don't overdo your welcome, my lord. I've come to pay a bride visit, of course. The news was devilish slow catching me, but once I heard you'd managed to get yourself leg-shackled, I had to pay my respects." He cast a glance around the hall. "Where's your bride?"

"Upstairs, I daresay," Darcy replied carelessly. "Do you stay to dine?"

Sir Nicholas laughed. "Dine! I hope to impose longer than that. I'm to collect young Colin for the long vacation at the end of the week. I'd as lief not go to Town and back again, if you don't mind."

"Suit yourself. Hope your tiger's prepared to see to your wants though, because I'm mighty short-handed at the moment, and Beck is going up to London for a day or so. Besides, he's already doing a good bit more than he's paid for."

"Does he get paid now?" Sir Nicholas asked innocently. "Must be a welcome change for him, since you'd never a feather to fly with before. But don't mind me. Dasher will be along soon enough with my gear. He'll look after me."

"Dasher! You still keep that clodpole?"

"Dear me," Sir Nicholas sighed, "I'd no notion you were so niffy-naffy in your ways. Dasher suits mine well enough, I assure you. Is there wine in this establishment? My throat could stand a wetting, if it's not too much to ask."

"Bring it into the library, Beck." Darcy sounded almost sullen as he stood aside to let his uncle precede him into that room. Sarah waited only until Beck had disappeared through the green baize door before hastening in search of Penny.

To her dismay, she found her companion laid down upon her bed with a sick headache. Penny's face was drawn and pale, and Sarah exclaimed aloud at the sight of her. "Penny! What on earth have you done to yourself?"

" 'Tis only one of my stupid migraines, my dear. I shall be right as a trivet by tomorrow, I daresay, if only I have a care for myself now. But don't get into a tizzy over it. You know these things pass quickly."

Sarah did know. Miss Penistone was rarely ever sick, but she had had such headaches several times in the past, and Sarah knew the only cure was complete bedrest until the thing had disappeared entirely. Clearly, no one had informed Penny of Sir Nicholas's arrival, and Sarah quickly decided that she must not do so now. Penny would insist upon getting up to help her dress for dinner at the very least, and that would be most unwise for her in her present condition. Therefore, she made soothing noises, promised to send one of the maids in later to be sure everything was all right, then tucked her in and wished her good night. "For you must be absolutely quiet, Penny, so that you will be your old self tomorrow. You have been working entirely too hard. We simply must have more help, so you won't feel obligated to do so much yourself. However, we shall say no more about it now. Just you go to sleep. Can I get you anything at all? A tisane, perhaps?" But Penny declined the offer and closed her eyes gratefully. Drawing the curtains to shut out the glare of the rapidly sinking sun, Sarah left her to her rest.

Sorry though she was for dear Penny, she readily admitted that the indisposition could not have come at a more inopportune time. Sarah wanted to look her best for dinner, and she simply could not manage the details by herself. On the thought, she set out in search of the most obliging of the three housemaids, finding her at last in one of the second-floor bedchambers.

"Betsy, quickly!" she urged. "Find out from Matty or Tom which of the bedrooms belongs to Sir Nicholas, and set one of the other girls to preparing it for him. Oh, and warn them both that they are to say nothing of his arrival to Miss Penistone. She must have her rest. Then I shall want a bath. And hurry! I'll need you to help me dress for dinner."

The girl bobbed a curtsy and fled, and Sarah returned to her own room to examine her wardrobe. Rejecting a lovely gown of virginal white silk embroidered with silver bugle beads at the bodice and another of cream-colored satinette embellished with a rose-pink sash, she chose instead a gown of which her aunt had disapproved strongly. Sarah had ordered it anyway and had had to submit to a blistering scold as a result, but she was glad now that she had held out. At least this gown would not make her look like a maid fresh from the schoolroom. She held it up and regarded her mirrored self with approval.

It was a simple affair of gold satin with a high waist, short puffed sleeves, and a slim skirt with a gathered demitrain. The neckline, scooping dangerously low both back and front, was trimmed with delicate Brussels lace, but there was no further decoration. Instinctively, Sarah knew that Sir Nicholas would like this elegant confection. She did not spare a thought for her husband's potential reaction.

Betsy returned with the news that Tom and one of the stableboys would soon be bringing hot water.

"Betsy, do you think you can do my hair?"

"I can try, my lady," the girl said doubtfully, "but I've not much know-how when it comes to London ways."

With a sinking feeling, Sarah looked at her. "Surely, you could contrive something!" She could not wear the golden dress with her hair all tumbled down her back. It would defeat the whole purpose. "Maybe I can help."

"Maybe. But 'tis an awful lot of hair, ma'am, if you don't mind me sayin' so."

"Well, I cannot cut it off," Sarah stated firmly. "And we've nothing to crimp it with even if I did. We shall simply have to contrive." But an hour later as she sat in her wrapper before her mirror, glowing warmly from her bath, she shook her head in frustration. Betsy had brushed her hair till the tresses shone like spun gold, but now she seemed to be at a loss.

"What does your woman do next, my lady?"

Sarah grimaced, trying to remember. Lizzie never seemed to do anything special. Her fingers just twisted here and tucked there until the thing was done. Penny was not nearly so clever about it, but the outcome of her labor was always neat and becoming. "I don't know, Betsy," she confessed forlornly. "I'm afraid I never paid much attention to the how of it—only the results."

"Well, I wears mine down me back or pushed into me cap, ma'am. Don't know much else 'cept plaitin', and I doubt you wants that."

"No . . . that is . . ." Sarah stared at her reflection as a glimmer of an idea came to her. She closed her eyes tightly, struggling to remember. When she opened them again, they sparkled. "Betsy, do you think you could make two plaits, braiding very tightly and pulled up as you go?"

Betsy nodded slowly, the expression on her face indicating that she thought it a rather odd notion. She began to part Sarah's hair down the middle.

" 'Tis a style I saw in *La Belle Assemblée* last month," Sarah explained. "They call it *à la Didon*, and it looks like a crown when it's done. The two plaits are wound so—" She indicated with her hand, drawing a halo around the top of her head. "—and they had it decked out with diamond pins and feathers and such, but I daresay it would look well enough plain. Do you think you could manage that?"

Betsy thought for a moment and then pronounced that she could, like as not. She was as good as her word, and the third attempt proved satisfactory. There were, as indeed there always seemed to be, various fine wisps of hair that refused to be confined. They curled instead around Sarah's ears and the nape of her neck, but she decided that these enhanced the style and left them alone. Slipping off the wrapper, she let Betsy help her into the silken chemise that went with the gown and then into the gown itself.

" 'Tis a lovely thing, my lady," Betsy breathed solemnly as she did up the tiny, satin-covered buttons in the back. "Makes you look like you was made of gold, it does."

Chuckling, Sarah thanked her, fastened a short strand of milky pearls around her throat, and slipped her feet into golden sandals. With a frowning look into the glass, she decided something was missing and, taking up a lacy shawl of Albany gauze, draped it so that it was caught up casually at her elbows. Satisfied that she looked the part of the elegant young bride, she dismissed Betsy and carefully seated herself to await her summons. It seemed only moments later that the young maid reappeared to inform her that she was wanted below.

As she descended the stairs, Sarah wondered how Sir Nicholas would behave. Normally, he had an abrupt way of ordering one about or of disapproving of one's behavior. And he was such a demon for propriety that, when she had realized it was truly he in the flashy curricle, she had thought there would be the devil of a row. But then, he had seemed completely relaxed when he spoke to Darcy, so now she knew not what to expect.

She found the gentlemen in the library. Darcy looked a bit glum, but Sir Nicholas was speaking quite amiably when she opened the door. His voice broke off at her entrance, and his gaze met hers. The look in his eyes caused her to tilt her chin a little higher.

"Good evening, Sir Nicholas," she said calmly. "How nice to see you again."

Both gentlemen got to their feet, and Sir Nicholas stepped forward to bow over her hand. "Charmed, Lady Moreland. Permit me to say that married life seems to agree with you."

"Thank you, sir." He released her hand immediately and turned away, much to Sarah's disappointment. How irritating of him, she thought, to show so little feeling. There had not been the faintest trace of jealousy in his tone. He had seemed, if anything, a trifle amused.

"Wine, Sarah?" Something in Darcy's voice made her look at him sharply, and she wondered if he were thinking of their earlier confrontation. But he did not seem angry or even annoyed exactly. His attitude was more like something she would associate with a child, though she was unable to identify it more closely than that. Consequently, she dismissed it as a mere case of nerves, for she knew he stood somewhat in awe of Sir Nicholas.

Smiling at him now, she moved to seat herself on the small settee near his chair. "Please, my lord, something light." Sir Nicholas leaned against the mantel shelf, watching them both. "Do you abide with us long, sir?" she asked him.

"A few days only, my lady."

"We missed you in Town." Darcy handed her her wineglass. "Thank you, my lord. I trust nothing was wrong, Sir Nicholas?"

"A minor irritation, ma'am, I assure you," he said evenly. "Family matters necessitated a brief visit to Yorkshire."

"Her ladyship's in the briars again, I take it," Darcy observed with a rather forced laugh. Sir Nicholas's gaze seemed to flick him on the raw, for his cheeks reddened, but the older man's voice remained placid enough.

"Not at all. My mother merely plans to follow your example."

"Mine!"

"Aye. And that of our beloved Princess. She means to get riveted again."

"Good Lord!"

"My sentiments precisely," Sir Nicholas agreed. "Hence, my bolt to Yorkshire. However, you will be as pleased as I was to learn that the match is perfectly eligible. She means to marry Packwood."

"What, that bag-pudding?"

"I'll thank you to show a bit more respect for my future father-in-law," said Sir Nicholas, grinning now. "He may be a bag-pudding, but he's very well to pass, you know."

"Oh, aye, he's rich enough, I suppose." Darcy's tone indicated that wealth was a minor asset, but beyond a glint of mockery in his eye, Sir Nicholas made no comment. Beck having already departed for Town, it was Tom who entered a moment later to announce that dinner was served, and Sarah wondered briefly whose arm she would grace. But Sir Nicholas made no move to claim a guest's privilege before Darcy took her hand possessively in his and placed it firmly upon his forearm.

Neither gentleman made a push beyond commonplace small

talk at dinner. Sir Nicholas commented appreciatively upon the progress made in putting the house to rights but was tactful enough, Sarah noticed, to say nothing that might indicate disapproval of Darcy's having allowed the place to go to rack and ruin in the first place. All in all, she thought, as she left them to their port, it was turning into a very boring evening. She wandered back to the library, certain that the gentlemen would soon join her there. They were a long time coming, however, so she had plenty of time to think.

She could not fathom Sir Nicholas's behavior. He seemed almost not to care a button that she had supposedly run away with his cousin. Aside from the one brief remark, he had not mentioned their marriage at all. Really, now she came to think of it, he could be most annoying!

But if Sir Nicholas had behaved oddly, so too had Darcy. He had seemed relaxed enough during dinner, but he had displayed moments of irritation and possessiveness toward herself that Sarah was at a loss to understand. She had put herself out to show Sir Nicholas that she was pleased to be Lady Moreland, not so much to placate Darcy, of course, as to show Sir Nicholas that he was nothing more than an ordinary guest to her. It was rather distressing, however, that he had accepted the role so easily. Darcy, on the other hand, seemed one moment to approve of her behavior and the next to view it with suspicion. Oh well, she thought now with a sigh, it was done. Sir Nicholas now knew her to be a happily married woman, and if she handled her husband right, there was no reason why she should not become just that. And why that idea should be such a depressing one, she was at a loss to say.

She sighed again, heavily. She would have liked to go to bed or at least to go upstairs to check on Penny. But she forced herself to remain where she was. To go at once, while the gentlemen still lingered over their port, might seem rude.

At that moment the door opened from the hall, and to her surprise, Darcy entered alone. It was clear from his uncertain navigation that he had had a great deal to drink and, from his expression, that he had come to her with a firm purpose in mind. Sarah gathered her resources to meet what was rapidly beginning to look like a difficult situation.

VI

"So here you are," Darcy said almost belligerently, his words slurring badly.

"As you see, my lord," Sarah returned calmly. "Where is Sir Nicholas?"

Dacry grimaced. "Aye, you'd like to know, wouldn't you? Trickin' yourself out like a damned trollop for him, as you have!" He kicked the door shut behind him.

Sarah's temper flared at his language, but she managed to suppress the stinging retort that rose to her lips, saying temperately instead, "I am sorry you feel that way, my lord. I thought only to spare us all embarrassment by making it appear that you and I are happy together."

"You didn't rig yourself out like a damned golden statue to please me, Sarah, and don't think you can cozen me into thinking otherwise. I'm not a bloody knock-in-the-cradle. You did it for Nick!"

"Why . . . how dare you, sir!" She was shocked by the venom in his voice, but even more so by his accusation. Surely, she had done no such thing! But then, honesty intruded, bringing a delicate flush to her cheeks. Perhaps she had not intentionally flirted with Sir Nicholas, but she could not deny having tried to stir his jealousy. From Darcy's point of view, would that not amount to the same thing in the long run?

He poured himself a glass of brandy, sloshing as much onto the desk as into the glass. When she fell abruptly silent, he sneered. "How dare I, indeed! As though it weren't enough that I must submit to a trimming from Nick——"

"A trimming!"

"A damned impertinent lecture! Harped at me like a blasted schoolmaster!"

"What did he say?" If Sir Nicholas had ripped up at him, no wonder he was so out of curl now!

"That's none of your affair," Darcy replied with great dignity. Then he rather spoiled the effect by muttering, "Said an elopement must cast a blot upon the family escutcheon, or some such addled rot."

"Well, neither an elopement nor an abduction is exactly the height of propriety," Sarah pointed out.

"Well, he don't know about any abduction!" Darcy snapped. "And don't you go putting any such notions in his head either, Sarah, or it will be the worse for you. Dash it! I'm your husband, ain't I?"

"You are, sir."

"Well, don't forget it. Just because I made some damn fool promises. . . ." He broke off, swallowed his brandy, and stared at her speculatively over the top of his glass.

His gaze made her nervous. She knew he had imbibed a great deal and wondered how much more he could hold. There was a scratching at one of the French doors, as Erebus asked politely to be let into the warmth. Darcy, still staring at Sarah, didn't seem to hear him, and Sarah ignored him. There was a new feeling in the air, and her defenses were aroused. She eyed her husband warily. He raised his glass in a toasting gesture. Then, noticing that it was empty, he banged it down on the desk again and attempted to refill it. But his hands shook, spilling brandy every which way.

"The hell with it!" he exclaimed at last, sending glass and decanter spinning to the floor. "To hell with stupid promises, too!" And despite his shaking hands and tipsy gait, there was a glint of purpose in his eye as he advanced upon her.

With a gasp of dismay, Sarah recognized his intent, and scrambling hastily to her feet, she moved away from him. "My lord, please consider! Your promise! You must not do this!"

"Must not, shall not," he mocked in a sing-song voice, following unsteadily as she backed away from him. "Everyone tells me how to behave. But I'll be damned if I'll stand peaceably by whilst you seduce Sir Blasted Nicholas under my very nose. Our agreement is at an end. I am your husband," he insisted, his words slurring, "and, by Jove, you shall honor the connection with no interference from Nick!"

Sarah had managed to get behind one of the chairs near the fireplace and was attempting to keep it between them. Darcy's eyes began to develop a glazed look, and he seemed to sway from side to side. Perhaps, if she could just keep him talking long enough, Sir Nicholas would come, or Darcy would simply pass out.

"You are raving, my lord," she said now, more calmly than she felt. "I am your wife and must, if you insist upon it, submit to your demands. But not like this. Your own sense of honor would make you sorry for it once you are yourself again. Besides, there is no reason for it. I have not tried to seduce Sir Nicholas, nor would he respond if I did. He would never interfere between you and your wife."

"Can't interfere," snickered Darcy, grasping at the single word. "Not here. Gone to visit our old Nanny Bates. All the way to the village. Won't be back for an hour or more." He swayed again, but then, as Sarah moved in the opposite direction, he suddenly lunged toward her, his hand clamping around her upper arm with incredible strength.

"Let me go!" she cried, trying to pull away. But it was no use. Inexorably, he pulled her toward him. But as she cried out again and began to struggle fiercely, there came a resounding crash against the nearest French door. Sarah's struggles ceased as both she and Darcy turned toward the sound. Erebus, plainly and vocally expressing his disapproval of the goings-on in the library, was already gathering his huge body for a second assault. Darcy's hold loosened, and it was all Sarah needed. Without a moment's thought or hesitation, she wrenched free of his grasp, planted both small hands firmly against his chest, and shoved with all her might. Toppling like a felled tree, Darcy struck his head against a hearthstone with a dull thud, then lay completely still.

Dismayed, Sarah dropped to her knees beside him. But a quick examination showed that he was breathing steadily, and although there was a rapidly rising lump on the back of his head, there seemed to be no blood. Letting out a deep sigh of relief, she got to her feet again, wondering if she ought to send for Tom. Darcy probably ought to be got to bed, but on the other hand, he would be coming to his senses soon, and she had no wish to be present when he did. Until he had shaken off the effects of the brandy, it would be far better that she play least in sight. Otherwise, he might still demand a husband's rights, and there was no one who would interfere if he did.

The noise at the door had ceased, but now there came a single, sharp bark, and she glanced over to see Erebus sitting patiently upon the flagstones, tongue lolling and tail thumping. Thus reminded, she moved to the French door, unlatched it, and let the huge dog in, taking a firm grip on his collar to prevent a curious advance upon his fallen master. A cold, wet tongue in the face was only too likely to bring Darcy to his senses before she was safely out of the way. But Erebus was pleased enough to follow her upstairs. Pausing briefly at Miss Penistone's door, Sarah looked in with a brief hope that that lady might be awake. But Penny was sleeping deeply. Sarah moved on to her own bedchamber, closing and automatically locking the door behind her. With Erebus trailing happily behind her, she stepped to the window to look out at the courtyard, thinking that Sir Nicholas or even Tom might approach from that direction. Whoever discovered him first would surely help Darcy to his bed, and with any luck at all, he would not, when he awoke, remember the events preceding his accident.

But twenty minutes later, there was still no sign of anyone, and there had certainly been no sounds to indicate that Darcy had been helped upstairs. Finally, her curiosity got the better of her, and she got up, adjusted the thin shawl carefully around her shoulders, and moved slowly toward the door. Except for the click of the dog's claws on the hardwood floor as he trailed behind her, the house seemed entirely silent.

She reached the door and hesitated. Having got herself out of a sticky situation, it would be sheer foolhardiness to put herself back in the lion's den, so to speak. But she could not sit still while her thoughts played merry havoc with the possibilities. The worst one, of course, was that perhaps Darcy had injured himself more seriously than she had thought, but the simple fact of the matter was that she could not bear not to know what was going on.

One hand on the latch, the other reaching for the key, she turned to gaze at her furry companion. "I am no doubt a fool, Erebus," she said softly, shaking her head with a wry smile when he wagged his tail. "All right, then. But I hope you know enough to protect me if I need it." A moment later, she pulled the door slowly open.

With Erebus at her side, she made her way to the first floor without incident. But she had taken only a step or two toward the gallery landing when suddenly the stillness was shattered by a barely muffled explosion of sound. Sarah froze, but the big dog's ears lifted, and surging forward, he began to bark as though he would rouse all the inhabitants of the Common. Bounding down the stairs, he came to a skidding halt at the library door, only to demand entry by scratching madly at the wooden panels.

Sarah followed more slowly. After that one loud noise, silence had fallen again except for the noise of Erebus's onslaught. She wondered why no one else seemed to have heard the explosion. The maidservants had, no doubt, retired to their rooms at the top of the house, but Tom at least ought to be about somewhere.

"Hush, Erebus." She laid a hand upon the dog's broad head, and he seemed to understand her, falling silent as she reached to open the door. Sarah gripped his collar to prevent him from bursting into the room as well as to keep him near enough to protect her against whatever or whomever she might find.

At first, since her gaze moved directly to the solitary pillow lying on the hearth, the room seemed empty. She noted briefly that the French doors were standing wide open. Then, she saw him. He was no longer lying in front of the fireplace, to be sure. Instead, he was lying, face down, in front of his desk.

Clapping a hand over her mouth, Sarah managed to stifle the scream in her throat as she moved closer. She loosed her hold on the dog, who promptly bounded into the night through the open door, but she scarcely noticed his barking. Her attention was focused on Darcy.

Did he breathe? She could tell nothing by looking at him. She knelt beside him and felt at once the sticky, wet stuff soaking through her skirt from the carpet. Her hand came away red with blood.

"Darcy! My lord, answer me!" As she grasped his shoulder, shaking it, trying to turn him, she saw the pistol. It lay between him and the desk, and dazed, Sarah reached to pick it up. She was as certain as she could be that he was dead. Still clutching the pistol and feeling rather sick, she got to her feet. A sudden chill shot up her spine, giving her gooseflesh, and without taking her eyes off the body, she clutched her shawl more closely around her shoulders.

"Foolish beyond permission, madam, but I must admit I wondered how long it would be before you murdered him."

Sarah nearly jumped out of her skin, whirling and dropping the pistol as though her fingers had been scorched. "Sir Nicholas!"

He stepped in through the open French doors, regarding

her with narrowed eyes. "I trust you had good reason for this, my lady."

She had been staring at him as though he were a specter, and it took a moment for his words to penetrate. Then, even though she knew what he meant, it was as though her brain refused to accept it.

"But . . . I . . . he . . . it's not as you——"

" 'Tis plain as a pikestaff what happened here," he said grimly, moving closer but eyeing her warily as a new thought struck him. "I don't suppose you've got the mate to that pistol in your possession? I've no wish to join Darcy in hell." She shook her head, still struggling with his original accusation. Why was it that that particular tone of his always had the power to reduce her insides to jelly, to deprive her of the ability to think clearly?

"Please, Sir Nicholas . . . I didn't——"

"Don't bother denying it, madam. What with that dog running loose outside, there's no way a footpad got in here to do this. I shall help you all I can, but we'll never wrap this business in clean linen." He moved past her to examine the body. "Shot through the heart," he observed, turning the body over. "A pretty piece of shooting."

Strangling a frustrated sob, Sarah turned away, bringing both hands to her eyes to blot out the brief vision of bloodstains across Darcy's white shirt. Sir Nicholas got to his feet, fastidiously wiping his fingers upon a linen handkerchief. He glanced at Sarah, and his eyes narrowed speculatively. She faced away from him, her shawl clutched tightly around her, anchored at the elbows, her hands still covering her face. The expression in his eyes softened, and without a word, he stepped nearer to lay a gentle hand upon her shoulder.

"I trust you don't mean to subject me to a fit of the vapors, my lady, for we must talk."

Sarah stiffened at his touch, but her hands dropped away from her face, and turning to face him, she made a serious attempt to regain her composure. The shawl slipped, and she twitched it back into place, finding odd comfort in the familiar motion. "There is little to discuss, sir," she said with only a slight tremor in her voice. "If you persist in this——"

"There is much to discuss," he countered sharply. "I had thought you cared for Darcy, and yet——"

"Please, sir," Sarah interrupted with careful dignity. "My feelings toward his late lordship are immaterial at this point——"

"The devil they are!" he growled. "They must have had a great deal to do with the matter at hand." He gestured toward the body. "No doubt, you would like me to believe you had nothing at all to do with this. But I am not such a fool, my girl. You'd do better to——"

Sarah stamped her foot. *"Will* you be silent, sir! You must *listen* to me!"

Sir Nicholas gave her a searching stare. "Very well, but I cannot imagine what you think you can tell me that I shall swallow. Why, with that dog running loose——"

"Erebus was with me."

"With you!" His eyes narrowed as the full impact of the simple statement struck him. "Then, how——"

"I let go of his collar when I saw the body. He went out through those same doors. He was growling. Barking, too."

Sir Nicholas let out a long breath. "I see. Maybe you'd better tell me the whole." And not before time either, Sarah thought with a sigh. He took her hand and led her to the settee, seating her so that she faced the fireplace, away from the desk. Then he moved to shut the French doors, pausing before he fastened the lock to open one again. "Well, come in then. I suppose you've cleared the premises of all intruders by now." And Erebus, tongue hanging again and tail wagging, galumphed into the room and collapsed, panting, in front of the fireplace.

Sarah watched silently as Sir Nicholas selected a pair of clean glasses from a tray on the side table before turning toward the desk, where someone had replaced the heavy cut-glass decanter from the floor. Miraculously, it still retained nearly a third of its contents, and he poured out two brandies, then returned to her side. She protested rather feebly when he handed one of the glasses to her.

"Drink it," he ordered, but with a gentle note in his voice. "You've had a shock, and whether you know it or not, you need this. It will help calm the trembling in your hands and bring some color back into your cheeks." He stirred the coals with his boot, an action which his valet would no doubt roundly deplore, and then seated himself opposite her. "Drink, Countess."

Her hands *were* trembling. She hadn't noticed before. Obediently, she lifted the glass and sipped. The heady wine burned her throat and nearly made her choke, but she could feel the effect of its soothing powers almost before the first fireball hit her stomach. She glanced at Sir Nicholas. He seemed relaxed as he swirled his own brandy, giving her a chance to collect her thoughts. She wondered how to begin.

"Why on earth did you elope with him in the first place?"

It was all she needed. The story seemed to pour from her as she explained about the abduction and Grandpapa's ridiculous will. She could not bring herself to explain why she had encouraged Darcy in the first place, so she glossed over those details, and he did not press her. She told him nothing about the afternoon's affair either, merely stating that Darcy had already been displeased with her when Sir Nicholas arrived, that her dress and behavior at dinner had angered him further, and that they had quarreled. "I think he must have had quite a bit to drink, too," she added.

"He did," Sir Nicholas agreed grimly. "Then what?"

She told him that there had been a struggle. Since she left out most of the details, he responded with little more than a grimace. But when she added that, later, she had feared she might have hurt Darcy seriously, even killed him, Sir Nicholas set his glass down and got up, moving with quick, athletic grace to kneel beside the body again. Carefully, he examined Darcy's skull.

"There's a beautiful lump there all right," he said, "but it didn't break the skin, let alone his head. He may have been groggy when he was shot, but I'd swear he was on his feet. He was certainly alive, at any rate. No bullet ever brought that much blood from a dead man." He returned to his chair with a further order to finish her brandy and continue her tale.

Flushing, Sarah took another sip. It felt smoother going down, so she tried another. "That's all, sir. I let Erebus in and took him upstairs with me. I was a little afraid that Darcy might come looking for me. And, even if he did not, I expected someone to find him and put him to bed. But no one came, and that's when I began to wonder if I'd killed him after all. I was just coming to see when I heard the explosion."

"Pistol shot," he corrected. "I heard it, too, down at the stables. Came as quick as I could." He looked at her sharply. "Where were you exactly?"

"On the landing. Erebus just lurched downstairs, barking, and scratched at the door."

"So you could see the library door when you heard the shot?"

"Yes."

"And those French doors were open to the terrace?"

"When I came in. I'm sure I shut them earlier."

"No matter. Just means Darcy let someone in. Be quiet a moment now. I must think."

Sarah watched him. He was still sipping brandy and leaning once again against the mantel shelf. He looked strong and capable and relaxed, for all the world as though the fourth Earl of Moreland still breathed. A new thought entered her head, and she stared at Sir Nicholas with great intent.

"You are his heir."

The sharp blue gaze encountered her own. "If that means you think I'm responsible for this, you can put that silly maggot straight out——"

"No, no!" Sarah protested, shocked that he would think such a thing. "I only just realized that you are the new Earl of Moreland . . . my lord."

He relaxed again, a tiny smile just touching his lips. "I suppose I am at that," he said, then eyed her more sharply yet, "unless . . . is it possible that. . . ." He hesitated. "Pardon the indelicacy, my lady, but could you possibly be with child?"

Sarah blushed, shaking her head. "No, my lord."

"How can you be so certain?"

Flushing painfully, she turned away. "I'm sure," she said firmly.

Nicholas's eyes narrowed, but he spoke calmly enough. "Then, I suppose I'm the new earl. Who would have thought it? Certainly not Darcy. Nor I, for that matter." He looked a bit dazed by the notion, but the effect was momentary. He gazed down at the body again, speculatively.

"What shall we do, sir?"

He looked at her again. "You are going to finish your brandy and go to bed. No, don't argue. I'll take you up myself, if necessary, and lock you in."

"You wouldn't!"

"Don't be melodramatic," he advised her. "Of course I would. I suppose Tom's gone off somewhere. Someone will have to find him. I'll send Timmy, my tiger, for the nearest magistrate. I assume Sir William Miles still holds that position." Sarah confessed that she had no idea. "Well, Tom will know.

At any rate, you would be well advised to play least in sight. There's little I can do to prevent your being suspected of this, but I'll do my possible. The less anyone sees of you now, the better. So drink up."

Glaring, she demanded, "Why should anyone else suspect me?"

"Because he was shot with his own pistol. I recognized it and so will Tom. So will Beck, if anyone shows it to him. How would a housebreaker manage to kill Darcy with his own gun?"

She swallowed. "I don't know. But I didn't do it!"

"I know that now. And you are not alone, Countess."

Sarah smiled gratefully. "Could we not remove the pistol?"

"No," he replied firmly. "We will tell the truth. The facts may tell against you now, but when the answer is found, they will tell against the real criminal even more. If we monkey about with the evidence, we can only help him escape."

Little though she liked it, his argument made sense, so Sarah drank the rest of her brandy and stood up, casting a last glance at her husband's body. "It is difficult to believe he is dead," she said, half to herself.

"Send for your maidservant," Nicholas said harshly. "You should not be alone up there."

Reluctant to admit to him that she had no personal maidservant, Sarah only nodded and turned away toward the hall. Erebus trailed after her.

"Lock your door, Countess."

Sarah glanced back at him. "I will. G-good night, sir."

He said nothing at all, but as she wended her way back upstairs, Sarah had little fear of being hailed before the magistrate, despite his rather pessimistic warnings. It did not occur to her to wonder why she should trust a man whom she had hitherto thought to be censorious, overbearing, and dictatorial. She only knew that she did.

By the time she had locked herself in her room, she had begun to wonder what would become of her and nearly chuckled at the thought that she was now a dowager, the Dowager Countess of Moreland. The title sounded perfectly stuffy. But the next thought sobered her quickly. She could not stay here. Surely, the new Lord Moreland would expect to take up residence at Ash Park, principal seat of the earls of Moreland since whenever, and even Penny's presence would not be enough to make living in his house with him an acceptable option. No doubt, he would expect her to return to her aunt and uncle. Sarah plumped down on the window seat, depressed at the very thought.

Her window was slightly open, and she soon heard the sound of hoofbeats on the drive. That would be Timmy going for the magistrate. She didn't know the exact time, but it was surely after eleven and would be midnight before they returned. It would be as well if Sir Nicholas—no, she must remember now to think of him as Lord Moreland—could claim that she was asleep by then.

Accordingly, she undressed herself, grimacing at the sight of the bloodstains near the hem of her skirt. She wondered if Betsy would be clever enough to get them out so that she might wear the flattering gold dress again. But of course she would not be able to wear it anyway, she realized, as her spirits plunged to a new low. She would be expected to mourn her husband's death for at least a year!

Snuffing the candles, Sarah crept into bed, feeling very sorry for herself. What had she done to deserve such a fate? It was not fair that, at the tender age of seventeen, she should first be stolen away from the gaieties of London, then forced into marriage with a man like Darcy Ashton, and finally cast into widowhood with all its attendant restrictions without so much as a thought by anyone for her own wishes. How had it happened?

A tiny voice deep within whispered that it had happened because she had played foolish games, had willfully disregarded her aunt's very sensible warnings, and had defied a cardinal rule of respectability by getting into a closed carriage with a gentleman. In other words, the tiny voice insisted, refusing to be stifled, the whole business was Sarah's own fault.

Knowing the voice spoke only the truth did nothing to make the accusations more palatable, but she virtuously decided then and there that in future she would heed the advice of those who had her best interests at heart, that she would never again give way to impulse, that she would strictly curb her willfulness. Sarah might have sunk even more deeply into the arms of self-pity, had she not suddenly shocked herself by gripping the pillow and wishing that whoever had murdered her husband had seen fit to do so before that damned assignation in Bond Street!

Caught up by the wicked thought, she came to her senses and began to think more practically about her situation. What were her options? At first, there seemed to be none, except to return to Berkeley Square and beg forgiveness for her sins. Then she thought that perhaps she might convince Miss Penistone that the two of them should find a cottage somewhere—not London—and set up housekeeping. They would need money, but surely Darcy had made arrangements for an independence—an annuity or something—or perhaps her grandfather's money would now come to her. These thoughts and others spun around her mind, and though she had been certain she would not sleep a wink, she soon drifted off.

No one disturbed her slumber, and she awoke much refreshed the following morning. The sky was clear, and birds sang cheerfully in the trees outside her window, so it was no wonder that she did not immediately recall the events of the previous evening. When she did, however, she jumped out of bed with a sense of dismay and a burning curiosity to know what had taken place while she slept.

Dressing quickly in a simple sprig muslin morning gown, she tied back her hair with a ribbon and sallied forth to find the new Lord Moreland in the breakfast parlor. Nicholas smiled at her and gestured toward a rather bulky gentleman standing near the sideboard.

"Good morning, my lady. May I present my man, Dasher? He has agreed to serve us this morning, since Beck is absent, and I thought it would be a deal more comfortable for you than if Tom were to do so. You may say what you like in his presence. As Darcy so inelegantly used to phrase it, Dasher's as close as an onion. Besides, I've very few secrets from him."

"How do you do, Dasher?"

"His lordship is very kind, my lady." With these brief words he turned his attention to the preparation of her breakfast plate, while Nicholas himself rose to seat her.

"I trust you slept well."

"Yes, thank you. But what happened? You must tell me everything."

There was little enough to tell. Sir William Miles, the magistrate, was reserving judgment for lack of telltale evidence. Pressed, his lordship admitted that the magistrate had asked a pointed question or two regarding Sarah's part in the affair but had accepted his request that she not be wakened. "I told him the truth," he added, "that you were in a state of shock and needed your rest. He wants to see you sometime today, however."

"Oh!" She had hoped never to have to think about the details again. "Must I?"

"You must. There's nothing to worry about. He is a gentleman and won't accuse you of anything. He merely wants to hear what you can tell him."

"Very well," she said meekly, thereby clearing the first hurdle of accepting someone else's advice. Nothing further was said while Dasher served her breakfast, but once he had poured out her tea, Sarah gathered her courage to broach the subject preying hardest upon her mind. "I suppose you will be wanting to send me back to London as soon as possible," she said, carefully casual.

VII

Nicholas set down his cup, his eyes narrowing. "Why the devil would I send you back to London?"

"Well, I certainly cannot stay here!"

"Why not?"

"I cannot believe you would ask, my lord," Sarah declared roundly. "You, who are forever preaching proprieties, should certainly realize that it would be most improper for me to remain here with you. Or do you not mean to take up residence here?"

"Certainly, I mean to take up residence. This place is crying out for proper management. But the one fact needn't preclude the other. You will naturally remove to Dower House."

"Dower House?"

"Of course. Surely, you've inspected it. I'm sure it needs a touch or two to make it habitable, but that needn't take long."

Sarah had a vague memory that Darcy had mentioned a Dower House, but she had assumed it must have fallen down, or burned, or suffered some other disaster, since she had never seen it. She was very much surprised to learn that it lay not fifty yards off the library terrace. The fact that she had never discovered it for herself was easily explained, since she had rarely left the house, and the thick growth of trees between the two dwellings rendered Dower House invisible from all but the uppermost windows of the main house.

Directly after breakfast, his lordship announced that he would take her over Dower House himself. Passing through the library doors onto the terrace, they soon discovered that Darcy's gardeners had evidently had no orders to clear the path, which was nearly overgrown. Nicholas went ahead, breaking branches in an attempt to make passage easier for Sarah, but she snagged her skirt more than once. Her curiosity

77

overcame any annoyance she might otherwise have felt, however.

The house itself, when it came into view, was a neat, three-story, white brick and half-timber structure with broad stone steps leading up to a wide veranda and double doors of heavy, carved oak. The entry was flanked by two projecting window bays.

Nicholas pushed open the front doors, clearly astonished to find them unlocked, but a hall floor thick with dust and walls hung with cobwebs seemed to indicate that no one had been next or nigh the place in months, if not years.

"This is disgraceful," he muttered.

Sarah could only agree as she followed him through a door on their right into what had been a drawing room in better days. Curtains hanging at the windows were so thin and faded that it was impossible to tell what their original color or material had been, and there was no furniture. Across the hall, the dining room was in similar shape. The floors were dry, cracked in places, and the whole place smelled of dust and mildew.

His lordship gazed at the peeling, green baize door leading to the kitchens and then at the cobweb-strewn staircase and announced that he had seen enough.

"So have I," Sarah agreed. "It is clearly uninhabitable, so you shall have to send me back to Berkeley Square after all."

"Nonsense. I shall do nothing of the sort. There is nothing wrong here that a proper cleaning, some wax, and some paint won't cure. I cannot permit you to return to London just yet."

"Permit! Who are you to talk of permitting me to do anything, my lord? You have no authority over me!"

"Perhaps not," he agreed equably. "Perhaps you have resources of which I am unaware."

"Resources?"

"Of course. Do you have money of your own, or do you expect Lord Hartley to frank you?"

"But, Grandpapa's money! Some of it must come to me now!"

"Not unless you have misstated the facts of his will, my lady," he said grimly. "As I understand it, the money was left directly to my nephew without qualification. Is that not so?" Sarah nodded. "Then that money comes to me, not to you. I am, as you noted yourself last night, Darcy's heir."

"You! But there must be something for me!" she protested.

"Grandpapa never meant me to be penniless, and he certainly never meant his money to go out of the family entirely."

Nicholas's voice held gentle scorn. "I personally think Sir Malcolm Lennox-Matthews was missing some links here and there, and you already know what I thought of my nephew. At least, you don't, but you may rest assured that I had little respect for him. He was a loose screw, but he did at one time or another make a will. Not only am I his heir, but he also commended his wife, should he die possessed of one, to my care and his children, ditto, to my guardianship. So you see, my lady, since I doubt he ever got round to changing things, I do have authority for my decisions."

"I see." Sarah gritted her teeth. "Does that mean that I shall be wholly dependent upon you, my lord?"

"I devoutly hope not," he asserted. "I shall go up to Town immediately and speak to your grandfather's man of affairs. Perhaps there is something or other of which we are unaware. However, should it prove to be as I fear it will, I shall settle enough on you to keep you comfortable here without having to come to me for every groat."

"Thank you, my lord. But must I stay here?"

"Where would you go?" he countered.

"Anywhere. Oh, not London, but away from here."

"I cannot permit it," he repeated, holding the front door open for her. "I don't mean to be harsh or unfeeling, and I hope you will try to understand. There will be scandal attached to Darcy's death, and there is already gossip about your unusual marriage. At least that was nearly made respectable, since there was no flight to the border, and your uncle made his little show of approval. But you must do nothing now to give that tale the lie. If you go haring off, who will believe you the grieving widow?"

"Could I not grieve just as well in Paris?"

He grinned down at her cynical expression. "I doubt it. And you are much too young to try such a thing on your own. I'm afraid that you must accept me in place of a guardian, ma'am, for you are under age yourself, and willy-nilly, you are now part of my family. I am legally responsible for your welfare."

Sarah saw that once again she would have to submit. The only person who had any power to take her side was her uncle, and she was certain he would be only too happy to let someone else accept the responsibility. "You will go up to London today, my lord?"

"Yes, and that poses another problem," he stated as they crossed the terrace. "You must have someone with you. A female companion. I would ask Nanny Bates, but she is getting on in years and has her husband to look after as well."

Sarah realized that Nicholas could know nothing of Miss Penistone's presence in the house.. There had been no mention of her at dinner the previous night, and since the maids had all been told to let her sleep, she had not yet made an appearance that morning. But already, Nicholas's air of command was beginning to irritate her, and she answered more brusquely than she might otherwise have done.

"I don't need your Nanny Bates, sir, nor any other female whose first loyalty would be to you." Hearing herself, she realized immediately how rude she sounded and broke off, glancing up at him uncertainly.

There was an awful silence. He had reached to open the door for her, but he straightened and looked down at her, his eyes like blue flints. "I shall grant you the benefit of the doubt, madam," he said grimly, "and assume that your rudeness stems from lack of sleep or aftershock."

Flushing deeply, she stammered, "I . . . I beg your pardon, my lord. It was childish and stupid. I should have explained that my own former governess has been here for some time now and acts as my companion. She has been laid down upon her bed since yesterday afternoon with a sick headache, and I gave orders that she not be disturbed. However, she should be perfectly recovered today."

"I see. Well, I shall want to meet her before I agree to leave you in her care. We shall discuss the matter more thoroughly later."

His manner was far from conciliatory, but Sarah was completely ashamed of herself and felt that she could scarcely blame him. Dismissed, she went slowly upstairs to find Penny, wondering how she could have allowed herself to be so unmannerly. What had come over her? The fact that she had automatically rebelled against his confident assumption of command over her life was no acceptable excuse. Nicholas was only trying to do what was best for her, and she ought to be accustomed to his overbearing manner by now. Would she never learn to curb her unruly tongue!

She found Miss Penistone fully dressed and on the point of leaving her room, mildly embarrassed at having been let to sleep so long.

"My dear, I can scarcely credit it. Past nine, and here I am just emerging from my cocoon. I protest, you let them spoil me."

"Oh, Penny, you'll never guess all that's been happening whilst you slept. It's been quite dreadful!"

"Has it, my love? Perhaps you had better tell me all about it, then."

Gratefully, Sarah shut the door behind her and sat down upon the only chair the room possessed. Penny stood placidly before her, showing no sign of distress as Sarah's tale unwound. The news of murder having taken place just downstairs was received with scarcely a blink. Sarah left nothing out, not even Sir Nicholas's suspicions regarding her own part in the tragedy, the current state of her finances, or his dictatorial attitude toward her future. When she had finished, she looked up into the serene face before her and waited.

"Sir Nicholas . . . that is, Lord Moreland . . . seems to think just as he ought," Miss Penistone said then with gentle, if somewhat maddening, practicality. "I hope you assured him, my love, that I shall remain with you as long as I am needed."

Sarah flushed. The one thing she had not mentioned was her rudeness in the matter of a female companion. She did so now, staring at her hands guiltily while she spoke, adding that she feared she might have set Nicholas's head against Miss Penistone by her thoughtlessness.

"Your behavior was certainly unwise," Penny agreed. "But Sir Nicholas is said to be a gentleman of superior sense, so we must hope he will not hold it against either of us. The best thing would no doubt be to get the matter cleared up at once. Therefore, I suggest we find his lordship immediately."

With a sigh, Sarah agreed, but she remembered rather uncomfortably that, according to her grandfather and, after his death, her uncle, dear Penny was quite outrageously expensive. She had no idea what arrangements, if any, Darcy had made for paying her wages, but Nicholas might be contrary enough to insist upon finding someone less costly. On the other hand, since Penny would not be required to do any teaching, she might not demand such an extortionate wage. Not that it mattered one way or another, she told herself staunchly, for Penny must stay. His lordship would simply have to pay whatever was necessary. He could afford it, and Sarah wanted Miss Penistone at any cost. Having more or less made up her mind to do battle, she led the way to the library with a nearly martial glint in her eyes. It rather took the wind out of her sails to find that no battle was necessary.

Nicholas was working at his desk when they entered, but he pushed papers aside and got to his feet, stepping forward to greet both ladies amiably.

"Penny, this is Lord Moreland," Sarah said, watching him warily. "This is Miss Emily Penistone, my lord, who was used to be my governess."

Miss Penistone dropped a dignified curtsy. "My lord."

Nicholas smiled at her. "I trust you are fully recovered from your recent indisposition, ma'am. No doubt, her ladyship has told you what happened here last night. 'Tis a pretty coil, is it not?"

"Indeed, my lord. A tragedy."

Nicholas gestured toward the chairs facing the hearth, and once the ladies had seated themselves, he took up a position in front of the fireplace in order to better his acquaintance with Miss Penistone. He exerted himself, and to Sarah's astonishment, Miss Penistone soon seemed to blossom under his deft management and even deigned to chuckle when he made a joke. She did not so far forget herself as to gossip about her previous employers of course, but his lordship soon managed to obtain a fairly clear understanding of the circumstances of Sarah's upbringing. Sarah herself contributed a great deal, for it was she rather than Miss Penistone who answered his more pertinent questions. So it was that when she rather firmly announced that Miss Penistone had agreed to remain as her companion, Nicholas raised no objection at all. In fact, he expressed his approval so cheerfully that Sarah ventured to mention the matter of expense.

"Are you dreadfully expensive, ma'am?" he inquired, smiling.

"So I have been led to believe, my lord," Miss Penistone replied calmly. "Sir Malcolm made regular and contumelious objections to paying one female for the express purpose of cultivating another, declaring it to be the height of absurdity."

Nicholas gave a shout of laughter. "So they made the old curmudgeon pay your salary, did they?"

"Yes, my lord. And he did so almost regularly until his unfortunate demise. However, my salary then had to come out of Lord Hartley's own pocket. He is a gentleman, so he refrained from grumbling more often than not, but he could scarcely be blamed for regarding Sir Malcolm's demise as an annoying inconvenience."

"He could afford it, could he not?"

"Of course, but it did seem a rather vexatious nuisance, what with Miss Sarah's come-out and the inevitable expense of a court dress rapidly upcoming, that Sir Malcolm's money should be so ridiculously tied up." At no time during her discourse did Miss Penistone make apology for her salary or suggest, as Sarah had hoped she might, that a companion's fees might be rather less than those of a governess. She did not mention Darcy at all, and Sarah did not quite like to mention the matter.

When Penny had finished, Nicholas grinned. " 'Tis my belief that none of your employers knew what a bargain he had, ma'am."

"As to that, I should not say, my lord," she responded primly. "It is not my place to comment upon my employer's knowledge or lack thereof." She did not need to comment, Sarah thought with amusement. Penny's expression said it all. She met his lordship's twinkling gaze and was nearly betrayed into a laugh.

"I do know a good thing when I see it," he said now, "and the expense will be well worth knowing that her ladyship is in good hands. I shall depend upon you to keep her out of mischief and to see she does nothing to bring the scandal-mongers down upon us."

Sarah, opening her mouth to protest, encountered a straight look from Miss Penistone, and subsided. Nicholas laughed.

"I see I have not mistaken you, ma'am. We shall discuss the details later and privately, but for the moment you may draw the bustle as much as you like to get her ladyship rigged out with proper mourning and to get the Dower House into a habitable state. I shall be leaving directly, but you may hire whatever servants you like, and if you need anything from Town, arrange it. However, her ladyship is not to leave Ash Park for any reason."

Again, Sarah would have liked to protest, but knowing it would be useless, she held her tongue. Miss Penistone said, "I foresee only one small difficulty, my lord, but perhaps it has already occurred to you. I presume, since her ladyship is wearing colors now, that she has nothing suitable to wear. As soon as the news is out and about, there will no doubt be a number of callers."

Nicholas caught her meaning at once. "I believe there is a

seamstress in the village," he said. "I shall inquire when I pass through and dispatch her to you at once."

"Perhaps if I might venture to supply you with her ladyship's measurements," Miss Penistone offered. "A good seamstress is generally prepared for this sort of request, you know, since it is generally a sudden and unexpected one."

"You think of everything, ma'am. I shall not fail you."

"And the funeral, my lord?"

"Saturday, if this cool weather holds," he said. "I hope to return Friday with my nephew. It means collecting him from Harrow a day or so early, but under the circumstances—"

"Certainly, the school authorities will not object, sir."

Nicholas chuckled. "That is very likely an understatement of the case. I daresay they will be only too pleased to be rid of him."

"A young gentleman of resourcefulness, I collect."

"Those are not precisely the words his headmaster might choose," Nicholas grinned, "but they will suffice. Now, if you ladies will excuse me, I must finish this business before I go." He indicated the untidy pile of papers on the desk. "Get me those measurements, ma'am. I'm off within the half hour."

Taking his words for dismissal, both ladies rose to their feet and stepped toward the door. But before they reached it, Sarah bethought herself of another problem and turned back hesitantly. "My lord, I wondered about Beck. He will be returning, and . . . well—"

"You may tell that rascal that his services will no longer be required in this establishment," Nicholas said shortly.

Sarah paled at the thought of confronting Beck with such a statement. Even with Penny to support her, she didn't think she could manage it. "My lord, I . . ."

He was watching her closely, and his tone gentled. "Perhaps I should leave Dasher with you when I go. He can handle Beck."

Sarah could believe it. There was something very solid about Dasher, as though it would take a good deal to put him out of countenance. "Thank you, my lord," she responded sincerely.

"Think nothing of it. Such an arrangement will answer very well. Give him whatever orders you like, and he will see your needs are met. You will find him to be a most resourceful person."

Thus it was agreed, and the two ladies retired to Sarah's

bedchamber, where Miss Penistone delivered a gentle rebuke upon the subject of widows in sprig muslin dresses, and Sarah was soon stripped of the offending garment. The required measurements were given to a housemaid to deliver to his lordship, and it was decided that a simple white muslin frock would have to do until the seamstress arrived from East End village. Sarah would have liked to relax with a cup of tea and a bit of conversation until that lady's arrival, but Miss Penistone declined to encourage her in such idleness.

"There is little time to spare, love, for I know you will wish to be settled in at the Dower House as quickly as possible. Let us find Mr. Dasher."

Dasher, with his bull-like shoulders, unprepossessing countenance, and air of reserve, did not at first glance seem to be a man of action, but it was clear that Miss Penistone quickly recognized a kindred spirit. When Sarah introduced them, they drew a little away, speaking quickly and obviously to mutual purpose. Miss Penistone then returned to her charge and spoke approvingly of his lordship's man, as they walked through the library and on down the path to Dower House.

Sarah was amazed to discover that the path had already been cleared, but that was nothing compared to her astonishment when they reached the house itself. Every window stood wide open, and dust seemed to fly everywhere under the energetic exertions of what seemed to be an army of servants. A manservant came out the front door carrying a wooden chair, which he added to a meager collection of furniture standing in the front garden.

"Merciful heavens!" Sarah exclaimed. "It has only been a couple of hours since his lordship and I were here!"

"They certainly seem industrious," Miss Penistone agreed. "Mr. Dasher said he had acquired some help to begin the task. It looks as though it won't take them long."

"There are so many of them!"

"Yes, indeed. A tribute, I am sure, to Mr. Dasher's skill as an organizer though he did mention that the locals are much more amenable now that his lordship has come into the title."

Sarah, remembering Darcy's petulant comments on the difficulties of finding servants, could well believe it, since Dasher seemed to have produced a whole battalion with a snap of his fingers. There were only three days to go before Nicholas would return, but the impossible now seemed probable. The work would not be finished, of course, but the house might at least be made habitable before then if she and Miss Penistone were not too nice in their requirements.

She was about to suggest that they go on inside to see what progress had been made, as well as to prepare a list of things to be done, when Dasher cleared his throat directly behind her, nearly causing her to jump out of her skin.

"Dasher! Don't *do* that!"

"Mr. Dasher," declared the unflustered Miss Penistone in the same breath, "you seem to be working a miracle here."

"Beg pardon, my lady. Thank you, ma'am. If you please, my lady, there is a gentleman by name of Sir William Miles says he's wishful to speak with you."

"The magistrate!" Sarah exclaimed. She had forgotten all about him.

VIII

The meeting with Sir William Miles was not nearly the ordeal Sarah had expected it to be. It took place in the library, and Sir William sat on the settee near the merrily crackling fire, while she sat in a chair facing him. With Miss Penistone there to support her, Sarah was not at all nervous and was able to answer his questions with poise and confidence.

Sir William was a bluff and cheerful man, clearly more at home in the hunting field than in a lady's parlor, but it was just as clear that he took his duties as magistrate very seriously, and the questions he asked were relevant and to the point. He took her carefully through her description of what had transpired in the library and showed no inclination to cross-question her. As Nicholas had foreseen, he merely wanted to hear what Sarah could tell him.

Sarah began her tale with the pistol shot, saying nothing of her earlier quarrel with Darcy. Therefore, nothing was said about the fall, and if Sir William was aware that Darcy had a large lump on the back of his head, he did not mention it. There was only one point that he asked her to clarify.

"Beg pardon, my lady," he said then, "but would you mind going over the bit about the pistol again?"

"I don't know what else I can add," Sarah replied. "I had knelt beside my husband and was shaking him when I saw it. I had got blood all over my skirt, and without really thinking clearly at all, I leaned over him and picked it up."

"You leaned over him?"

"Yes. The pistol was between him and that desk."

"I see. Was it under his body or just alongside?"

Sarah closed her eyes, repressing a shudder as she tried to visualize the scene again. "Alongside, I believe. I know I didn't have to pull it out from under him."

Sir William stared into the fire for a moment, working his lips as he considered her words, Then suddenly, he shot a singularly piercing gaze at her. "Have you considered the possibility, Lady Moreland, that the late earl, for reasons unbeknownst to us, might have elected to put a period to his own life? In a word, madam, might your husband have shot himself?"

It was tempting. Indeed, it was very tempting, and Sarah knew that such an interpretation by Sir William would make things a good deal easier for all of them. She glanced at Miss Penistone to find that lady's expression as bland as ever. However, just as Sarah was about to agree to a vague possibility, Nicholas's words echoed in her mind. It was as though he were right there speaking to her, sternly warning her that they must do nothing to aid the real criminal. So, regretfully, she shook her head.

"I am quite certain, Sir William, that my husband would never have done such a thing. There could have been no reason for it. He had no financial worries, and I can think of nothing else that might have driven him to such an act. Someone k-killed him." The break in her voice rather caught her by surprise, and she realized she had been holding herself under very tight control. Before, when she had discussed Darcy's death, with Nicholas or Miss Penistone, she had kept her thoughts on the surface of things, merely describing what she had actually seen and heard. Oddly enough, this was the first time she had actually put the matter into such simple terms, and she paled at the vision her words brought to mind. She hadn't particularly liked Darcy—she certainly hadn't loved him—but it was altogether dreadful to think of his dying at the hand of another in such a violent fashion.

Watching her, Sir William nodded, and his response was gentle. "That's the way I figure it, too, ma'am, not believing the lad to have had the bottom for that sort of thing. Still and all, I was curious to know what you would say." Resolutely pushing the unsettling visions aside, Sarah breathed a sigh of relief. Though it had been a very small trap, it was nevertheless gratifying that she had escaped it. Perhaps there were advantages to taking other people's advice now and again. Sir William stayed only a few moments more, but before taking his leave, he asked that she have someone notify him when Beck returned from Town. "He may be able to shed some light on this matter," he said. "Ought at least to know one or two of his master's enemies." Sarah agreed and passed the message along to Dasher.

The East End seamstress arrived late in the afternoon, bringing several gowns with her that had already been cut and pieced to Sarah's approximate size. All that was necessary was a final fitting and a few minor alterations. The seamstress spent the night, and with the help of Miss Penistone and the maidservant, Betsy, two mourning gowns were ready for Sarah the next day. Besides Betsy and the other two girls hired by Darcy, several more maidservants had taken up residence in the servants' quarters by then, and Dasher had also managed to find four young men to serve as footmen in the main house. Since they were chosen as much for size as for ability, the uniforms that arrived from London on Thursday fit them perfectly.

Sir Nicholas had first thought to hire his servants in Town, Miss Penistone informed Sarah, having gained her information firsthand from the worthy Dasher. "But he concluded that it would be better to use local people in order to better the Park's image." Sarah remembered these words when the little seamstress mentioned a shop in the village that could provide materials for curtains and upholstery, as well as bedding and linens, if her ladyship was of a mind to bestow her patronage there. She added diffidently that no doubt her ladyship would prefer to order such stuff from Town.

"No such thing," Sarah declared, smiling. "I should be most obliged to you in fact, Mrs. Potter, if you would ask that shopkeeper to visit us with samples from which we might choose. Such an arrangement will be a great deal more convenient than to be forever having to run up to Town."

Seeing the light her words brought to that good lady's eye, she knew she had made the right decision. Even if the shop could not provide exactly what was wanted, it was important to improve relations with the local people. She was sure Nicholas would agree, and it *would* be more convenient.

Beck did not return from London until well into the following day. She saw him as she was returning to the library from Dower House. He seemed surprised by all the activity and was clearly about to approach her when Dasher intercepted him. She could have no exact idea of what was said, but the expressions playing across Beck's face piqued her curiosity. First, there was shock and dismay. Then, however, there was surprise and disbelief, followed by anger and belligerence. He

moved as though to push past Dasher, but the other man
forestalled him merely by laying a hand upon his arm. Beck
was the taller, but there could be no doubt as to who would
win a match of strength between them. Dasher reached into
an inner pocket of his black coat and pulled out a thick enve-
lope which he passed to Beck. Then he gestured toward the
stables and said something further. Beck was clearly receiving
his *congé*, and he was not at all pleased about it. Glaring
angrily, he turned on his heel, casting a malevolent look at
Sarah in passing that caused her to be certain that he, at
least, believed she had murdered his master.

She did not dwell on it, however, merely being glad that he
had gone. Her days were much too busy to allow any time for
thinking of the past or worrying about what Beck thought or
didn't think.

It seemed that she never had a moment to relax. Work
progressed rapidly, and while servants washed, waxed, polished, and painted, she and Miss Penistone scoured the main
house and the attics of Dower House for furniture. The cellars
there had long since been closed off for one reason or another,
and those at the main house seemed to contain only dusty kegs
and bottles of wine, but they managed to collect an assortment
of the bare necessities.

By Friday morning, the weeds had been cleared from the
front garden, and the trees nearest Dower House had been
pruned. Ivy had been cleared from walls and windows, and
the outside walls had been crisply whitewashed and trimmed
with black paint. Inside, the smell of bee's wax and lemon oil
had replaced that of dust and mildew. The drawing room now
contained several chairs, a small sofa, two side tables, and as
an extra touch, a fire had been laid in the newly cleaned
fireplace, ready to light. The windows were bare, waiting for
new curtains, but a blue and red carpet lay upon the highly
polished floor, and a bowl of fresh flowers on one of the side
tables added a note of cheerfulness.

Across the hall, the dining room boasted little more than a
table and four chairs, but at least, Sarah reflected, it was not
bare. They would have to take their evening meals at the main
house anyway, until a cook could be found for Dower House.

Upstairs, the bedchambers contained only dressing tables
and a chair or two. Sarah had taken the patchwork coverlet
and the French seat from her room in the main house as well
as the cheval glass from the downstairs saloon. The beds

would be moved later. All in all, she thought with satisfaction, they had done rather well.

Dasher had also been busy, and the main house gleamed from attic to cellar. He had disposed of Matty and Tom by pensioning them off, and a widow from East End had been installed as cook, her first presentations proving to everyone's satisfaction that the standard for dining had vastly improved.

By the time the yellow curricle rolled up to the front door in grand style on Friday afternoon, Sarah felt as though mountains had been moved. She was arranging flowers in the pewter vases on the library mantel shelf when she heard the arrival and moved to the window to watch. Timmy leaped down and ran to the horses' heads, while Nicholas descended in a more leisurely fashion, followed immediately by a tousle-haired lad of about thirteen years. The boy looked up at his uncle, laughing, and she could see a clear family resemblance between the two. But though Colin boasted the same crisp fair curls and firm chin, his eyes were a lighter blue, and his face was dusted with freckles. He was thin and wiry, rather than broad-shouldered and muscular, but no one could doubt he would fill out and grow taller, given a few more years. The two wasted no time before bounding up the steps and into the house, and Sarah stepped to the hall to greet them.

"Good afternoon, my lady," Nicholas said, smiling. "May I present my nephew, the Honorable Colin Bessling, who will be staying with me for a time."

Sarah nodded and made the proper welcome while, with an engaging grin, the boy managed a very creditable bow. Nicholas asked immediately about the progress of Dower House and seemed pleased to hear that the ladies intended to spend the night there.

"But I thought Dower House was haunted," mused young Master Bessling idly.

"Nonsense," Nicholas responded sternly. "You thought nothing of the sort."

"I distinctly recall that Gram once said she left Ash Park rather than be relegated to that ghost-ridden monstrosity," Colin insisted blandly. But his twinkling eyes gave him away.

"I don't believe she ever said any such thing," Nicholas declared roundly, "and you, my friend, had best think twice before starting any ill-conceived rumors where I can hear them. Forgive him, my lady. 'Tis mere boyish high spirits, all on account of being let out of school early."

"I shall keep my wits about me, my lord," Sarah assured him with a chuckle. "I have never been particularly missish, you know, and I am afraid that, were I to encounter a ghost at Dower House, I should simply invite him to acquaint me with his name and history."

Nicholas grinned appreciatively, but she noticed that the boy gave her a rather measuring look. It was forgotten a moment later, when Dasher hurried into the hall and bore young Colin off to show him to his bedchamber, and Nicholas invited Sarah to show him what had been accomplished at Dower House.

Miss Penistone met them in the entry hall, expressing her pleasure at his lordship's safe return. Then, the three of them toured the house. Nicholas commended them without reservation for the work that had been done and chuckled when Miss Penistone handed him a list of further requirements. He seemed especially pleased when Sarah told him that she had decided to acquire as much as possible locally.

"I am glad to hear you say that, my lady, for it can only be beneficial to us all." He glanced at the list. "I see that your first priority is to install your own cook. I should have thought a lady's maid would be more welcome."

"Well," Sarah began doubtfully, "if you don't object, sir, Betsy has agreed to work for us."

"An excellent notion," Nicholas agreed. "She is a good worker. But she is no lady's maid. I think you will agree that a proper dresser should be brought from London. I have, in fact, already arranged it, and she will arrive later this afternoon."

Something in his tone told Sarah more than his words had done. "Lizzie!" she exclaimed.

"The same, and delighted to come, I might add."

"Oh, splendid! But that means . . . that is, I collect that you must have seen my uncle, sir."

"Indeed. *And* your aunt. And she, I might add, is as formidable as ever."

"Are they still furious with me?" Sarah asked in a rather small voice.

"A bit. I think your uncle will come round eventually, but Lady Hartley is undecided as to whether she should be more enraged by the impropriety or by the stupidity of your actions."

"I see. Then you told them the truth?"

"I thought they deserved to know," he said gently. "Would you rather I hadn't?"

"Of course not," she replied quickly, then in answer to a gleam of mockery in his eye, she added, "I don't really know, sir. All I know for certain is that I've no wish to confront her ladyship for a good long while!"

Nicholas chuckled. "I don't doubt it." He glanced at Miss Penistone. "And you, ma'am? Have you quite settled in now?"

"Indeed, my lord. The house is coming about rapidly, thanks to Mr. Dasher's extraordinary powers of organization."

"I'm delighted to hear it, though not surprised. Dasher's greatest talent is his ability to conjure up the impossible at a moment's notice. It made him an indispensable asset in the Peninsula, I assure you." A few moments later, they glimpsed a party of menservants under Dasher's personal direction carrying two bedsteads, and Nicholas left them to finish putting their house to rights, observing that he would see them both at dinner.

Lizzie arrived as promised about four o'clock and, after a rapturous reunion with her mistress, exclaimed and scolded over the state of Sarah's wardrobe. But when she declared that she would like to have a few moments alone with the person who had been caring for her mistress's clothes, Sarah called her to order, explaining that, though Betsy had never been trained to it, she had done her best.

"She has been very kind to me, Lizzie, though she was hired as a housemaid, and I shan't allow you to scold her. Now, do put off your cloak and never mind my affairs until you have quite settled in. Then I shall ask you to help me dress for dinner, so the gentlemen will stare!"

"And so they shall, m' lady," Lizzie promised in her soft Irish lilt as she hurried out the door to see to the bestowal of her own things. She was soon back, ready to go to work. She had changed her gown for a fresh one and bundled her fiery red hair into a snood at the nape of her neck. Her blue eyes twinkled, but her pert little nose expressed distaste for Sarah's black gowns.

"I know, Lizzie, but nothing can be done about it," Sarah said. "He was my husband, after all."

"Aye," replied Lizzie tersely, "and 'tis none of my place to say what I think about that!"

"Certainly not!" Sarah agreed, but she smiled. "I know

what you think, Lizzie, and I apologize for deceiving you as I did. All I can say now is that I made a foolish mistake."

"Well, as to apologizing to the likes of me," Lizzie said sharply, indicating that Sarah should sit in the dressing chair, "there's no call, m' lady. My faith! If only you could have seen her ladyship's face when I told her you'd gone!"

Sarah grimaced. "I heard about it, thank you. You might have chosen a time when Lady Jersey was elsewhere."

Lizzie chuckled. "And didn't I hear about that later! The very instant m' Lady Jersey took her leave. 'Miss O'Hare, you are never again to burst into my drawing room in such an unseemly way.' My sainted Patrick, but she was in a snit!"

She mimicked Lady Hartley's tones exactly, and Sarah couldn't help laughing, though she knew she ought to reprove her instead. It was certainly not proper for her to allow her maidservant to make jest of her aunt. But she was glad Lizzie was here. She said so, adding, "No one else could ever do my hair so well."

Lizzie just grinned, and her nimble fingers went right on working. Sarah watched closely but, even so, could see nothing unusual. Just a twist here and a tuck there. Nevertheless, the result was wonderful and vastly becoming. Her bronze tresses were piled atop her head like a tumble of curls arranged any which way. Tendrils curled around her ears and down the nape of her neck, and the style gave her height and an extra touch of elegance as well.

She pinched her cheeks to give them extra color, while Lizzie inspected the dress she had chosen to wear, flicking imaginary bits of lint and smoothing a tiny wrinkle before holding it ready for her to don. Once the buttons had been fastened and the skirt twitched into place, she stood back to view the results.

"Well, 'tis passable," Lizzie sighed, "but not what we like. Black is *not* your color, my lady. There just isn't enough of you to carry it off. It overwhelms you."

"I know, Lizzie." Sarah smoothed her skirt, hating the feel of the bombazine and wishing the dress needn't be quite so plain and priggish. With a low-cut bodice and short sleeves, she would not seem so enveloped. But it could not be. She slipped her feet into a pair of silver sandals, for she had not thought to do anything about proper shoes and had been wearing her dark green kid boots till she was heartily sick of them. A few moments later, when she entered the library with Penny beside her, Nicholas eyed her approvingly from the top of her head to the gentle folds of her floor-length hemline.

"I am glad you were able to secure proper attire so quickly," he said. "Of course, you will not wish to sport so frivolous a hair style at the funeral, but amongst us here, it does not matter."

Colin had been eyeing a tray of wine glasses and sherry when they entered, but his uncle's remark brought a grin to his face. "He might at least mention that the style becomes you charmingly, Lady Moreland," he observed sweetly.

"That will be quite enough out of you, my lad, if you wish to dine with the grown-ups," his uncle warned. "You may make yourself useful, if you please, by pouring a small glass of sherry for each of us."

"There are only three glasses," Colin mentioned suggestively.

"So there are," Nicholas agreed. "Pour, brat."

The boy obeyed and seemed not the least cast down by his lack of success. Later, over dinner, Sarah asked him about school, and he obliged with several amusing anecdotes, seeming quite at home in adult company.

"Will you not miss having your friends about you?" she asked, once the laughter following one of his tales had died away. "I should think Ash Park would seem rather lonely after Harrow."

"Not at all, my lady," Colin replied. "I shall have my horses here, and there are streams nearby for fishing. I like the Park. Besides, Uncle Nick has said I might invite one or two of my friends for a visit if I like or perhaps go to visit some of them later."

He seemed perfectly content, and although he cast an indignant look at his uncle when told after dinner that he might now take himself off to bed, he went without argument. Once Colin had gone, Sarah and Miss Penistone would have left Nicholas to enjoy his port in solitary splendor, but he requested that it be served in the library and asked them to join him there.

"I wanted to speak to you both about the funeral," he said quietly, when they had seated themselves. "It is to be very private, without any grand fuss, but there is no telling who might come from Town. Dasher will be ready for anything, of course, but I wanted you to be prepared as well. What on earth have you got on your feet!"

Sarah, though listening conscientiously, had idly held one foot out to the fire. She snatched it back, tucking it primly under her skirts. "I'm sorry, my lord, but I didn't think about shoes before. Nearly everything I have is of a color to match a gown. I thought these would be the least offensive."

"Well, you certainly cannot wear silver sandals to your husband's funeral," Nicholas declared flatly. "Have you any suggestions, ma'am?"

"No, my lord," Penny replied. "My own shoes are black, of course, and I should be pleased to lend them, but my feet are of a larger size than her ladyship's, so they would not answer."

"Well, don't be silly, Penny," Sarah said acidly. "We could always stuff the toes, if his lordship will insist upon every propriety being met."

"An excellent notion," applauded Nicholas. "I am glad to hear you propose it. That will do very nicely indeed."

Sarah stared at him, dumbfounded. "You are joking!"

"Indeed I am not, madam. You should have thought of the need for shoes before I left for London, where I could easily have seen to their purchase. But since you did not, and since Miss Penistone has offered to lend you a pair, you will have to make do."

"Well, no one else thought of them either," Sarah declared, her temper flaring, as usual, at his authoritarian attitude. "And you cannot truly expect me to attend a funeral where you admit you don't know whom I might meet in stuffed-up governess shoes!"

Nicholas swallowed the last of his port and got to his feet. " 'Tis a pity we didn't think to hire someone to do your thinking for you, Countess, since you seem unable to accept that responsibility for yourself. However, we did not. And since I very lamentably failed to realize that you would need black shoes, you don't have any. Nevertheless, you will be properly dressed tomorrow or be prepared to answer to me. And whatever the reason for this," he added, looking down at her grimly, "there is no cause for you to speak so insultingly of an offer that was kindly meant."

Flushing to the roots of her hair, Sarah opened her mouth to answer him in kind, but encountering the cold anger in his expression, she faltered, stammering an apology instead.

"So I should hope," Nicholas replied uncompromisingly. "But you would do better to make your apology to Miss Penistone, rather than to me. Now, if you ladies will excuse me, I have work to do." He held the French doors open for them and, her eyes filling with sudden, burning tears, Sarah flounced past him, the placid Miss Penistone following in her wake.

"That abominable man!" Sarah muttered wrathfully, after striding for some moments in irritated silence.

"Well, he was perhaps a trifle severe, my dear, but you cannot deny provoking him," Miss Penistone observed fairly as they mounted the steps to the house. "I am sorry you do not like my shoes."

Sarah was immediately contrite. "Oh, Penny, don't be absurd. It has nothing to do with your shoes, and I am truly sorry if I offended you. Indeed, I don't know what it is about that man that makes me fly into the boughs like I do." She pushed open the front door to the sight of Erebus sprawled at the foot of the stairs, his tail thumping the floorboards in greeting. "Dogs sleep outside," she said firmly, pointing out into the night. With a heavy sigh, the huge dog lumbered to his feet, his soft brown eyes brimful of reproach as he treaded ponderously to the door. On the threshold he turned back with a final plea for mercy. "Out," said Sarah, and defeated, he plodded down the steps and melted into the darkness beyond. "Where was I, Penny?" she asked, shutting the door.

"Something about not knowing—"

"Oh, I remember. That was silly. Of course I know. Sir Nicholas—that is, Lord Moreland—is so puffed up in his own arrogance that it just makes a body boil. I've a strong notion to wear my gold dress tomorrow, just to teach him that I am not to be ordered about like a lackey."

"I shouldn't advise it, love."

Sarah remembered the cold fury in his lordship's eye and unaccountably shivered. "No, perhaps not." She sighed. "I suppose we'd best have a look at your shoes, Penny."

A pair of black leather slippers was found that could be induced to stay on Sarah's tiny feet, and so it was that she appeared at the funeral in strict widow's wear from tip to toe, with her hair swept back severely from her face and all but hidden under a black lace veil. There were very few mourners. Beck was there, but he made no attempt to approach her and, accosted by Sir William Miles, left with that gentleman as soon as the coffin was lowered into the ground. As expected, several people did arrive from town, but they were all men, and as it transpired, they were men to whom Darcy owed money. Once the ceremonies were over, they accompanied the family back to the house and disappeared, one after another, into the library with Nicholas.

Sarah did note one familiar face at the funeral. It was the strange man who had visited with Darcy in the library the afternoon before his murder. He stood to one side of the gathering at the churchyard and, later, seemed to have followed the small procession back to the house. Sarah's curiosity was aroused by the way he seemed to peer at each of the guests in turn, with a particular interest in the men who accompanied Nicholas to the library.

At last, his lordship finished his business and came out to join the dwindling company. Dasher, on the lookout for him, promptly presented a glass of wine. "Thank you." He turned to Sarah. "I hope your shoes are not pinching, my lady."

There were lines etched around his eyes, and she thought he looked tired. But whether he was or not, she had no intention of quarreling with him. A night's rest coupled with the solemnity of the day had convinced her that she had been wrong to take exception to his reproof the night before.

"The shoes are fine, my lord," she said quietly. "And if they did pinch, 'twould be no more than I deserve for taking snuff at your remarks last night. I hope you will forgive me."

"Very prettily said, Countess. Did you practice?"

Her eyes flew wide, and all her good intentions dissipated. "You are insufferable, my lord!"

"That's better," he approved. "I like the way your eyes hold fire when you are angry. They were a trifle insipid before."

"Oh!" Suddenly aware that other eyes were turning toward them, Sarah managed to keep from stamping her foot, but she could no longer stay beside him without causing a scene. So she dropped a barely civil curtsy and moved away. When she looked back a moment later, he was talking to the man she had observed earlier.

They disappeared toward the library, and all the mourners had gone by the time Nicholas reappeared. Sarah was still out of charity with him, so although she was nearly consumed with curiosity, she refused to question him. No doubt the man had come to demand payment of some debt or other as the others had done, which would also explain his previous long meeting with Darcy and the latter's subsequent argument with Beck on the subject of money. Or partially explain it, she tempered. Nonetheless, her ears pricked up when Colin asked the question uppermost in her mind.

"Who the devil was that queer nabs, Uncle Nick?"

Nicholas fixed his nephew with a pointed stare. "If you mean to ask the name of the person who was just with me in the library, I wish you will phrase your question in a more civilized manner."

"Well, then," said Colin, unabashed, "that is precisely what I wish to know. Who is he, if you please?"

"I am afraid I cannot imagine how that might be any concern of yours," pronounced his uncle in quelling tones. "So if you will excuse me, I have matters that must be tended before dinner." And he left the room, leaving at least two of the three remaining persons to stare at each other in no little consternation.

IX

Sarah's curiosity was well and truly aroused by Nicholas's attitude toward the stranger. If he had simply provided the man's name and added that their business was of a private nature, she would very likely have thought no more about it. But his abrupt dismissal of the subject piqued her curiosity and stimulated her imagination. The stranger had, after all, visited Darcy on that fatal day. At the least, he might be able to cast some light upon the mystery. At the worst, he might prove to be the murderer. The notion caught her unawares while she was walking back to Dower House to refresh herself before dinner. She stopped quite still in her tracks, turning the idea over in her mind, examining it from all sides.

"Sarah, love, whatever is the matter?" Miss Penistone inquired gently at her side.

Filled with an excitement completely out of keeping with the horror of her idea, Sarah turned with sparkling eyes, fully prepared to explain the matter. But something in that gentle, alert expression caused her to think twice before laying her accusation.

"Nothing, Penny," she replied vaguely. "Just a silly notion, not at all suitable to the day." Miss Penistone said nothing at all to this, and they soon arrived at the Dower House. Pleading a need to rest before dinner, Sarah soon found herself tucked up on the French seat in her own room, alone with her thoughts.

Who was the mysterious stranger? The question sounded as though it had sprung directly from Mrs. Radcliffe's pen. Surely, such occurrences belonged in the world of her Udolpho and were out of place at Ash Park! Nevertheless, she was certain that her mysterious stranger could cast a light on Darcy's death.

A sharp movement in the garden below caught her eye, and she turned to see young Colin waving frantically. He made other odd gestures once he had her attention, and she quickly came to realize that he had something of a private nature to impart to her.

Sarah did not doubt for a moment that Colin wanted to speak to her about the mystery, so she quickly slipped on her horrid shoes, smoothed her skirt, and hurried downstairs to join him in the front garden. He did not disappoint her.

"That man we saw," he began urgently, "the queer one Uncle Nick wouldn't speak of . . . he's down at the stables. I saw him!"

"Are you sure, Colin? Maybe he left his horse there whilst he spoke to your uncle."

"That was ages ago," the boy scorned. "I'm sure Uncle Nick thinks he left. That fellow's up to no good, my lady. Mark my words."

Sarah smiled at his intensity. "Why did you come to me, Colin? Why not inform your uncle?"

"He would only say I was interfering in matters that are not my concern," was the candid reply. "But I think there's more to that fellow than meets the eye. And I'll wager you agree with me."

She couldn't deny it. "Perhaps, if we were just to stroll down toward the stables," she began tentatively.

He grinned. "I knew you were a right one, ma'am. We'll soon see what he's up to."

But when they arrived at the sprawling stables, it was to find that their quarry had flown. Sarah stifled her disappointment and agreed that Colin should question one or two of the stableboys. She watched intently as he spoke first to one and then another; consequently, she did not hear the approaching footsteps behind her.

"What the devil are you doing down here?"

She spun around to face Nicholas. He was frowning, and she found herself without a plausible answer. "I . . . that is, we . . . we were just . . . some exercise before dinner!"

"Surely, you didn't mean to go riding, my lady!" His gaze drifted from her shoulders to her feet. "You are hardly dressed for it. Or do you generally keep company with stableboys? I should have thought your tastes a trifle more elevated than that."

Her cheeks burned at his tone, but Colin had heard his voice and now ambled toward them, speaking before her unruly tongue could betray her again. "Have you the time, Uncle Nick? We don't want to miss dinner."

With a sharp look at the boy and a rather rueful one at Sarah, Nicholas obligingly drew out his watch and flicked open the gold case. "You have approximately twenty minutes to make yourself presentable. Do you make it a habit to drag your lady friends along when you visit the stables?"

Colin met his gaze unblinkingly. "Do you not like her being here, sir? If so, I must apologize, for it is indeed my fault. I wanted to ask Jem about having one of my horses reshod with lighter shoes, and it seemed a good time. Her ladyship and I were walking when the notion struck me, and she said she wouldn't mind a stroll to the stables." He paused, eyeing his uncle carefully. "If you do not care for it, I shan't bring her again."

Nicholas glanced again at Sarah, who was exerting iron control over herself. But if her color was a trifle high, he no doubt put it down to his earlier words and did not hesitate to apologize.

"I should not have said what I did, Countess. I didn't realize Colin was with you, but I should have known you would not have come here unattended. I beg your pardon." His tone was stiff, and he turned away immediately, striding off toward the house.

She looked at Colin, who was grinning unabashedly, and dissolved into laughter. "Of all the plumpers!" she exclaimed when she could draw a breath. "How did you dare to offer him such a tale! And now you will have to have one of your horses reshod besides!"

The boy shrugged. "It was the first thing I could think of when I saw he didn't like you being here. Do you suppose it's on account of thinking you were here alone or because he didn't want you finding out about Jeremy Oakes?"

"Jeremy Oakes?"

Colin nodded. "Our mysterious stranger. Jem told me his name. Said he asked about Tom and Beck, how long they'd been here, if they were around when the old earl was done in. Asked a lot of silly stuff, Jem said. Did we have any priest holes and such? Like he was looking for treasure or something, he said."

"Treasure!"

Colin nodded again with a musing frown. "That's what he

said. You don't suppose there could be a buried treasure around here somewhere, and Cousin Darcy found it and got murdered for it, do you?"

Sarah stared at him. Buried treasure on Finchley Common seemed utterly ludicrous, but just as flat denial reached her lips, she remembered the contradiction of Darcy's attire and London life style to his supposed poverty. Surely, he must have had some means of supporting himself. His clothes were the height of fashion, and despite the creditors at the funeral, she didn't think he had been very deeply in debt, or his reputation would have been quite different when she met him. But wherever the money came from, it was clear he hadn't spent much of it here, so he must have wanted his possession of it kept secret from the local people.

"Lots of families hid valuables during the Cromwellian period," Colin said thoughtfully, breaking into her thoughts. "Perhaps our family treasure was never recovered, and Cousin Darcy found it."

"But I should think he would have told everyone he could tell!" Sarah protested.

"Not if he was afraid he might have to share it or prove his claim to it," Colin said. "That would have cost a great deal of money. Better to keep mum and have it all to himself."

It was farfetched, but Sarah could believe that Darcy might have been devious enough to have kept such a matter to himself. "How would your Jeremy Oakes have discovered about the treasure?" she asked.

"He's hardly *my* Jeremy Oakes," Colin chuckled. "I don't know how, but he did, and it's my belief he's the murderer. Killed Cousin Darcy and then couldn't find the lolly. So now he's skulking about."

"What did he learn from the stable boys? Did they tell you?"

"Not much. They're all new, you know. Couldn't tell him a thing, except that Beck left in a snit." He paused, thinking. "Jem also seemed to think that Oakes had Uncle Nick's permission to be here, but I don't see how that could be." He didn't seem to expect Sarah to respond, and she was grateful, for her mind was suddenly struggling with a thought that had sprung up totally unbidden. "Why do you suppose Uncle Nick didn't want you down here?" Colin asked, his words following her own train of thought so nearly that she almost answered him with that dreadful, encroaching idea.

Taking herself forcibly in hand, Sarah replied carelessly,

"Oh, I expect, as you said before, that it was because he thought I had come alone. He's a rare stickler for propriety."

"Don't I know it!" Colin laughed.

"Then how did you dare to tell him such a whisker?" she demanded, glad enough to change the course of her own thoughts.

"Oh, that one was nothing," he scoffed. "I can tell much better ones if necessary. I've had a good deal of practice."

"Colin! How can you be casual about such a thing? Surely, you cannot boast about telling falsehoods!" She stared at the boy, shocked at such a possibility.

"Are you going to pretend you've never told a whopper?" Colin teased. Sarah opened her mouth to deny it before she remembered one or two episodes that would not bear repeating. He read the answer in her expression. "Just as I thought! I do not tell any that would hurt anyone else. Mostly, I tell them to save my own skin. The masters at my school are rather strict, you know."

"I have heard it said," she admitted. "But do you tell them often, Colin? I should think it would go much worse for you when you are caught out."

"Ah, but I am never so foolish as to get caught," he replied simply. "When there is no hope for it, I take the consequences. But my imagination, thankfully, is rather fertile," he added with a twinkling look.

"I have a feeling," she advised wryly, "that it would be wise to avoid telling falsehoods to your uncle. He has an uncanny way of reading one's very thoughts."

Colin chuckled. "I know. I very rarely try it on with him, but today it was to protect us both. I've a feeling he wouldn't appreciate our investigation of Mr. Jeremy Oakes."

They fell silent after that and soon parted company to prepare for dinner. Sarah's thoughts were such that she felt an urgent need for solitude. Why would Nicholas dislike their discovering more about the ubiquitous Mr. Oakes? Could he possibly know something about the man that he did not wish them—or more particularly, Sarah herself—to know? Could Oakes have had something to do with Darcy's death? Was he, in fact, the murderer? And if he was the murderer, did Nicholas know it? Had Nicholas perhaps even . . .

But here she forced herself to stop, appalled at the course her thoughts were taking. She could not—would not—think such a thing of him. She turned her thoughts instead to the possibility of treasure. That was almost exciting. She had a brief vision of herself and Colin discovering buried treasure in the garden or perhaps in the thick woods near the main house. Chuckling to herself now, she pushed open the door to her own bedchamber.

"Ah, here you are at last, love," Miss Penistone said calmly, while in the same instant Lizzie demanded in strong Irish tones to know where in the name of the blessed Saint Patrick her ladyship had taken herself.

"For how I can be doin' your hair when you're nowhere to be found, I haven't a notion!" she declared roundly. "Now, sit ye down, your ladyship, for we've little enough time, and you've been out and about in that wind, I see."

Resigned, Sarah apologized and abandoned herself to their ministrations. Some ten minutes later, she was ready, and she and Penny walked over to the main house, entering through the library.

Nicholas had poured himself a glass of wine and, rising, offered one to each of them as well. He smiled at Sarah when he handed her her glass, making her wonder just how she was supposed to know what to expect from him. Half an hour earlier he had been annoyed. Now, it was as though he had no memory whatsoever of the incident.

A few moments later, Colin entered, his shirt changed, his hands and face scrubbed to a rosy glow. Following closely upon his heels came Dasher to announce dinner, and they adjourned to the dining room, where the delicious smell of roast pork greeted them. The meal was simple, two courses only, but there were enough side dishes to tempt anyone's appetite, and it was clear the new cook was to be a success. Conversation ambled lightly from one topic to another, until Colin suddenly turned to his uncle and announced that his form had been making a study of Charles I and Cromwell.

"Indeed," remarked his uncle.

"Yes, sir. It must have been very difficult for the noble houses during the transition."

"I daresay. Do try some of these creamed onions, Miss Penistone. They are delicious." Sarah hid a smile.

"Well, I was just wondering," Colin persisted patiently as he passed the dish on to Miss Penistone, "how so many of them managed to retain family treasures—you know, art work and silver and such stuff—when Cromwell's army was dashing about confiscating it for the good of the state?" He watched

Nicholas hopefully, and despite the common sense which told her Colin's notion was ridiculous, Sarah found herself waiting impatiently for the answer.

"They hid it, I suppose," Nicholas replied. "Those old houses had no end of priest holes and hidden cellars. I daresay that's where most of it went." He turned his attention to his plate, and Colin cast Sarah a speaking glance.

"What about the Ashton family, sir?" he asked innocently. "Did they hide their treasures?"

Nicholas grinned. "I doubt there was much to hide, brat, but if there was, it was dug up long since to pay some Ashton's debts. What are you about now, anyway? Trying to cozen her ladyship into believing in buried treasure since she scorned your ghost tales?"

"Not at all, sir," Colin smiled. "I just wondered."

"Well, it's the first interest you've shown in your family history that I know about."

"But if her ladyship does meet a ghost and insists upon hearing his pedigree," Colin returned sweetly, "I would certainly like to know enough to prove or disprove his information."

Nicholas chuckled, then eyed his nephew more sternly. "I thought I told you to put that ghost nonsense out of your head."

"Yes, sir. And had you not mentioned it first, I should not have brought it into our conversation."

"You are impertinent, Colin. I'd advise you to have a care."

The boy subsided immediately with a murmured apology, and Sarah stepped bravely into the breach. "Don't scold him, my lord. I've told you, I have no fear of ghosts. You refine too much upon boyish jesting."

"Perhaps. Suppose we change the subject. Have you thought how you will obtain suitable shoes? You cannot wish to continue with what you are currently wearing."

"No, my lord. I have my own shoemaker in London, of course, but until someone goes to Town . . . perhaps, there is someone in the village."

"Perhaps," he agreed, "but there is no need to carry local patronage to such extremes. Give a list of your requirements and the address of your shoemaker to Dasher. He will see to it. What sort of riding boots do you have?"

"York tan."

"Then you will need a new pair. Have you ordered a habit?"

"I didn't know if you would approve," she confessed.

"Don't be nonsensical, Sarah! Of course you may ride, but you must be suitably attired. If you are referring to my displeasure this afternoon, your attitude is spurious, for you know perfectly well why I was annoyed. And I have already apologized for it." He spoke as though they were the only two in the room, and a small silence followed his words.

Then Sarah cleared her throat. "I shall order a habit at once, sir. It will be pleasant to be able to ride again. By the way," she added, deeming that a new subject was desirable, "I saw Beck with Sir William Miles at the funeral. Was he able to provide any useful information?"

"None at all, according to Sir William," Nicholas replied evenly, "but you needn't worry about Beck any longer, I daresay. Dasher surprised him later this afternoon, walking through the wood near Dower House, and sent him off with a flea in his ear. I have given orders that he is henceforth to keep away from Ash Park entirely."

Sarah felt a strong sense of relief but made no comment, and Miss Penistone took up the conversation, remarking upon the fine bursts of scenery she supposed could be found in the neighborhood and drifting from that point to a concise description of her journey from Cornwall. By the time she finished, it was a simple matter to revert to the sort of small talk they had indulged in earlier. Soon, Nicholas called for his port and ordered Colin off to bed, and Sarah and Miss Penistone excused themselves to wander back to Dower House.

Their days fell into a sort of pattern. Betsy prepared their breakfast and a light luncheon, while they continued to take their evening meals at the main house with the earl and Colin. There was still much to be done before Sarah would consider the Dower House comfortable, but she rather enjoyed the work of setting it to rights. The new materials soon arrived and patterns were selected for curtains and bed hangings. New linens and blankets were likewise acquired, and the rest of Sarah's clothing and footwear were finally delivered. She was particularly pleased with her new riding habit, for although it was black like everything else, it was made of light wool and fitted her exquisitely. The buttons were silver, and daringly, she had had her hat made without a veil and embellished with a jaunty silver feather. To Miss Penistone's gentle hint that a veil was expected, she rejoined lightly with the necessity for unimpaired vision. Thankfully, nothing was said about the feather. Her first opportunity to wear the new outfit occurred when she met Colin, his eyes brimming with excitement.

"I say, my lady, that Oakes bounder has been round again!"

"Are you certain?" Sarah asked. "I've not seen him."

"Well, Jem did," he replied. "On one of the tenant farms. He must be nosing about everywhere. But this time maybe we can discover just what he's about. It's the Randolph place, and that family's been here since the Conqueror."

"The Conqueror?"

"Well, near enough," he grinned. "But what do you say, ma'am? Shall we investigate?"

She was eager to do so as much for the ride as for the possibility of discovering anything and quickly ran upstairs to change. Moments later, she rejoined him, and they hurried to the stable, where a fresh problem awaited them.

"His lordship has said nothing further about my riding," Sarah said then. "I've no idea which mount would be most suitable."

"We'll ask Jem," Colin decided. "How well do you ride?"

"Competently," Sarah replied. "I'm not a neck-or-nothing, mind you, but I daresay I can contrive to stay on any animal that's had a modicum of training."

Colin was perfectly satisfied with this response and spoke to Jem immediately. The result was that Sarah was soon mounted upon a spirited young ginger gelding. She was very well pleased with him, and he soon proved to have a smooth, even gait and strong forward action. They let the animals have their heads down the main drive and were soon galloping across the Common itself. When Colin signaled a halt at last, Sarah was nearly breathless.

"That was wonderful!" she cried. "It has been donkey's years since I have ridden like that, for you must know that to do so in Hyde Park, where I usually ride, is not at all the thing. One is expected merely to ride along sedately, stopping now and again to pass the time of day with one's acquaintances."

"Sounds devilish slow to me," pronounced Master Colin.

"Oh, indeed it is," Sarah agreed fervently. "This is ever so much more stimulating. Are we near to the Randolph place yet?"

"Over that hill yonder," he replied. "We could have taken the woods path. It's a bit shorter, but we couldn't have had our gallop. The path there is not conducive to speed."

Ten minutes later they rode into a tidy farmyard. It looked

as though the little cottage at one end had been newly thatched and painted, and three men were in the process of repairing the gate leading into a paddock of sorts. Colin rode up to the group and hailed one of the men, a burly and ruddy-faced fellow with bristly gray hair and side whiskers, who detached himself from the others at once and came smiling to meet them.

"Master Colin, as I live," he bellowed. "Welcome. Get ye down, lad, and come in to see Marthy. She'd not forgive me an I neglected t' show her how big ye've growed. Servant, ma'am." He ducked his head at Sarah.

"This is Lady Moreland, Sam," Colin informed him, whereupon Mr. Randolph's complexion became a deeper shade of red and he bowed lower, effusive in his apologies.

"I'm pleased to meet you, Mr. Randolph," Sarah said politely, jumping down from her horse. "How nice everything looks."

"Thank 'e, my lady. Feels good to be puttin' it t' rights again. The missus would be honored to make yer acquaintance, if ye'd condescend to enter our cottage."

Sarah happily complied and discovered Mrs. Randolph to be a feminine replica of her husband. Gray-headed, slightly florid, and a bit on the plump side, she exclaimed cheerfully over their entrance into her tidy kitchen and sought to wipe the flour from her hands.

"There now, if you didn't just catch me settin' my bread to rise," she chuckled. "Another few hours, and you could have had a slice still warm from the oven with butter meltin' all over it, like I know you likes it, Master Colin. 'Tis unusual for me to be adoin' it so late, but with all the extra work goin' on, I seem to get behinder every day. And we had a visitor this mornin' to boot."

"Mr. Oakes," Colin responded promptly. "Heard he'd been here. What did he want?"

Sarah was taken aback by his blunt approach, but it didn't seem to bother the Randolphs. Sam pulled up chairs right there in the kitchen, and Martha quickly set out sweet biscuits on a platter and poured a small glass of her own elderflower champagne for them each before she answered.

"Sam'l thinks the man's touched in his upper works. Not sure, m'self." She settled her bulk upon a small bench near the stove and sipped her wine.

"Man's got to be daft," Sam put in. "Couldn't keep to a subject two sentences runnin'. Asked about changes up t' the house, then about that Beck fellow what called hisself his lordship's valet, then about the house itself—priest holes, passages, and what-not. I ask ye, Master Colin, did ye ever hear the like?"

"Sounds a curst rum touch to me," Colin agreed. "What then?"

"Says he's doin' a history of old houses on the Common," Sam said. "Collectin' fer a book. Doubt the fellow could write one. Talked more cant than flash. Need t' be flash t' write books, I'd say."

"Right." Colin fell silent after a speaking glance at Sarah. "Did he say anything else? I must say, he seems a curious rogue."

"Aye, he does that, lad. Asked a few questions about the fourth earl—where he got his money—like that."

"What did you tell him?"

"What *could* he tell him?" Martha snorted. "Didn't know t' last earl *had* any money till he got hitched, beggin' your pardon, I'm sure, my lady. Couldn't prove his wealth by this place, that's certain enough."

Sam agreed, adding that things looked to be much better under the fifth earl, who seemed to have a good sense of what was needed as well as the blunt to pay for it. From there, the conversation drifted to roofs and repairs and livestock, and Colin made no effort to turn it back again. When Sarah taxed him about it on their return trip, he explained that the subject had plainly played out.

"If there had been more, Sam would have said so. My guess is they couldn't tell him what he wanted to know either."

Sarah could only agree, but she had been thinking. "If he murdered Darcy, why does he continue to stay so near?"

"The treasure, of course."

"But, Colin," she protested, "if that treasure is so large that Mr. Oakes is willing to risk his neck to find it, why on earth would Darcy have abducted me?" Colin stared at her, awe-stricken, and Sarah quickly realized her error. "You didn't know. Well, I probably should not speak of it to you. In fact, I'm quite sure that to do so is most improper, but it's true, nevertheless. He abducted me on account of my grandpapa's fortune. Why on earth would he have done so if he had already discovered a fortune of his own?"

Colin was silent, digesting this new tidbit and striving to force it into conformation with his theory. "Perhaps he felt he needed a cover for his own sudden wealth," he suggested finally. "Would people not have wondered about his affluence otherwise?"

Sarah opened her mouth to state that there had been nothing sudden about it, that Darcy had always *looked* affluent enough, that it hadn't been until her uncle's investigation that there had seemed to be any mystery about its origin. But, the words never came. Her attention was diverted instead by the view of a rapidly approaching horseman. Colin saw him, too.

"Why, it's Uncle Nick!" he exclaimed, waving. "Mind now, my lady, not a word to him about our discoveries!"

X

Sarah had no intention of confiding in Nicholas, but she could not repress a smile of appreciation, for he rode as though he were part of his magnificent bay stallion. He reined in. "Good morning, Countess. Have you not wandered rather far from home?"

"We've been visiting Sam and Martha Randolph," piped up Colin before she could speak. "Martha gave us cake and elderflower champagne. Only a small glass," he added hastily.

Nicholas turned to him with a smile. "So I should hope! Sam says two glasses of that brew will make the paths go all boggly. I must hope you are both still able to navigate properly."

Sarah chuckled. "It was very good," she said, "and it certainly didn't taste very dangerous."

Nicholas had turned his steed, and the three of them continued back toward Ash Park. There was a momentary silence following Sarah's light observation before he spoke again. "As to the danger," he said then, "I doubt you'd find it with Sam and Martha, but there is danger, my lady, when you ride outside the confines of the Park with only this young rattle for an escort."

"I can take care of her," Colin put in stoutly.

"Perhaps," his uncle replied kindly, "but I should be much easier in my mind if you had taken one of the grooms along as well. One who is not afraid to carry a sidearm."

"A pistol! Whatever for?" Sarah demanded. "Surely you exaggerate the dangers, my lord!"

"You may be right, Countess," Nicholas agreed with a rueful smile. "I know I must seem censorious to you at times, but I am trying not to seem so now. My first thought was to forbid your riding out altogether—"

"But, it was you who encouraged me!" Sarah protested.

"That is perfectly true, although it was against my better judgment. However, I realize I cannot keep you locked up—"

"So I should hope!"

"Steady, Countess. I have said I cannot. Nonetheless, there is danger and will be until Darcy's killer has been caught."

"Oh!" Sarah had not considered that the murderer might be a threat to herself. "But, why? I am no threat to him!"

"I daresay that's true," Nicholas agreed. "However, it is possible that he does not know that. There may be reasons unknown to us for his considering you a threat to his safety. Now, don't fly into a pelter," he advised when she stiffened. "I can protect you well enough at Ash Park. I've sent Tom, Matty, and Beck away, and everyone else is either answerable to me or well-trusted by you. But once you stray beyond the gates, I cannot offer that same protection."

Sarah gazed at him, wishing she could ask about Jeremy Oakes. But she was certain it would do no good. He would only fob her off with one Banbury tale or another. At least, he seemed to be making an attempt, however feeble, to be reasonable. Thinking it would be wise to encourage him to continue in that vein, she smiled.

"We did not mean to worry you, sir. I shall certainly take a groom in future. Perhaps I should take Erebus as well."

His eyes narrowed, as though such prompt capitulation gave him cause for suspicion, but Sarah couldn't help that. She knew he was perfectly capable of giving orders that would make it impossible for her to ride at all if he didn't trust her to obey him. Then she would be a virtual prisoner.

Nicholas left them as soon as they reached the stables, and Colin watched him go, a musing look in his eye. "I believe Uncle Nick knows more about this business than he's telling us," he said slowly. "It would definitely be one in the eye to him if we could solve the mystery."

Sarah agreed that she would like to surprise his lordship by finding the murderer, but she pointed out that he had rather effectively restricted their opportunity. "For we can hardly ride out to investigate Mr. Oakes with an armed groom. We should have to take him into our confidence, and that would never do."

Colin shrugged it aside. "I daresay if worse came to worst, we could rely on Jem not to split. But there are things we can do right here, you know."

"Here?"

"Certainly. That treasure is bound to be nearby. I doubt Cousin Darcy would have let it far out of his sight. We can search for it. I've already done a bit on my own."

"Where?" Sarah asked, interested in spite of herself.

"In the main house, mostly. I look after Uncle Nick sends me off to bed. I've searched Cousin Darcy's bedchamber and the one you had—most of that floor, actually."

"Colin! You haven't!"

"But I have. I am never tired so early as that, and it seemed a very good notion. You should do the same at Dower House."

"Nonsense," Sarah replied with a touch of asperity. "That house has been cleaned from attic to cellar—well, nearly anyway—and nothing out of the way was found. I shall certainly not go about poking and prodding at the paneling. I am by no means as positive as you are that such a treasure even exists."

Colin shot her a very speaking look but refrained from comment, allowing her to change the subject as they wandered back toward the main house. Sarah left him at the library terrace and returned to Dower House to partake of a light luncheon with Miss Penistone. She described their visit to the tenant farm, observing that things seemed to be moving along at quite a good clip.

"If improvements on the other farms have kept apace of the Randolphs', his lordship can expect to begin receiving quite decent rents next year."

"It would certainly seem so," agreed Miss Penistone. "Mr. Dasher commented only this morning that things seemed to be going very well. I think his lordship must be well-pleased."

Sarah had no notion of whether his lordship was pleased or not. He still seemed to be always either displeased or critical where she herself was concerned, but she let Penny's comment pass unchallenged and maintained her end of the light conversation without difficulty. After luncheon, Miss Penistone retired to the drawing room with a pile of linens that needed to be mended and counted, and Sarah wandered out to the garden. Lizzie had brought Miss Austen's *Emma* with her, atoning for her earlier oversight by having kept it safe from Lady Hartley, and it seemed a very good time to get on with that tale.

Settling comfortably against a magnificent oak and soon chuckling at Mr. Woodhouse and his comments upon the horrors of matrimony, she sat long into the afternoon, interrupted only once, when Erebus plumped down beside her and pressed his head into her lap. It was thoroughly relaxing, so deciding that she had earned a respite from chores, she stayed until the afternoon grew chilly. Rolling cumulus clouds drifted overhead, now and again obscuring the sun, and a wind rose, stronger than it had been in previous days. Finally, even the warmth of the great dog curled beside her was insufficient, and with a sigh she shut her book and returned to the house.

Lizzie was busy doing unknown things with Sarah's wardrobe, so she went back downstairs to the drawing room, where her services were gratefully received, and counted and tallied until it was time to dress for dinner.

Nicholas seemed to exert himself to be charming at the dinner table and told several interesting anecdotes, both about life in the Peninsula and about his adventures on the London scene.

"You are a member of the Corinthian set, are you not, Uncle Nick?" interjected young Colin at one point.

"I have been accused of it," replied his uncle with a smile, "though I trust my interests include other things than mere sport."

"But it's true that you once won a wager by driving your sporting curricle to Brighton in under four hours, is it not?"

"Three hours and forty-eight minutes," affirmed his uncle, "but it was a racing curricle. How the devil did you come to hear of it?"

"Oh, Antony Baldridge's father wrote him about it. Said he dropped a pony on account of it. Risked it only 'cause he said you were well-foxed at two at the Great Go, so he never thought you'd make it out of bed the next day, let alone to Brighton."

Nicholas frowned. "I think this conversation has gone beyond what is pleasing. We will change the topic, if you please."

"Do you attend cockfights, too, my lord?" Sarah inquired sweetly. Colin chuckled but fell silent again when he encountered a straight look from under his uncle's lowered brows.

"Upon occasion, my lady, but I draw the line at dog fights and bull-fighting."

"I am delighted to hear it, sir. What else amuses such a noted Corinthian as yourself?"

"A number of things, not many of which are intended to provide subject matter for the dinner table."

"Ah, yes, Jackson's Boxing Saloon, Cribb's Parlor—you are

no doubt a member of the exclusive back-room set there—
Angelo's Fencing Rooms, White's, Watier's, Boodle's, Brooke's.
No doubt, you think nothing of driving twenty miles or so to
see a good mill, and naturally you go to Newmarket for the
races and dread settling day at Tattersall's. Let me see, have
I omitted anything?"

"Just the ladybirds," offered Colin, carried away by Sarah's
banter and not looking at his uncle. There was a markedly
heavy silence before Nicholas directed his frowning gaze at his
nephew.

"You may be excused, sir," he said pointedly.

"Yes, my lord." Biting his lower lip, Colin slid from his seat
and made a rather hasty departure.

Sarah glared at Nicholas. "There was no need to send him
away, my lord. He merely followed my lead."

"That is quite true, but he should not have done so."

"Perhaps you should send me away, too."

Nicholas's lips twitched and he said wryly, "It is not my
place to teach you manners, Countess. Besides, I confess that
I encouraged you, however unwisely. Nevertheless, the boy
was impertinent. I could not let it pass."

Miss Penistone nodded in agreement, and Sarah dropped it.
She knew he was right. She had carried matters too far, but
Colin had crossed the line between the acceptable and the
unacceptable.

Directly after dinner, she retired to her room with a branch
of working candles to finish her book. By the time she turned
the last page, it was fairly late, the fire had gone out, and the
candles had burned low. Shivering, Sarah quickly changed to
her nightdress and pulled down her quilts. The candles began
to gutter, so she snuffed them carefully, then remembered her
window was still shut and went to open it.

A movement in the garden caught her eye and she paused,
peering into the darkness below. There it was, a flicker of
white amongst the trees. She remembered Colin's warnings
about the Dower House ghost, and a shiver went up her spine.
There it was again! Carefully, silently, she opened the window, straining to catch the least movement, very conscious of
the stillness. Not a cricket or nightbird stirred.

Suddenly, there came a low growl, then a woof followed by
outraged barking, and the white creature flitted from the
thickest part of the wood, across the main garden, and up the
giant oak beside the path. Erebus exploded from the shrub-

bery and attacked the foot of the tree, loudly expressing his indignation.

Repressing a chuckle, Sarah quickly found a wrapper and thrust her feet into sheepskin slippers before making her way hurriedly to the ground floor and out the front door. As she approached the oak tree, she could hear the dog's furious barking, punctuated by desperate whispers from above to "hush!" The whispers ceased when she drew near.

"Erebus! Come here!" she called sternly. It took several more similar commands before she was heeded, but at last the great dog lumbered to her side, and the barks gave way to low, menacing growls. "You may come down now," she said quietly.

There was no response. The branches of the oak were thickly foliaged, but catching a glimpse of white about a third of the way up, she moved closer, peering up through the densely growing leaves. "Come down now. I have him, so it is quite safe, you know."

Still there was only silence. She had kept her voice low, but she was certain the intruder had heard her, and she was wondering what might be the best approach to the situation when she was startled by a familiar voice from behind.

"What the devil is going on now?" Nicholas demanded.

Sarah turned to him in consternation. " 'Tis nothing at all, my lord. Erebus merely treed some poor beast or other. I am sorry if he disturbed you."

Nicholas glared at her and moved closer to the oak, peering upward as she had done. "Some poor beast indeed," he muttered. Then, in a louder voice, he added, "Come down here at once." The leaves rustled a bit, but otherwise there was no sound. A cloud cleared the moon just then, and the leaves glittered silver. The white figure was more clearly seen, and Nicholas spoke angrily. "Come down at once, young man. I'll not tolerate much more of this."

Slowly, the white figure descended, helped along the last few feet by his lordship's firm grip, and the sheet was twitched off to reveal a rather sheepish Colin. He glanced up at his uncle only to look quickly away again.

"What is the meaning of this?" The boy shifted his feet but made no reply. "I see. Well, I don't suppose I need an answer after all you've said about ghosts. 'Tis plain as a pikestaff that you meant to frighten her ladyship." Colin looked up in protest, but the expression disappeared almost immediately, and he looked away again. "Just so," pronounced his uncle grimly. "It will do you little good to deny it. We shall continue this discussion back at the house. You may await me in the library, if you please. And, as for you, my lady," he went on in the same grim tone, when the boy had turned glumly away, "I've a word or two for you as well."

Sarah turned to face him, surprised. "But what have I done?"

"I'll tell you what you've done! Whatever possessed you to come out here, unprotected, to take on an intruder by yourself?"

"It was only Colin! I was hardly in danger from a thirteen-year-old boy!"

"So you knew it was Colin?" Sarah nodded, thinking that now he would scold her for trying to deceive him earlier. "How did you know, Sarah?" His eyes were like flints.

"I . . . I just knew. After the things he said . . ." She broke off. She hadn't really known. She had only assumed it to be Colin. It might have been anyone. The thought showed itself as she raised widening eyes to his, and Nicholas nodded, his lips folded tightly.

"Just so, Countess." He took her by the arm and began to lead her back into the house.

"Erebus was there, sir," Sarah said quietly, making a last-ditch effort to retain some dignity.

"An armed intruder could have killed both the dog and yourself, quick as winking," he growled, pushing her through the front door. "Now, mind well what I say to you." He took her chin in his hand, forcing her to look him in the eye. "If you ever do so cork-brained a thing again, Countess, I shall make you wish you had never been born. Do I make myself clear?"

Her knees threatened to give way at his tone, but Sarah managed to nod, and he released her. She turned quickly toward the stairs and started up, holding tightly to the hand-rail, but halfway up, she looked back. Nicholas stood watching her, and his expression nearly caused her to miss her step.

Colin entered the dining parlor next morning before Sarah had even finished her breakfast. She was alone, for Penny had already taken herself off to attend to the myriad details with which she managed to occupy herself each day. Sarah indicated an empty chair. "Sit down, Colin, and help yourself to whatever strikes your fancy."

He obeyed, sitting carefully, and began spreading marma-lade on a slice of toast. Betsy peeped in and reappeared a moment later with a pot of chocolate, which she set down by his elbow before taking herself off again. Colin remained silent, concentrating on his toast, until he was sure they would be undisturbed. Then he looked straight at Sarah, a touch of amusement in his eye. "I am to apologize for my reprehensible behavior last night."

"So I should hope." But she grinned at him.

"It was not as he thought."

"Was it not?" She sipped her tea, watching him.

He shook his head. "I never meant to frighten you. You had said a ghost wouldn't, but I thought if anyone else saw me creeping about, they might think twice about investigating. I forgot about Erebus."

"What were you doing?" Sarah asked, though she was nearly certain she could supply the answer for herself.

"Searching for the treasure," he responded predictably. "I thought there might be an outside entrance to your cellars, and you said you wouldn't look."

"Dolthead," she said affectionately. "Those cellars have been closed off for years. Damp and dry rot made them unsafe, according to your uncle, so they were sealed off when he and your Cousin Darcy were children, as a safety measure to keep them from coming to grief there."

Colin looked skeptical. "Do you know where the entrance was used to be?" he asked.

"Of course. There is a passage off the kitchen, but the door has been bricked over. I assure you, it is perfectly solid, no secret latch or hinges, just solid brick."

Colin shrugged. "There might be another entrance you know," he insisted. "One that has not been bricked over."

"Well," Sarah replied practically, "if there is one, it seems odd that no one discovered it whilst we were refurbishing the place." The boy still frowned, so she sought for a means to divert his interest. "I think we are more likely to discover the solution to our mystery by acquiring information about the elusive Mr. Oakes. If he visited one tenant farm, he very likely visited others. I believe it would be a good plan to ride to some of them this morning. We could take your Jem along as a sop to your uncle, and perhaps, we might gather some new information."

Colin hesitated, and Sarah was surprised to note the light flush spreading over his face. He carefully adjusted his cuff, not looking at her. "Not today, I'm afraid," he said with studied carelessness. "Perhaps tomorrow."

"But why not today?" she demanded. His color deepened, and she suddenly realized what was wrong. "Oh dear! That brute!"

That drew a reluctant grin. "Fact is, he was pretty thoroughly angry, you know. Read me the devil of a scold before . . . well, you know. Anyways, it wasn't so bad. I've had worse at school. Daresay I'll be right as a trivet tomorrow."

Sarah still thought his lordship had overreacted, especially since he thought the thing only a boy's prank. She had a strong desire to give him a piece of her mind, but she was afraid to confront him lest she reveal Colin's true intentions. Then, the cat truly would be among the pigeons, and she had no notion how his lordship would react.

With a sigh, she decided she must leave well enough alone, though it meant a day of forced inactivity as far as the mystery was concerned. Not that she need be bored, because Penny would have a dozen suggestions for constructive use of her time. Just the thought spurred her thinking. A glimmer of a notion came to her.

She gazed at Colin. "Listen. I think I have an idea." He gave her his full attention. "Your uncle said before that I might be in danger. Could we not put that possibility to good use? What if I were seen out riding alone? I wouldn't really be unprotected, of course," she added as he moved to protest. "It would only seem so. Would the murderer not have to show himself in order to get me?"

Colin's eyes lit, but then he frowned heavily. "It would be too dangerous. Uncle Nick wouldn't like it at all."

"Well, of course he wouldn't. Which is why," Sarah said patiently, "we shan't tell him. We will enlist the aid of your friend Jem. He will escort me, armed to the teeth, out onto the Common. But then he will drop back until I seem to be alone. Tomorrow you may come with us, and then I shall have two guardians."

Colin hesitated. "It would be better if you were to take the woods path, I think. It would be difficult out on the Common to get Jem to drop far enough behind. Tomorrow, we can go the other way, and I will be able to divert him and still come up to you soon enough to effect a rescue."

"Very well," Sarah agreed. "Although nothing will happen today, for it will catch the villain unawares and unprepared.

But if he sees that it is become a habit, he will, sooner or later, make his move. Then we shall have trapped him."

Colin considered the plan but finally shook his head. "It may be a good notion, ma'am, but it is too dangerous."

"You cannot stop me," she said gently. "Or you could do so, of course, by laying information with your uncle, but I am convinced you would never do anything so shabby."

"Well, of course I would not!" Colin declared, indignant at the very thought. "However, I daresay Jem will not agree to lag behind either. Very likely, he has had his orders from Uncle Nick."

But Sarah wisely said nothing to the groom about her intentions. Colin strolled to the stables with her, once she had changed to her habit. He smothered a grin as she asked Jem if he would accompany her so that she might indulge in some much-needed exercise. The groom agreed at once and had clearly had orders from his master, for when he reappeared, leading their two mounts, Sarah saw the stock of a shotgun sticking up near his saddle bow.

Jem helped her to mount, and she waved to Colin as they set off at a brisk trot down the path leading to the main drive. A few moments later, they emerged from the Park, and with a quick glance around, Sarah drew rein. Jem pulled up beside her.

"Where would you like to go, my lady?"

Sarah hesitated. "I don't really care, Jem," she said at last, "but I wish I did not need an escort." He looked puzzled, and she hastened to add, " 'Tis not that I don't appreciate your protection, Jem, only I should prefer to be alone with my own thoughts. Surely, you can understand that." He nodded doubtfully. "I knew you would. Look here, perhaps we can manage it so that I may have my solitude and you can obey your master. If we take the woods path, and you allow me to ride a little ahead, you would still be near enough to protect me, but I should be alone with my thoughts."

Jem eyed her warily. "How far ahead, my lady?"

"Oh, not far," Sarah said with an airy gesture. "Just far enough so that you are out of sight but near enough to hear me if I shout." She watched him hopefully, knowing she had set him a problem. No doubt Nicholas had made his orders quite plain. Then she saw hesitation in Jem's eye and quickly pressed her advantage. "You know there will be no danger. 'Tis only one of his lordship's starts. You wouldn't worry if your sister wanted to ride alone on that path." Jem had no sister, but it was clear that he had never thought of the trail through the woods as a source of danger before. His expression relaxed.

"Very well, my lady. We'll do as ye say. Only perhaps we ought not to explain the matter to his lordship."

She chuckled. "Never fear. If he asks about my ride, I shall tell him you did your duty exactly as he would have wished."

A gap-toothed grin was her reward, and she kicked her mount into an easy lope, soon leaving the groom well behind. Once into the woods, Sarah maintained the pace only long enough to make sure he was well out of sight. A tremor of excitement made her shiver. Despite what she had told Colin about setting up a pattern of behavior, she thought it just as likely that the villain, if he truly wanted her, would be looking for any possible opportunity.

The wooded area on either side of the narrow path was silent, though she heard an occasional bird's trill. In some areas the shrubbery was dense right up to the path, while in others, the ground seemed barren underneath tall trees. Shafts of sunlight beamed down through the foliage here and there, lighting the carpet of dead leaves with glints of orange and gold. It seemed peaceful enough, and Sarah's thoughts turned, as they had done before, toward London and what she would be doing, had she not chosen to play her foolish games with Darcy Ashton.

The season was drawing to a close, now that the Princess Charlotte was safely married, and most of the Beau Monde would have followed the Prince Regent down to Brighton. Her uncle had hired a house there on the Marine Parade, and Sarah had been looking forward to a sojourn in that famous seaside resort. Lord Hartley was not a member of the notorious Carlton House set, but she had been invited to a ball and a musical evening there and had hoped to receive at least one or two invitations to visit the fabulous Brighton Pavillion. Now, it would never be.

Instead, here she was, hemmed about with restrictions once again, but perhaps Nicholas would relax some of them once the murderer had been caught. And, if she could be the one to catch him—well, that would make his lordship sit up and take notice. He might even, for once, approve. With a sigh, Sarah came back to earth. Whatever else he did, Nicholas would *not* approve. If she were to capture the murderer single-handedly and deliver him bound and gagged to Sir William Miles, Nicholas would no doubt censure the act as conduct unbecoming a lady of Quality.

Her horse shied a bit, startling her, but she brought him back to order. Jem was still out of sight, and she could see no other reason for her mount's odd behavior. He settled down almost immediately, but his ears continued to twitch, and Sarah looked around again a bit nervously.

She wondered how long his lordship meant to keep her at Ash Park. Perhaps one day she would return to London. Certainly, she would like to visit Paris and Rome. Colin had had two letters from his mother, and the bits he read aloud had stirred Sarah's blood with yearning to see the cities she heard described.

Lost in her thoughts, she was unaware of the thickening shrubbery, unaware that she was entering a section of the wood where sunlight seldom pierced, except in an occasional trickle on a breeze-tossed leaf. The gelding maintained its even, hypnotic pace, while Sarah envisioned herself at a Viennese ball or making her curtsy at the French court. Perhaps, she might meet a dazzling Russian prince or a gay Italian count. But then, suddenly, thoughts of counts and princes vanished, as a great bay stallion plunged out of the dense shrubbery immediately to her right. A hand of steel clamped bruisingly across her mouth before she could scream, and she was swept struggling from her saddle by the unseen horseman.

XI

Unable to see her captor, Sarah experienced a moment of sheer terror. His hand still tight across her mouth, he urged his horse back into the shrubbery then turned so that, well-hidden, he faced the path once more. A moment later, Sarah saw Jem ride around a bend in the path, and a new fear welled up within her. The murderer clearly meant to trap Jem as well, to kill him, so as to leave no witnesses. No matter what became of her, she must prevent that.

Jem saw her horse standing in the path and urged his own mount forward with a muttered oath. Sarah felt the man behind her stiffen. It was now or never. Forcing her mouth open against his hand, she snapped her teeth shut upon his little finger.

"Ow! You little vixen!" He snatched his hand away, but though the opportunity was clear, Sarah held her tongue. The voice was only too familiar, and as he swung to the ground still holding her firmly, she was conscious of a devout wish that she were the sort of sensible female who could faint dead away in a crisis.

Nicholas dragged her with him onto the path as he moved to intercept the hapless Jem. "I will see her ladyship home," he grated. "You get back there as fast as that beast will carry you, and I suggest you use the time you have before my return to concoct an acceptable explanation for daring to defy my explicit order!"

Sarah gasped at the fury in his tone. She had never meant for Jem to suffer; indeed, the possibility had never crossed her mind. The rapid hoofbeats were soon lost in the distance, and an uncomfortable silence descended upon the wood. Nicholas's hand was heavy on her shoulder.

He drew a long breath and turned her to face him. "So help

me," he growled, "if you were wife, daughter, or sister, I'd lay you across my knee and blister your backside."

Sarah drew herself up, squaring her shoulders under his grip. "Pray do not let the lack of a proper relationship deter you, my lord. You have already made it clear that you hold yourself my guardian." She glared at him, adding angrily, "And you proved last night that you prefer violence to reason when it comes to dealing with disobedience from those under your charge!"

"Nonsense!" he snapped. "It was nothing like the same sort of thing, and you know it. You'll only catch cold trying that line on me. If you've got an explanation for this, I'd advise you to trot it out, instead of doing your possible to make me lose my temper."

"How did you find out?" she evaded.

"Heard you'd gone for a ride and thought you'd prefer even my company to that of the groom, so I followed. Saw the lad riding alone and figured that, one way or another, you'd managed to give him the slip, so I circled through the woods. But we digress." There was another pause, while Sarah examined his top boots. "I am waiting."

He didn't sound prepared to wait very long, and she wondered fleetingly what he would do if she refused to answer him. But then, she looked up, and the expression she encountered gave her quickly to realize that her courage would not long withstand his temper. She forced herself not to look away, to meet that stern gaze.

"You will not like my answer, sir."

"That is a foregone conclusion," he replied uncompromisingly. "I am determined to hear it, nonetheless."

"Very well." Sarah heaved a sigh. "You said the murderer would probably be looking for me, so I thought if I could draw him out, Jem would be able to capture him, and we could all be comfortable again." In view of what had actually transpired, it sounded lame even to her own ears, and she looked away again, bracing herself for the explosion.

"Did you tell Jem what you expected?" Nicholas asked harshly.

"No." This should help Jem's cause. "I simply ordered him to fall back. I said I wished to be alone with my thoughts."

But this explanation did nothing to mollify his lordship's temper. Indeed, it seemed to exacerbate things, for his frown grew heavier and the grip on her shoulders began to hurt.

"Of all the crack-brained, idiotic women! In other words, having convinced your escort that no rescue would be necessary, you expected him to be ready to fly to your defense in the wink of an eye. By God, madam, you try me too far." His grip was bruising her, and she struggled to free herself, but all at once he was shaking her. "I warned you, Sarah, last night in the garden. I don't know what you deserve for this defiance, but 'tis plain as a pikestaff you've no notion of how to protect yourself, so I shall have to manage the business for you." He seemed to realize what he was doing, because the shaking stopped, but he did not release her.

"What will you do?" She felt breathless and could barely force the words out.

He glared at her. "The first thing is to get you home. Come, I'll toss you up." Her horse had stood quietly and paid little heed now as Nicholas gathered the reins. Sarah took them silently, and he placed his hands on her waist, preparing to lift her. But suddenly he spun her around again and, before she had any idea what he was about, lowered his head to hers, gathering her to his broad chest in a crushing embrace. She fought briefly, but his lips seemed to burn against her own, and almost against her will, her body melted to his. She had never felt such feelings before, had never dreamed them possible. He kissed her lips, her cheek, and then muttered harshly against her curls, "Oh God, little Sarah, how could you be so foolish?"

Released by those words from what must have been a spell, Sarah stiffened and began to struggle again. "Let me go, damn you!" Nicholas released her immediately, and she stumbled but recovered herself sufficiently to deliver a resounding slap across his cheek. "How dare you, sir! To preach propriety on the one hand and treat me like a chambermaid on the other! 'Tis you who are foolish, my lord, to think that I should submit blindly to *any* decision of your making!"

With that, she turned away indignantly, but she had barely taken a single step before strong hands clamped her waist again, and she was hurled, skirts flying, onto her saddle. Such was his savagery that she nearly continued head over heels, but she managed somehow to keep her balance. Nicholas held her horse's bridle.

"We will return to the Park together, my lady. I'll not release you without your word to that effect, for I have no desire to chase you over the Common, and I doubt you wish to discover what I'll do if you decide to defy me again."

It was as though, once more, he had read her mind, but there was a new and chilling note in his voice which led her to suspect that if she opposed him any further, Nicholas would not hesitate to punish her as he had threatened. She certainly had no wish to discover if he were bluffing or not.

"I shall obey you, my lord," she said quietly.

Nicholas said nothing more but released her bridle and swung into his own saddle. The ride back to the stables was accomplished in silence. When they arrived, he helped her to dismount, but when she would have turned away toward Dower House he held her arm.

"One moment, my lady." He called to the head groom and, when that worthy stood before him, gave strict orders that in future no horse was to be saddled for her ladyship unless he personally gave the command. Nicholas spoke loudly enough so that Sarah was certain everyone in the area could hear him, and then, satisfied that he would be obeyed, he turned back to her. "You may go up to the house now, Countess, but I shall want to speak to you again shortly."

Utterly mortified, Sarah could feel the warmth flooding her cheeks as she turned away, but conscious that even the lowliest stable boys were watching her, she managed to hold her head up until she reached the shelter of the trees. Then, the tears began to flow. She heard Nicholas shouting for Jem, but she scarcely spared a thought for the poor groom, so wrapped was she in her own shame and fury. How dared he speak to her so! She could not understand him at all. First, to scold her, then to kiss her, then to humiliate her in front of the stablehands. The man was clearly unhinged! And to think that earlier she had been hoping to discover some means by which to make him approve of her. She must be as daft as he was himself!

She was kicking rocks from the path in a savagely unladylike manner by the time she reached Dower House, tears streaming unnoticed down her cheeks, obscuring her vision. Thus it was that she failed to observe the figure perched on the top step.

"My lady! Cousin Sarah, what happened? Oh, I was afraid something would happen when I saw him ride out!"

Colin hurried down to meet her, and Sarah made an attempt

to collect herself, rubbing her eyes with the back of her sleeve. "Your uncle is altogether abominable!" she fumed.

"What did he do?" Colin demanded. "Surely, he didn't—"

"He sent me up to the house like a child!" Sarah muttered, "and in front of them all! And he said that I am no longer to ride without his express permission! I am his prisoner!"

"Miss Sarah, I believe your feet are damp. Surely, you will want to come up at once and change your boots." It was Miss Penistone, standing in the open doorway, her features unruffled, her voice perfectly calm, and her words brought Sarah back to earth with a thump.

"Yes, Penny," she said at once, striving to achieve that same ladylike calm. "I am just coming. Excuse me, Colin."

"But I want to know what happened!"

"Her ladyship will speak with you later, Master Colin," Miss Penistone interposed kindly. "But, just now, you must run along and allow her to change her dress."

"Yes, do go, Colin. Your uncle will be here shortly, so you'd best make yourself scarce, else he'll know you've had a hand in this." The boy needed no further urging but took himself off immediately, leaving Sarah to seek comfort from her companion.

Miss Penistone listened calmly to the recital of woe, asking a pointed question or two and receiving answers that were, at times, a bit stilted. But when Sarah declared angrily that Nicholas was an insensitive brute and cruel besides, she dared to take exception.

"I think you owe him a sincere apology, my dear."

"Penny! How can you say so, after I tell you of his abuses to me!"

"His behavior was not exemplary," Miss Penistone agreed gently, "but he has been sorely tried. I truly believe he fears for your safety and is displeased only because you have defied orders meant to protect you." She gave Sarah a straight look. "I think you had better go upstairs, Miss Sarah, and wash your face. And whilst Lizzie is helping you change, I trust you will think seriously on my words and try to see matters from his lordship's point of view."

Sarah was dismissed just exactly as she had been dismissed to think on her sins as a child. And if anything was needed to put the final touch to her misery, it was having Penny revert to governess. It was enough to set one's teeth on edge! Nevertheless, she let Lizzie change her dress and went downstairs again half an hour later, when Betsy informed her that his lordship wanted a word with her in the drawing room.

Penny was in her favorite chair near the window, occupied with more of the interminable mending. Observing gratefully that she showed no inclination to leave her alone with Nicholas, Sarah dropped a stiff curtsy and waited mutely for him to say his piece.

"I wanted to speak with you, my lady, only because I feared you may have thought me a trifle harsh."

Sarah looked up into his eyes, widening her own in mock innocence. "Harsh, sir?"

"I have no wish to seem so, ma'am," he went on doggedly, "but it is my duty to see you safely through this business. I am certain you find my orders restricting, and I am sorry for it; however, until that villain can be brought to book, you will have to abide by them."

"And if I do not?"

His features hardened. "I trust you will find it difficult to flout them, ma'am, and I should certainly not advise you to try it. My patience is limited. I should be sorely tempted, should you continue to be reckless of your own safety, to deliver you to Lady Hartley with my compliments. I believe I could trust her to keep you safe enough."

Sarah's jaw dropped, and the color drained from her face, for although she was nearly certain he would never carry it out, the threat alone was enough to curb any inclinations toward further rebellion. No matter how restricted she felt at Ash Park, it would be much worse in London. Her aunt would scold, her uncle would be made uncomfortable by her very presence, and they would certainly never let her keep Penny. In short, it would be utterly dreadful.

"I hope you would never do such a thing, my lord," she said tightly. "I shall endeavor to give you no cause for it."

He smiled, his eyes softening. "Then I am sure I shall have no further reason for complaint, Countess. Come, do not look so gloomy. 'Twas not my wish to frighten you. Well," he amended, "perhaps that is not quite true. I do mean for you to understand that I am determined to protect you. There may be no cause for it, as I have said before, but I would prefer not to risk it." He stood to take his leave, and obeying a gesture, Sarah walked with him into the hall. He pulled the front door open but stood looking down at her. "Sarah . . ." He paused, and she looked away. The tender look in his eye and the matching note in his voice were nearly as unsettling to her nerves as his anger had been.

"Uncle Nick! Uncle Nick!" Colin was fairly flying down the path, his eyes alight with excitement, and the moment was broken. "You'll never guess who's here! It's Gram! Gram's here! Her coach is still at the front door!"

Nicholas smiled ruefully at Sarah. "I think you are soon to experience the privilege of meeting my mother."

"Your mother! But she is in Yorkshire!"

"Not, it seems, at the moment. Indeed, unless Colin has gone round the bend—which I'll grant you his present behavior would indicate—she appears to be on the premises. Would you like to come along now to meet her?"

But this Sarah could not agree to, despite Colin's adding his persuasion to his uncle's. Her mental state was still anything but calm, and she was certain that Nicholas's mother would wish to be private with him at least long enough to catch up on all that had occurred at Ash Park. But she agreed that she and Miss Penistone would come a little early so as to make her ladyship's acquaintance before dinner.

In honor of the guests, dinner was put back to the more civilized hour preferred by town folk, and as she dressed for the meal, Sarah was conscious of a wish that she could appear to better advantage. She wished it even more when she entered the library with Penny to discover the presence of two strange gentlemen. Colin grinned at her from his place near the fire, as the earl and the two strangers got somewhat hastily to their feet.

"My lady, may I present Sir Percival Packwood and his son, Lionel. Sir Percival is recently become my father-in-law. This is Lady Moreland, Darcy's widow."

Sarah made a brief curtsy to Sir Percival, but her eyes returned involuntarily to his son. Lionel Packwood wore bright yellow pantaloons under a coat of bottle green, but it was primarily his waistcoat that made Sarah stare. That startling article was fashioned of bright yellow-and-red-striped satin and was certainly a wonder to behold. Lionel himself had more nose than chin, auburn hair, and eyebrows a shade or two lighter above pale blue eyes that were set a touch too close together. The generous nose and his cheeks were daubed with liverish freckles, and though his teeth were fairly even, his lips were too full for Sarah's liking, particularly the lower one, which Lionel had a tendency to push into greater prominence whenever he wished to appear meditative.

His lordship's actual words finally penetrated, and she dragged her eyes away from Lionel, who was grinning fatuously at her. "I beg your pardon, my lord, but did you say Sir Percival is your father-in-law?" Nicholas nodded with a glint of amusement, and she turned to the older gentleman, her hands outstretched. "Then, congratulations are in order, sir. I collect you have married Lady Moreland."

"Lady Packwood now, ma'am," corrected Sir Percival with a smile rather unfortunately like his son's. There the resemblance ended, however, for where Lionel put Sarah in mind of a bantam rooster, Sir Percival looked much more like an emperor penguin. He was a biggish gentleman, conservatively dressed in buff pantaloons and a dark coat, and broader amidships than above or below. His round, pale face was framed by dark, tufting sidewhiskers and bristling, salt-and-pepper eyebrows. Now that she thought about it, perhaps it was a walrus he reminded her of. She would ask Penny for her opinion later. Sir Percival, still talking, informed the room at large that, her ladyship having taken it into her head at long last to get riveted, he hadn't given her time for a second thought.

"Quite right, my love!" trilled a voice from the library threshold, and they all turned to greet her ladyship. Lady Packwood might have been buried for years in the wilds of Yorkshire, but one would never know it to look at her. Though Sarah knew the woman to be nearing the half-century mark, she was dressed in the height of fashion and looked ten years younger in a copper-green satin dinner gown that would have looked very well on Sarah herself. On her ladyship, it was stunning. She had kept her figure, and the color of the gown was particularly good with her hair, which was light brown with deep golden highlights. The puffed sleeves were perhaps a trifle fuller than Sarah would have had them, the lace trimming a trifle longer, but on the whole, she decided as she made her curtsy, Lady Packwood was a very well-preserved specimen.

"How do you do, my lady?"

"Very well, I thank you. So you are Sarah. How pretty you are, my dear, and how lucky to be rid of the deplorable Darcy! You must be ever so much more comfortable without him. And don't look at me like that, Nicholas, for I am still your mother, and that scowl is definitely impertinent. You may pour me some Madeira instead."

"As you wish, ma'am," he replied stiffly.

"Oh, isn't he impossible?" she twinkled at Sarah, as she took her seat with a graceful swish of satin. "Here, sit beside me, my dear. I wish to become better acquainted. I must say at the outset," she added as Sarah obeyed, "that I hope you don't hold me responsible for Nicky's absurd sense of propriety."

"Certainly not, ma'am," Sarah said quickly, then feeling his lordship's eye upon her, she flushed, adding, "that is, I—"

"Oh, don't give it another thought," laughed Lady Packwood. "I assure you I have been listening to him prosing on most of the afternoon, and I cannot for the life of me think how he came by such starched-up notions."

"Can you not, ma'am?" Sarah encouraged sweetly, avoiding Nicholas's eye and Colin's as well, albeit for vastly different reasons.

"Not at all," replied her ladyship, "for you must know that I am not at all nice in my notions, and his father, may he rest in peace—though I doubt he'd find a peaceful situation very amusing—was a rake of the first stare."

"He was!" Sarah was astonished, for she had thought of Darcy's grandfather as rather a stuffy old man, an early replica of Nicholas at his most censorious.

"Indeed," chuckled Lady Packwood. "He was dashing, outspoken, and outrageous right up to the end. I daresay he would have abducted me, had I not been entirely willing to marry him."

"Mother!" Nicholas expostulated. "Surely, we might change the course of this conversation. It is not at all suitable for either Lady Moreland or Colin."

"Oh, fiddle-faddle," replied his mother. "You are becoming positively fusty, my dear. I daresay you hadn't noticed, so you will thank me for dropping a hint in your ear. And pray do not call poor Sarah Lady Moreland in that stuffy way. It sounds positively puritanical. What a good thing I thought to marry Percy before coming down. It would have been quite dreadful otherwise." She glanced around brightly at the circle of puzzled faces. "Well, my dears! *Two* dowager countesses of Moreland! It wouldn't have done at all. Too, too confusing!"

Noting the storm warnings in Nicholas's eye, Sarah hastily inquired about the recent nuptials and discovered them to have been very recent indeed.

"Four days, my dear," informed her ladyship. "Why, as soon as I received word of the deplorable Darcy's death—dear me, what a brat he was as a child, a whining, puling brat, I promise you. Where was I? Oh, yes. Well, as soon as word reached us, I ran to Percy and said, 'The time has come, my love.' Those were my very words, were they not, my love?" She turned to her spouse, who had moved to stand behind her chair. He patted her shoulder comfortably.

"Indeed, yes, my sweet. Your very words, indeed."

"There, I knew he would remember! But it had to be immediate. You understand that, Sarah. One simply cannot be married in black gloves, so I had to accomplish the deed before ever the tattle-mongers had the tale."

"They must not have had it yet," stated her son ironically, "since you still have not put on your black gloves or any other sign of mourning."

"Do you truly think I should wear mourning for the deplorable Darcy?" inquired her ladyship, wrinkling her lovely nose at him. "I cannot think why. I am only his grandfather's second wife, no kin to him at all, which I always counted among my blessings, of course. I daresay I shall unearth my black gloves for the brief time we shall be in London, as a sop to the tabbies, you know. I think I must have packed a pair somewhere or other. At least, I daresay my woman probably remembered to do so."

"Do you go to London, then, ma'am?" Sarah asked, in another hasty diversionary attempt.

"Indeed, yes," replied her ladyship on a note of *ennui*. "It is too bad of Percy, but he insists that he has matters of business to attend before we can leave for the Continent. And, of course, we will leave Lionel there. He would be a trifle *de trop* on our honeymoon, don't you agree?"

Sarah nodded, refraining from speech for fear of overstating the case. The idea of Lionel on anyone's honeymoon, including his own, was nearly more than her sense of the ridiculous would tolerate. Lady Packwood watched her closely, and her merry hazel eyes began to twinkle.

"Just so, my dear. I expect he will get into all manner of mischief, but he can only learn from his mistakes. Percy is leaving his finances in the hands of a very competent man of affairs, so Nicky will not be expected to tow him out of River Tick as he did, more than once, I'm sure, for the deplorable Darcy."

"I wish you will stop calling him 'the deplorable Darcy'!" snapped Nicholas.

"Pish tush. He *was* deplorable—grew from a detestable child into a contemptibly insignificant little dandiprat—and Sarah is very much better off without him, as I am certain she would agree, were anyone to inquire."

"Damn it, Mother, that has nothing to do with the matter—"

"Begging your pardon, my lord, and no wish to shove my oar in. Bad form, don't you know." It was Sir Percival, and the astonishment Sarah felt at his voluntarily putting in a word of his own seemed to be shared by everyone. Even Nicholas stopped midsentence, as Sir Percival went blandly on. "Well, stands to reason, don't it? Oughtn't to speak to your doting mother that way. She is doting, y' know. Told me so herself. Well, anyway, free country, ain't it? Lady can say what she wants. Particularly, if you'll pardon my sayin' so, about her own relatives. Lot of dirty dishes, more 'n likely. Stands to reason, don't it? Most folks' relatives—" He turned a jaundiced eye toward his heir. "—well, most of 'em put one to the blush at best." He paused, looking around for confirmation.

"Don't they just!" exclaimed Colin. "Well, uh—" He stammered, as his words caught him up. "—I mean to say, not you, Gram, or Uncle Nick or Cousin Sarah—Lady Moreland, I mean—I suppose she's one of mine now since she married Cousin Deplor—"

"Colin!" Nicholas half rose from his chair, but as Colin began to back away from him, stammering a hasty apology, Lady Packwood burst into merry laughter.

"Do, for heaven's sake, relax, Nicky! The boy merely suffered a slip of the tongue, and it was my fault entirely. I know you'd dearly love to tear a strip off me, but that is no reason to rake poor Colin over the coals."

"Well, it's the *very* reason I wanted you to stop all that improper talk," retorted Nicholas, taking his seat again, much to Colin's visible relief.

"Of course it is, and I daresay you were perfectly right. I expect it comes of not having to worry about proper conversation. Your father said most other females talked nothing but missish drivel, and Percy doesn't mind my unruly tongue at all. Do you, my love?"

"Not at all, my sweet," he responded gallantly, adding with more truth than tact, "Don't notice it."

But her ladyship was not offended in the least. She merely

chuckled. "There, you see, Nicky! It does not unsettle the people I care about, except you, of course, dear boy. But it needn't, you know. And, come to think of it, it never used to do so."

Her son did not respond to this gambit, so she looked at him closely, then directed her gaze at Sarah and smiled a little smile. It disappeared almost immediately, however, and she turned to Penny, who was quietly working a bit of elegant petit point.

"Pray forgive our manners, Miss Penistone," she said cordially. "It must be difficult to pretend that one's mind is otherwhere during a family quarrel."

"But my mind was not otherwhere, your ladyship," replied Penny in her usual placid way, as she set another stitch. "It would be quite impossible to ignore speech in a room as small as this one is, you know. But I promise you I shan't regard it."

"Indeed?" Simple respect dawned in her ladyship's eyes, and Sarah, finding it impossible to repress a chuckle, was grateful that Dasher chose that particular moment to announce dinner in tones stentorian enough to compete with the most experienced London butler.

XII

After she had said good night to Lizzie, Sarah thought back over an evening that had been a good deal livelier than its predecessors. She was quite certain that Penny disapproved of Lady Packwood, for were not Penny's watchwords, "poise, posture, and propriety"? The three P's. And no matter how much her ladyship possessed of the first two, she certainly had little notion of the third. What was more, she seemed proud of it!

Sarah snuggled under the coverlet, found the perfect place for her head on the down pillow, and thought about Lady Packwood. She had been prepared to like Nicholas's mother, but she had never expected Lady Packwood to be exactly the sort of woman she would like to be herself. And, she had set them all by the ears!

Heretofore, their conversation at the dinner table had been, for the most part, polite and conventional. Sarah chuckled, thinking that tonight had been neither. Lady Packwood had barely taken her seat before she demanded to know why Sarah was dressed as a crow.

"Darcy was her husband," Nicholas said sternly into the stunned silence. "It is expected that his widow wear deep mourning."

"Poppycock!" announced her ladyship with bland disregard for his subtle gestures toward Dasher, the footman, and two maidservants who were serving the first course. "Anyone with sense knows how poor Sarah came to marry that lobcock, and no one believes she really mourns his loss. No one with sense," she repeated. "Well, I mean, how *could* they? How could anyone mourn the loss of such a ninnyhammer?"

"Nevertheless," Nicholas pronounced stonily, "Lady Moreland

will not flout convention. She will appear appropriately garbed for the customary year."

"Gothic! That's what you are! Isn't he, my love?"

"If you say so, my sweet," replied her amiable spouse, applying his attention to the succulent pigeon pie upon his plate.

"Relicts always wear black for at least a year, just as Cousin Nicholas says," declared Lionel in accents perilously near a lisp.

"Rot!" retorted his stepmama, rounding on him. "You keep your tongue between your teeth until you've learnt some sense. Nicky is *not* your cousin, and you shall address him by his title until he gives you leave to do otherwise. And you are *not* to call Sarah a relict. Abominable word!"

"Papa!" protested Lionel.

"He's right, my sweet," mumbled Sir Percival through his pie. " 'Relict' is a perfectly respectable word."

"Well, I don't like it. Never did."

"Ah, now that's another matter entirely," responded her love, turning a withering eye upon his son. "She don't like it, Lionel. Don't use it again."

Flushing, Lionel muttered, "She shouldn't speak to me so. *I* don't like it."

"Nonsense!" Sir Percival retorted. "Daresay it's good for you. May learn sense yet, if your stepmama pounds it into you."

"Yes, that's very true, Lionel," added her ladyship, "for whatever has been said against my own children, no one has ever yet accused them of lacking sense. But I shan't have time to do it properly, you know, for your papa and I shall soon be leaving for the Continent, and you will be quite on your own. I daresay you'll make a muck of it, but that cannot be helped. Pass me that dish of dressed salmon again, Dasher, if you please."

Lionel looked slightly cheered as a result of what Sarah thought to be a rather daunting speech, and she glanced at Nicholas, surprised to see amusement in his eyes. His gaze met hers, and a delicate flush tinged her cheeks. She looked away only to encounter a direct and rather speculative look from Lady Packwood. But her ladyship had not finished with Nicholas.

"I daresay he's right, you know," she mused, "and it would be another matter entirely if black were a color that flattered you, Sarah, but it don't. Makes you look old-cattish when you've not seen eighteen yet. Your skin looks pasty, and your hair looks dull. You need colors with a bit of warmth to 'em. Isn't that right, my love?"

Thus appealed to, Sir Percival dragged his eyes from the truffled rice and creamed squab and even went so far as to lift his eyeglass, the better to examine Sarah. "I daresay. Damned pretty piece though, whatever color she be."

"This discussion is pointless," said Nicholas, jaws clenched. "She will wear black because I want no more scandal. It is the color she is expected to wear to show proper respect for her husband."

"Respect for that—" But Lady Packwood broke off the sentence in response to a wrathful glint in her son's eye. "Oh, very well, my dear. I suppose I have plucked that crow quite bald. But is it necessary that Sarah wallow in her mourning when there is none to see her save ourselves?"

Sarah caught her breath as Lady Packwood's intent became clear. It would be wonderful if Nicholas would allow her to wear colors, even dull colors, at home. She looked at him, willing him to agree. But he was frowning.

"I cannot believe hyprocrisy is the answer, madam."

"Piffle! 'Tis the height of hypocrisy to dress a lie. Better she should do it as little as possible. I see no reason why she should not dress as usual here. If she goes elsewhere, she can don her respect."

"And if we have callers? A fine thing it would be for someone to encounter a recent widow dressed in colors!"

"Fustian! What on earth do you keep Dasher for, if not to delay or get rid of unwanted company? If he cannot arrange it so that she has adequate warning of callers, he's not much of a butler. He's not much of a butler anyway, come to think of it. You really ought to get yourself a proper one, Nicky, to puff up your consequence."

"He'll do for the present. He knows my ways," Nicholas said absently. He glanced at Sarah. "Would you prefer to wear your other clothes, Countess?"

"Oh, yes," she breathed.

"Well, I shall take the matter under consideration," he said finally.

Lady Packwood asserted that she, for one, was glad she would soon be in Paris where English manners and customs were thought to be mildly amusing and where no one would expect her to mourn her first husband's grandson. Declaring that she would rig herself out in the first style of elegance, she drifted easily from that topic to details of the honeymoon itinerary and the latest letter from the Lady Honoria, whom she was planning to meet either in Brussels or Rome—she could not recall precisely which.

"How she will stare when she sees Percy!" her ladyship chuckled. "I merely wrote that I should be going over, never a word about him. Do you think your mama will be surprised?" she asked Colin.

"I should say!" the boy exclaimed. He had been staring, awestricken, as Sir Percival methodically devoured the contents of one plateful after another.

When they left the gentlemen to their port, Sarah thought privately that Nicholas looked a bit harrassed, but whether it was a result of his mother's forthright speech or the prospect of sharing his excellent port with Sir Percival and Lionel, she could not tell.

In the library, she was able to sit back and relax, while Lady Packwood exerted herself to become better acquainted with Miss Penistone. The conversation was more restrained, and there was little in it to put anyone to the blush, but Sarah was not at all amazed by this phenomenon, for there was something about Penny's placid, ladylike demeanor that usually put others on their best behavior.

They had been speaking for some ten minutes or so when the library door opened and Colin slipped inside. "Is it all right, Gram?" he asked in an undertone. "May I come in?"

"Of course, dear boy. Come in and tell us how you have been amusing yourself since you left school." She patted the cushion beside her invitingly, but Colin looked toward Sarah instead.

"If you like," he said absently, "but I didn't come for that. That is . . . well, I came to find out what happened this morning. I didn't want to go to bed."

"I'm sure that's not to be wondered at," observed his grandmother, giving him a curious look. "Your uncle never wanted to go to bed directly after dinner either. But then, he was rarely allowed to dine with the grown-ups. What about this morning?" Sarah flushed, and Colin looked conscious of having spoken out of turn. Miss Penistone's expression did not change. "Come, come, children, what's toward here? I thought Nicky had told me everything, but he said nothing about this morning. Cut line—as old Moreland used to say."

Sarah glanced at Colin and then at Penny. She had intended to tell Colin exactly how outrageously his uncle had behaved, but somehow with both Penny and Lady Packwood watching her, she could not do it. She knew suddenly that Penny had been right, that he had been angry because she had sidestepped his arrangements for her safety. She had been foolish. As for the other thing that had happened in the wood, she would say nothing about it.

Briefly, she described her plan and Nicholas's reaction, including his prohibition of her riding without his express permission, but she recited the facts calmly and without any comment as to her own feelings. There was a small silence when she had finished. Colin broke it.

"I suppose it wasn't a very good idea," he said quietly.

"No, it was not," agreed Lady Packwood, "but it shows you've got spunk, my dear, and so I shall tell Nicky. He needn't have been so harsh."

"Oh, please," Sarah begged, aghast that the incident might be revived and, with it, his lordship's temper. "Please, my lady, I was wrong to go out by myself, and I feel dreadfully that Jem got into trouble through following my orders. Please, say nothing."

Lady Packwood smiled at her but would not promise to keep silent; therefore, Sarah greeted the entrance of the gentlemen with some trepidation. After a nod from Dasher, moments before, Colin had slipped quietly out the French doors onto the terrace. She supposed he would get in again through the kitchen door.

Nicholas did not seem restored to his normal self but, instead, was nearly sullen. Lady Packwood greeted him cheerfully, saying he looked exactly like an undertaker's mute. "And that puts me in mind of something I meant to ask you, dear boy," she added thoughtfully, "whom did you get to build the deplorable Darcy's coffin?"

Nicholas raised an eyebrow. "One of the tenants," he replied. "You probably remember him. A man named Randolph."

"Of course, and I'm glad to hear it. An excellent man. Sure to have done a proper job of it. We had our own carpenter when your father died, you know, and he was buried in solid oák, polished to perfection and lined with silk pillows. But when William and Maria went—Darcy's parents, you know," she added for Sarah's benefit, "that Tom did up two pine boxes that were little more than crates. Leaky, I'm sure, and certainly none too comfortable. I am certain Mr. Randolph did better by the deplor—well, for Darcy. Not that he deserved better," she added with a challenging look at her son.

But he had relaxed at last, amused, and let the comment pass. The conversation drifted after that, until her ladyship proposed a game of lottery tickets, saying she hadn't played since Nicholas's last holiday from school. But her notion was squashed flat by both her spouse and stepson, before anyone else had an opportunity to comment.

Lionel said, "Lottery tickets!" in tones of deep loathing, while Sir Percival merely observed that such a game was not his style, adding that he wouldn't mind taking a hand at whist. Lionel seemed to feel the same about whist as he did about lottery tickets, but he allowed as how he would very much like to teach Sarah—Lady Moreland, that was—how to play piquet.

Sarah, who already played better-than-average piquet, thanks to Penny's having a fondness for it, declined politely, whereupon Lady Packwood advised her stepson not to be a ninny.

"If your papa wishes to play whist, then you should be graceful about it, Lionel—not that you possess much grace, of course, but one never knows what a little practice may achieve."

"But I don't *wish* to play whist," complained Lionel.

"Then don't! Take a turn in the garden instead. I daresay Miss Penistone plays an excellent hand and will oblige. I do not wish to do so myself, for I wish to pursue my acquaintance with Sarah."

But Lionel, who had clearly hoped to do that very thing himself, pointed out that it was dark outside and very likely damp as well, which wouldn't suit his constitution. At that point, Lady Packwood lost her patience with him and recommended that he cease his nattering and decide for himself what to do, since she could not be bothered racking her brain for his amusement.

Miss Penistone, after a glance at Nicholas, promptly agreed to take a hand, and a card table was soon set up for the three of them near the fireplace. Rather sulkily, Lionel stood watching the play, first over one shoulder, then over another, until ordered sharply by his father to busy himself elsewhere or take himself off to bed. He had been gazing at Sarah even more avidly than at the cards, much to that young lady's discomfort, and now shot her a look of helpless frustration that made her long to smack him. Evidently, Lady Packwood was similarly affected.

"Yes, do go away, Lionel. You are making your papa nervous, which is a thing he don't like when he's trying to concentrate, and the way you have been making sheep's eyes at poor Sarah is enough to give anyone a blue megrim. Go to bed."

Lionel might have protested had Nicholas not suddenly raised his eyes, but something in that look caused him to shrug his shoulders and slump off. Lady Packwood turned back to Sarah.

They were seated away from the others, toward the back of the room in a cozy little corner, and Sarah was ruthlessly being made to tell her ladyship all about herself. Surprisingly, it was not difficult, for Lady Packwood proved to be a very good listener. She sympathized over the death of Sarah's parents, nodded understandingly when told about Lord and Lady Hartley's sense of duty, and exclaimed indignantly over the eccentricities of Sir Malcolm Lennox-Matthews. Sarah even found herself relating the tale of one of the few times during her upbringing that she had come to her aunt's attention.

"I was eleven, I think," she confided. "At any rate, it was not so very long after I went to live with them. There was a child next door who looked to be near my own age. I saw him over the garden wall, but I didn't wish to call out for I had been forbidden to climb the trees next to the wall. I tried whispering. You know—psst, psst!—but it did no good, for he was facing away from me. Finally, I pulled a walnut from the tree and launched it at him. Unfortunately, I missed and broke a window instead. I don't think I ever scrambled down from a tree so fast in all my life."

Lady Packwood laughed heartily, drawing brief notice from the cardplayers. "I daresay the attention you received was not in compliment to your aim."

"No," Sarah agreed with a twinkle, "and it was no laughing matter then, I assure you. The woman next door complained to Aunt Aurelia that I had been throwing *rocks* at her nephew, and I was promptly summoned to Aunt's dressing room. I was not even granted an opportunity to explain, for Aunt Aurelia was absolutely livid!"

Her ladyship chuckled again. "Well, you seem to have survived your childhood well enough, though I don't envy you such encounters with your aunt. I was always turned over to my governess when I misbehaved."

"Oh, well, Penny would never have been so severe," Sarah

said, casting a fond glance at that placid lady. "Did you love your governess, too?"

"Dear me, no! She was a dried up prune of a woman with a face like a split cod. Her favorite pastime was building card castles, and she was very strict. My father got her because he thought all girls of the first circles had them. I would much rather have gone to school, but he was determined to do things properly. He was in trade then, you know."

"In trade!" Sarah couldn't help it. She simply couldn't believe Lady Packwood came from a family with its roots in trade.

"Indeed," replied her ladyship with a grin. "Though he became nearly respectable later on through having made pots of money at it. When he sold out he owned thirteen textile mills in Yorkshire. Nicky inherited his money, and it served as the foundation of his own fortune. He is as rich as Golden Ball, you know."

"He is! That is, no, I didn't know. Is he really?"

"Certainly, though he doesn't puff off his consequence, so I daresay very few people realize it. If the deplorable Darcy had known, it's likely Nicky would have been the murder victim. It was on account of Waterloo, you see."

"Waterloo!"

Her ladyship nodded, glancing at the card table as though to be certain they were not being overheard. "Yes, you see when Nicky went with the Duke, he left all his money invested in the Funds. He had a man of affairs, of course—same one as my Papa always had in London—but Nicky went off without leaving Mr. Thompson any real authorization to handle the money. When the Funds started slipping I went myself to see him—Mr. Thompson, that is. He was nearly frantic, and I must admit, so was I. Both of us saw poor Nicky coming home a pauper. But there was nothing to do. Mr. Thompson wrote him, of course, but received nothing in reply, and without proper authorization he simply couldn't sell out. Nearly everyone else did, you know, thinking Napoleon would win the war at last. But when Wellington held the day at Waterloo, the Funds soared, and the few who were left in made what old Moreland was used to call a real killing. Nicky came out of it worth five or six times what he had been worth going in."

"Merciful heavens!" Sarah tried to imagine what the proceeds from the sale of thirteen textile mills multiplied by five or six times might amount to in current terms and failed miserably. "I can tell you one thing, ma'am," she confided in an undertone. "My aunt and uncle knew nothing of it, or they would never have encouraged me to set my cap for Darcy instead of his lordship. The title would have meant nothing compared to wealth like that!"

"Good gracious!" exclaimed her ladyship. "Did they encourage you to pursue the deplo—no, I must stop that," she scolded herself. "Nicky is perfectly right. But did they?"

"Well, only until Uncle Barnabas discovered that he hadn't a feather to fly with. I must say, though, that no one else guessed it, for he always looked to be rather plump in the pockets. But I suppose, if his lordship was franking him, as you indicated earlier, that would account for it."

Lady Packwood looked at Sarah rather oddly, but Dasher entered just then with a footman and the tea tray, so she made no comment. The cards were put away, and the discussion became general again when her ladyship began to pour out.

"What do you do for amusement in the daytime, Nicky?" she asked. "'Tis hardly the season for hunting, nor warm enough for picnics."

"I hadn't thought about providing entertainment for you," he replied smiling. "I was under the impression that you were on your honeymoon and could scarcely wait to reach the Continent. Do you plan an extended visit?"

She raised her brow and looked down her nose at him. "Don't be impertinent, young man. I daresay we shall stay a few days. No doubt, dear Percy can put off his business that long. Can you not, my love?"

"Certainly, my sweet," came the reply, muffled though it was by a mouthful of cheese tart.

"So there we are. What shall we do to amuse ourselves? Sarah informs me that you have stabled her horse more or less permanently, or I should suggest riding. 'Tis excellent exercise."

Intercepting his heavy frown, Sarah flushed deeply and turned away again. She tried to maintain her composure, but her teacup rattled in its saucer, and for one crazy moment she felt perilously near to tears. How ridiculous, she scolded herself, to feel like a limp weed whenever Nicholas seemed disapproving. His mother was right. He was positively fusty, and she ought not to let his moods trouble her.

"I did not mean for her to think I was forbidding the *exercise* entirely," he said, watching her. "For that matter, I doubt she did think it. I merely wish to know where she is going and to be certain she is adequately protected. I've no objection to her riding with you or Sir Percival, though if you and she go alone, I will insist upon your taking a groom or two. I will also beg that you not ride out across the Common itself, since there have been nearly daily reports of highwaymen accosting travelers there. Only a week or so ago, a man was killed for the sake of his watch and ring."

"But that's disgraceful!" exclaimed her ladyship. "Things were never used to be so bad as that."

"No, but since the patrols have been reduced or eliminated, things have become much worse. We've asked for the Army to send in a unit or two, but so far our requests seem to fall on deaf ears."

Something in his expression made Sarah think Nicholas was either dissembling or neglecting to tell the whole tale, but she didn't feel that she had enough courage at the moment to call him on it, and his redoubtable mother didn't seem to notice.

Sarah and Miss Penistone did not normally stay so late at the main house, so after they had finished their tea, Sarah responded immediately to her companion's subtle signal and began saying their good-nights. Nicholas stood when they did, of course, but it quickly became clear that he meant to accompany them.

"It isn't necessary, my lord," Sarah protested. "Our front door is scarcely more than fifty yards from here!"

"It is a good deal later than usual, Countess, and the woods are very dark. I shall be easier in my mind if I know you have arrived safely." He spoke calmly and even smiled, but Sarah knew it would be useless to argue with him.

"I own it will be comforting to have your lordship's escort," Miss Penistone said serenely. "One never knows what might be lurking behind the next tree."

Lady Packwood chuckled. "Most likely, my grandson would be the only bogey out there, Miss Penistone, and I doubt he has it in him to frighten you. Besides, after what I hear about last night, I daresay he has gone very sensibly to his bed."

"He better had," observed his lordship with a grim smile. "It would do him no good to let me catch him in the woods tonight."

"What's that?" Sir Percival seemed to have slipped into a doze and been startled awake again. He brushed crumbs from his neckcloth and reached for his snuffbox. "Who's in the woods? Not murderers again, I hope. Told you to be careful, my sweet," he added accusingly, opening the case with a practiced flick of his thumbnail. "Don't hold with murderers. "

Lady Packwood patted his knee comfortingly. "No murderers, my love. Nicky is merely preparing to escort Sarah and Miss Penistone to the Dower House, because the path is a trifle gloomy."

"Dower House?" He helped himself to a generous pinch of snuff. "Thought you said the place was a wreck. Pretty young thing like that oughtn't to live in a rat trap. Speak to Moreland about it. Might listen to you. Daresay he wouldn't to me."

Sir Percival seemed to be still half asleep, and Sarah nearly laughed when Nicholas left the task of explaining matters to his mother and escorted them outside. The moon shone brightly between drifting clouds, and she was very conscious of his presence. Once, when she nearly stumbled on a tree root, his hand was at her elbow immediately to steady her. He took it away again at once, but she could still feel the warmth of his hand where he had touched her.

They reached the broad stone steps, and Betsy opened the door to greet them, spilling light from the front hall onto the porch.

"You should have a manservant to tend that door," Nicholas said suddenly, his voice loud in the night. "A houseful of women—there should be at least one man. That Betsy would be no match for an intruder."

"As you please, my lord," Sarah said meekly, though she was thinking that Lady Packwood was very likely right and Colin the only probable intruder. It seemed hardly possible that Erebus had treed his ghost only the night before. She smiled at the memory, as the big dog lumbered forth from his place under the stairs to greet them.

"He seems very much at home," Nicholas commented as he reduced him to abject slavery by scratching between his ears and down the center of the broad back.

"He sleeps outside," Sarah said firmly. "Come on, dog. Out!" She turned to say good night to his lordship but was confounded when he simply escorted her inside and shut the door on the long-suffering Erebus.

"I wish to have a word with you, Countess, if Miss Penistone will excuse us." He glanced at Penny, and to Sarah's astonishment, her protectress merely nodded acquiescence and turned away upstairs. "In the drawing room, my lady?"

He opened the door for her, and still in a state of shock from Penny's desertion, she obeyed him silently. The lamps were still lit, and their light cast a rosy glow over the comfortable room. Sarah turned to face him, squaring her shoulders.

"If you are displeased with me for telling your mother about this morning, my lord, I apologize. She is very easy to talk with, and I told her without thinking how you might feel."

"That doesn't matter," he said brusquely. "Did you really think I would forbid your riding altogether?"

So that was it. She turned away, biting her lip, amazed that he would care what she thought about his arbitrary orders.

"Well, did you?"

She shook her head. "Not really, I suppose, though I wasn't sure, of course."

"My God, Sarah, I am not your keeper, nor am I a brute!" His words were gruff, as though he were really shaken. "How could you think for a moment that I should be so harsh with you?"

"You were angry," she muttered. "You behaved so strangely, I didn't know what to think. And then . . ." Her voice faded. She caught her breath. He was standing right behind her. ". . . and then, it was so humiliating . . . what you said in the stableyard."

At that, she felt his hands gently upon her shoulders, and to her own amazement and his lordship's consternation, Sarah's eyes overflowed and tears streamed down her cheeks.

XIII

"What a beast I am," Nicholas said gently, dislodging a large linen handkerchief from his waistcoat pocket and dabbing at her cheeks with it. "I am truly sorry if you were humiliated. I only meant to be certain my orders were obeyed. As for the other, I can only ask your forgiveness. I don't know what came over me, but I had no right." He paused and seemed a bit uncertain. Sarah took the handkerchief and rubbed her eyes and cheeks. She could not quite bring herself to blow her nose on Nicholas's handkerchief, so she sniffed instead, handing it back to him.

He shook his head at her. "Poor, foolish little Countess. Your world has indeed been turned upside down. I shall try not to make matters any worse." But he stood looking down at her in a way that made Sarah avoid his eyes entirely. He was being gentle and kind for once, and it unnerved her a little, although she was perfectly certain that it was only because he had made her cry. Sarah knew very well that most gentlemen were unmanned by feminine weeping. She had used it to her advantage upon more than one occasion.

"Miss Sarah!" It was Penny calling from the top of the stairs. "Has his lordship gone? Betsy must be longing for her bed."

Nicholas stepped away. "His lordship is just leaving, Miss Penistone. Good night to you both, ladies." And he was gone.

"He stayed rather longer than I anticipated, love," said Penny, as Sarah climbed the stairs. "I hope nothing is amiss." She wore a woolen wrapper and thick slippers, and her fine, glossy hair had been brushed till it shone and tied back with a narrow, white ribbon. The effect would have been rather startling to anyone but Sarah, for she looked twenty years younger.

Sarah smiled at her. "Dear Penny. Nothing is amiss. He merely wished to apologize for his behavior this morning. He did nothing out of the way, I promise you."

"Oh, it never occurred to me that his lordship would transgress the bounds of propriety here under your own roof. He has too great a sense of what is pleasing to go beyond the line. I only feared you might somehow have vexed him again, and I worried lest another scold overset you. I well remember how her ladyship's recriminations used to do so."

That brought a chuckle. "Why, Penny, I do believe you are curious, for I've never heard such humdudgeon from your lips before. You know perfectly well what it meant each time I was summoned to my aunt's dressing room, for you used to do your possible to protect me from such confrontations. I promise you his lordship's scolds are much less physical!"

Miss Penistone smiled. "So I should hope, and I never meant you to compare the two in such a way. But get you to bed, child. Lizzie is waiting."

Sarah dropped off to sleep, idly asking herself how a rake and a lady with very little elegance of mind could have produced a son quite like Nicholas, and Lady Packwood wondered the same thing aloud next morning as the two of them rode together slightly ahead of Sir Percival and his son. Nicholas had permitted them to ride with only these gentlemen for escort, though Sarah had seen from his expression that it went against the grain for him to do so. But to have sent a pair of grooms along might have set up the collective Packwood backs, and Nicholas resisted. He repeated his instructions that they not venture out onto the Common itself, however, adding that the highwaymen had been known to attack groups of horsemen.

"I don't know how he got so fusty," Lady Packwood complained. " 'Tis something about Moreland's sons, perhaps, for William was just such another, only worse—a pompous prig. And that woman he married! Well, I tell you, the deplor—Darcy turned out well, considering."

Sarah grinned. She was wearing her black riding habit because she knew it would displease Nicholas if she were to leave the Park dressed in colors, but she firmly intended to change into one of her favorite morning gowns when they returned, despite the fact that he had not yet actually given his permission. "Was he always so, ma'am?"

"Oh, my, no!" laughed her ladyship. "He was a serious little boy at times, but always ripe for a lark. There was a period of time when he and Darcy actually got along rather well and even got into mischief together. Whenever that happened, Moreland used to take Nicky into the library and give him a good sound thrashing, and that would be that; whereas, William would prose on and on about whatever wrong had been committed until Darcy must have nearly gone mad. William insisted it was wrong to beat children, that one should reason with them, explain their errors and so forth. Fortunately, Darcy's schoolmasters didn't agree, or he might have turned out even worse than he did."

"But surely, ma'am, you don't think it wrong to explain things to children when they misbehave!"

"Certainly not. But there has to be a limit. William used to bring the same matters up again and again, till there was no end to them. I think a child should have the security of knowing that once he has been punished the matter will not be referred to again. Otherwise, he either learns to let things prey upon his conscience, or else, like Darcy, he learns not to heed his misdeeds at all, to do simply as he pleases."

Sarah nodded. "Yes, he was like that. But it seems that your first husband's methods must have turned out types who worry too much about propriety."

"Dear me, did I give you that impression? I never meant to. William was indeed a prig, but I've no notion what made him so. I expect it was something or other he read. As for Nicky, again I cannot say what did it, though I am beginning to have my suspicions." She smiled enigmatically at Sarah and then added airily, "I daresay it was something to do with the war—all those young things under his command. He got into the habit then, I expect, of ordering others about."

"Here, my sweet, ride with me. I didn't follow you to Yorkshire just to suffer that young whelp's conversation in a gloomy wood."

"Very well, sir. He did, too," she added to Sarah, as she drew rein. "Follow me to Yorkshire, that is. I shall tell you all about it later. Here, Lionel, come up and bore poor Sarah with some of your idle chitchat."

The younger man obeyed, lifting an ironic eyebrow for Sarah's benefit. But she paid him no heed then and very little as they meandered along the wooded path. The sunlight danced through the leaves as it had done the previous morning, and the air was warm and clear. The taste of summer was on the breeze that gently stirred leaves here and there, and summer wildflowers were replacing their spring sisters in the occasional grassy clearings.

Sarah took a deep breath, savoring the woodland smells, until Lionel's words pierced her consciousness, and she realized that he was suddenly waxing poetic over her hair, her eyes, her lips, her skin. Since he compared the latter two to cherries and strawberries respectively, she was nearly betrayed into a chuckle when she envisioned herself suddenly transformed into a bowl of fruit. However, she restrained herself and turned on him sternly.

"Do talk sense, Lionel! The things you have been saying are very improper and nonsense besides."

"You didn't seem to mind," he replied, to her astonishment nearly leering.

"Don't be absurd. I wasn't even attending. I found your initial conversation deadly dull, and I simply turned my mind to more interesting things." Harsh words, perhaps, but the young man seemed thick-skinned.

"You are merely being coy, Sarah. I can tell, you know. 'Tis because of Cousin Nick, of course. You think he means to order your life henceforth, because of that awful Darcy. But he shan't, for I won't let him."

"Oh, Lionel, do hush before you say anything more absurd than you have already said. I don't need any protection from *Lord Moreland*, and if I did, I shouldn't look to you. No, hush, or I shall tell your stepmama that you are annoying me." Flushing deeply, Lionel lapsed into uncomfortable silence, which allowed Sarah to return to her daydreaming.

The morning rides became a daily occurrence, and Sarah could only be glad when Nicholas sometimes took Lionel's place. The younger man continued to cast sheep's eyes at her and was guilty of a knowing wink or two, but he behaved himself after Sarah's threat, and she soon ceased to worry about him, although Colin teased her unmercifully about her "newest conquest." Every once in a while, the boy looked a bit mischievous while he was "ragging" her, as he called it, and she wondered what he had been up to, but she did not press the matter.

Lady Packwood, visiting Sarah in the Dower House drawing room and complimenting her generously on the changes that she had wrought, made good her promise to tell about Sir Percival's pursuit, and Sarah was amazed to discover that the lady she thought had been buried in Yorkshire was a seasoned traveler. Having spent time in Paris, Rome, Baden-Baden, and Lucerne, among other places, her ladyship had met Sir Percival in Bath and realized that he would suit her to a nicety.

"For he didn't care a straw about my odd ways. He liked the way I look and said it was refreshing to meet a female who spoke her mind and didn't converse according to the given formula."

Sarah chuckled. "Dear me, I suppose that's exactly what we're taught to do, isn't it."

"I daresay. Moreland said so, said most girls were mealy-mouthed and threatened to beat me soundly if I even looked like conforming to the pattern." She grinned. "I never did. That's why Percy is good for me. He truly doesn't care. Other men have told me they like the way I speak—when we were alone—but it embarrassed them to have me speak frankly to others. Prodigiously uncomfortable, I assure you. So I cast my lures to Percy. He was clearly interested, but it wasn't until I returned to Yorkshire that I was certain of him. He arrived less than a fortnight later. Of course, it was rather disconcerting that he had Lionel with him, and then Nicky came haring up, having heard some rumor or other out of Bath, but it was Darcy's death that brought things to a head. I quit dithering then, I can tell you."

They had other conversations, and Sarah came to feel very fond of Lady Packwood. For once, she felt she could confide in someone without being condemned for speaking of personal things. She even told her ladyship in detail of Darcy's peculiar ethics and listened contentedly to an articulate castigation of his character.

Nicholas made no comment when Sarah first appeared in a morning gown of pale blue sprigged muslin, its satin sash tied high under her breasts with a cheerful nosegay of blue silk rosebuds, so she happily went on ignoring her blacks except for their daily rides or the presence of an occasional caller. One morning, nearly a week after the Packwoods' arrival, Sarah donned a charming frock of lilac muslin with a sash and satin-covered buttons in a deeper purple and stepped out into the garden for some fresh air. A lilac ribbon had been threaded artistically through her curls, and she knew she was looking very well. She walked carefully in dainty lilac sandals, skirting the library terrace and crossing the main drive to the forecourt. Moss roses were beginning to bloom in the herbaceous borders, and she wanted to see what other interesting varieties might be preparing to make their presence known. The morning was not so bright as its predecessors had been, for there were puffy clouds scudding across the common, now and again dimming the sunlight.

The drumming of hoofbeats on the drive diverted her, and she looked up to see Mr. Randolph approaching, mounted on a horse that would have looked more at home pulling a plow. She waved, and he swung the animal toward her.

"Good day to ye, my lady!" he called cheerfully. "I was just coming fer 'is lordship, cause that sow he's been watchin' has produced a fine family. Ten of 'em, and she looks to be knowing her business, which they often don't first time round. His lordship'll be right pleased, I'm thinkin'."

"I'm sure he will, Mr. Randolph. Oh, look," she added as the familiar figure came into sight from the library side of the house. "There he is now, so you may tell him at once."

Randolph rode off to meet Nicholas, and Sarah continued her round of the borders, then climbed the front steps to the entrance, just as earl and tenant parted company. Nicholas turned toward the steps at once, but Randolph's news notwithstanding, his expression was anything but cheerful.

"Come into the library," he said sternly. "I've a deal to say to you."

Sarah stood her ground, her courage bolstered by continued association with Lady Packwood. "Don't bark orders at me, my lord. You may say whatever you wish to say right here."

"Don't be impertinent, Countess," was the crushing retort. "And believe me when I say you would prefer to hear me in the privacy of my library, rather than here, where anyone might chance to listen."

That could not be denied, but though she followed him, Sarah was determined to retain her dignity. A startled footman sprang to open the library doors, but Nicholas scarcely waited for him to shut them again before snapping without preamble, "I said nothing when you began wearing colors, but by heaven, I expected you to practice some discretion! Instead, I find you preening yourself in front of Sam Randolph as though you hadn't a thought in your head for your dead husband."

"Poppycock!" said Sarah, borrowing one of her ladyship's favorite words.

"What!"

"I said, 'poppycock,' my lord, for I *haven't* a thought in my head for Darcy, and I don't particularly care who knows it. What I do to satisfy propriety, I do because you say it is necessary. But if you mean to tell me that I must keep to my own house and not venture out of doors at all, then I might just as well keep to my blacks. It was the purest misfortune that Mr. Randolph saw me, and he was full of his sow's news, so I doubt he noticed anything untoward. He would have thought it odd indeed, however, had I turned and run from him."

"Nothing was said about flaunting yourself in the front court or on the main drive," Nicholas replied severely, "and you know it very well. The point was that you would wear your dresses where none but the family would see you, that you would be protected by the servants and your own discretion from chance meetings with those who might be offended by such behavior. I'll agree that Randolph's mind was not on your clothing, but it might just as well not have been Randolph. My mother's presence here is known throughout the neighborhood," he went on in that same harsh tone, "and she has already had several callers. There will be more. If something like this happens again, you will return to your blacks permanently, so I suggest you give careful thought to my words."

He did not grant her an opportunity to reply, but turned on his heel and left the room, shutting the door behind him with a firm snap. Sarah stood where she was, her fists clenched against her skirts. Once again, she was close to tears, and she knew she had brought it on herself.

A hand touched her shoulder and she nearly screamed. "He should not have spoken to you so, Sarah!" Lionel said, breathing fiery indignation.

She had been so wrapped in her own thoughts that she hadn't heard his approach, but she realized he must have been in the library the whole time. "Lionel! You nearly frightened the wits out of me! What are you doing here?"

"Reading," he answered simply, indicating the high, winged chair that faced the fireplace. "Nothing else *to* do. I heard him though, and I shan't allow him to abuse you so ever again."

"Don't be silly, Lionel. How could you stop him?"

"I'll marry you."

"Marry me!"

"Oh, Sarah, you are wonderful," he breathed. "So beautiful, so pure, so sweet." He moved to take her in his arms.

"Lionel!" she gasped, eluding him with difficulty. "What can you be thinking of? I am a widow in mourning. I cannot be married for at least a year. Even a year would be questionable to some."

"Take you to France," he replied, making another effort to capture her. "Nobody cares a button about such things there. Stands to reason," he added. "We wouldn't tell them."

"Oh, you're demented!" Sarah cried, escaping his clutches once more only to come up against a corner where two bookshelves met. "I wouldn't marry you under any circumstances! You're . . . you're too young!" she finished triumphantly.

"Older than you," he pointed out. "Heard my stepmama say you wasn't eighteen yet. Well, I am. Got money, too—at least, Papa has, which is by way of being the same thing. I'll cherish you."

"I don't *want* you to cherish me," Sarah wailed, trying ineffectually to push him away when he boxed her into her corner. "I want you to leave me alone!"

"No, you don't. I know better," he muttered huskily, bending his head to try to kiss her, his hands pressing into her shoulders. Her bodice was of the sort known as *à l'enfant*, and one sleeve slipped away under his fingers. Sarah began to struggle more wildly.

"Let me go, Lionel!"

He was holding her with his body pressed against hers, and the shelves behind were digging into her back painfully. He was much stronger than she would have thought, had she given the matter prior consideration, and she feared for a moment that she might suffocate. She twisted her head from side to side, crying out against him and trying to push him away, but the way he was holding her made her arms and hands seem useless. He even began to caress her bare shoulder, but she was too busy trying to elude his thick, wet lips to worry about that. Being kissed by Lionel would be exactly like being kissed by a fish! She screwed her eyes shut and twisted her face as far around toward the corner as it would go.

"Don't fight me, beautiful Sarah. You know you will like it. It's only a matter of time." He pressed against her even harder, bringing the hand that had been caressing her shoulder up to turn her head. "No need to be missish," he murmured. "Come to think of it, you already know all about such things. Stands to reason. Married to that Darcy fellow." His hand was forcing her chin around, and Sarah could scarcely breathe. Then, suddenly, he gave a startled gasp, and she was relieved of his weight.

She opened her eyes to see him spun around by a grip of steel just before he was floored by a wicked right jab to what there was of his chin. Nicholas rubbed his knuckles and glanced briefly at Sarah before he lunged forward and yanked Lionel to his feet again. Since he chose the younger man's neckcloth as his handle, she thought it no wonder that Lionel gave a terrified shriek.

"We'll finish this business in the stableyard, by God!" Nicholas growled furiously. "You just come with me, you young Casanova. Either on your feet or not, as you please. I'm perfectly willing to drag you the distance."

"No! No, you don't understand!" Lionel squeaked. "She wanted it. She is mad about me!"

Nicholas still clenched the neckcloth, forcing Lionel up onto his toes, and Sarah feared briefly that he meant to throttle the younger man then and there. She cried out to the earl, but he gave no sign of hearing her. His attention was focused entirely upon Lionel.

"What on earth is going on here?" Lady Packwood pushed the hall door wide and took in the scene in one swift, comprehending glance. Sarah, flushing to the roots of her hair, was attempting to restore her gown to its proper order, and Nicholas retained his grip on Lionel as he turned to face his mother. "Release him, Nicky," she said steadily.

"Not on your life, madam," Nicholas grated. "I intend to teach him manners. He is coming with me to the stableyard, where I mean to introduce him to the business end of a horsewhip."

Lionel blanched, going perfectly still in Nicholas's grasp, much like a terrified rabbit, and Lady Packwood regarded him with undisguised contempt. Then she turned her direct gaze on her angry son.

"I sympathize with your feelings, dear boy, but I cannot allow it," she said with a touch of regret. "It would upset his father. Lionel," she went on brusquely, "I am completely disgusted with you. Go upstairs to your bedchamber at once, until I speak with your papa about this." Lionel looked willing enough to obey her, but since Nicholas had not yet let go of his neckcloth, he was helpless. Lady Packwood met her son's stubborn gaze with one just as determined. "Release him, Nicholas. At once." She held his gaze while her will clashed with his, and Sarah felt a tension in the air so tactile it seemed something must snap before it would ease.

Nicholas sighed. "Very well, madam, since it means so much to you." He let go, and Lionel scrambled away to the door. But then, he nearly ruined everything, for he paused on the threshold, safely behind his stepmother, and turned back.

"Sarah wanted it, my lady. I know she did. She——"

Nicholas took a threatening step toward him, and he fled. Lady Packwood laid a restraining hand on her son's arm. "Let him go, Nicky. I'll attend to him, never fear. He shan't annoy her again."

"No, that he will not," Nicholas confirmed in a tight voice, "for he is going to pack his bags and get out just as fast as he can manage it. I'll not tolerate that puppy's presence here one second longer than necessary." He paused and gave his mother an apologetic look before proceeding. "I don't mean to cause difficulties for you, Mama. If it can be managed in such a way that you and Sir Percival need not go with him, I should like you to remain as long as it suits you to do so."

Lady Packwood smiled at him. "It would have been very improper for you to horsewhip him, you know, though I am glad to discover that, in certain instances, you can still be swayed by emotion and not always ruled by propriety. Let me talk to Lionel and then to his father. I shall have to contrive a bit, perhaps, but I doubt it will be beyond my talents."

"I doubt anything is beyond your talents, ma'am," her son said, lifting one of her carefully manicured hands to his lips. "If it will help, I will place my post chaise at your service."

"I shall keep your kind offer in mind," she said with a wink. "Sarah dear, don't stand like a stock. Go wash your face, and get that Betsy of yours to fix you a cup of tea."

She left and Sarah, still in her corner, watched Nicholas warily. He made no move to approach her, merely wiping a hand across his brow. "How did it happen?"

She realized she had been holding her breath and let it out slowly. "He was here, in that chair, while you . . . while we were talking before."

"I'm sorry."

"I didn't see him. He said he wanted to marry me."

"What!"

She nodded. "To protect me from you. He said he would take me to France, that no one would care about the proprieties there." Her lips twitched as she remembered Lionel's exact words.

Nicholas stared as though he thought she might be mocking him, but she nodded again, and he frowned. "Coxcomb!"

"He was very sure of himself, sir. He seemed to think I would welcome his advances, that I was just flirting when I tried to rebuff him."

"Where would he get such a notion?" Nicholas demanded, staring at her suspiciously again. Sarah's temper flared.

"Well, he didn't get it from me!" she retorted hotly. "He tried playing off his stupid tricks once before, whilst we were riding, and I said I would speak to your mama if he didn't behave himself. *That* stopped him cold, I can tell you, and he *can't* have thought I would say such a thing just to lead him on!"

There was amusement in his eye now. "No," he conceded, "that is not the usual strategy. But you cannot deny, Countess, that he has been watching you these past days like a hungry puppy, whilst you have done little to dissuade him."

"No, for he was not bothering me—only watching, as you say—and I had no wish to cause a scene that would upset her ladyship or Sir Percival."

"It might have been better for all of us if you had," he suggested gently.

"It might have been better for all of us," she retorted, "had you been content to say your piece on the front steps instead of hailing me before *such* an audience!"

Nicholas put back his head and laughed. "Oh, Countess, you take the honors this time. What a thing to say!"

Sarah only grinned at him in passing, as she made her way to the terrace door, intending to follow Lady Packwood's advice. She felt Nicholas's eyes on her back as she left, but she did not turn, nor did she see him again before dinner.

Lady Packwood announced then that, since Lionel was pining for the delights of London (having, in fact, been too blue-deviled to come down to dinner), Sir Percival had agreed to take him up to the metropolis himself on the morrow and see him established while, at the same time, attending to the business that awaited him there. Her ladyship, feeling that she would only be a nuisance to gentlemen intent upon gentlemen's matters, meant to stay on at Ash Park, if dear Nicky would have her, until Sir Percival returned, at which time they would, if the mood was right, set off directly for the Continent.

Thanks to Lionel's absence, the mood at the table was not nearly so strained as Sarah had feared it might be; nevertheless, the gaiety of past evenings was missing. She noted Colin's gaze upon her more than once and thought he looked a bit under par, but she assumed idly that it must be her own attitude and everyone else's affecting his.

The ladies adjourned to the library, and Nicholas followed soon after, informing his mother that Sir Percival had stepped outside to blow a cloud. The conversation seemed to lag, and Sarah was just thinking of bidding everyone else good night when the hall door opened and Colin stepped in, looking very uncomfortable indeed. His eyes sought out his uncle, who was leaning against the mantel shelf, and he swallowed hard before blurting, "Please, Uncle Nick, it was all my fault!"

XIV

There was a moment of stunned silence while the four adults looked at the boy in astonishment. He had been sent off to bed as usual after dinner, and although several of those present might have suspected he would not be asleep, none expected him to seek out his uncle in such a way. Nicholas recollected himself first.

"*What* is all your fault?" Colin hesitated and looked so miserable that Sarah wished she could help him but, knowing she could not, kept silent. He glanced at her, then back at his uncle. "Would you prefer to speak to me privately?" Nicholas inquired gently.

"Yes . . . no, sir," the boy amended, lifting his chin. "It wouldn't be right. Cousin Sarah should know, and I don't mind Gram or Miss Penny. But you're going to be angry," he added bluntly.

"Then you'd best get it over with so that we may all be comfortable again, don't you agree?"

Colin nodded slowly, one hand rather nervously plucking at a coat button. He opened his mouth once or twice and glanced at Sarah again, but no words came.

"Has it to do with Lionel?" Nicholas asked quietly.

Colin's eyes flew to his, and his mouth opened slightly. He swallowed again and nodded. "Yes, sir. He said he has to leave and that it's my fault, that because of me he insulted Cousin Sarah." This time he looked toward his grandmother, but his gaze quickly returned to his uncle. Nicholas was frowning, and Colin bit his lip.

"How does he think it your fault?" Nicholas asked finally. "What did you do?"

Colin took a deep breath. "It was just ragging, because he

was so nutty on Cousin Sarah, and I never meant anything to come of it. I guess he's a bit sillier than I thought."

"Lionel is *very* silly," inserted his grandmother calmly, "but you have not explained things very well, you know. I expect your uncle wishes to know precisely what you said to him."

"Precisely," Nicholas agreed, shooting a speaking look at his mother. Sarah realized that Lady Packwood had spoken up in hopes of preventing Nicholas from barking at the boy, and it was clear from his look that Nicholas also realized it. Miss Penistone seemed to be giving all her attention to the piece of fancy work in her lap.

Colin swallowed again, then looked manfully into his uncle's eyes. "I told him that Cousin Sarah was nutty about him, too," he confessed. "I said she had told me so, that she thought he had beautiful eyes, that she was partial to red hair, that . . . that she dared not speak to him for fear of you." He had opened the budget, and now he avoided Sarah's eyes and his uncle's as well.

"Wretch!" Sarah muttered angrily under her breath, but then she glanced at Lady Packwood, who was having difficulty stifling merriment, and the humor of the situation was brought home to her. She looked at Nicholas. His lips were pressed together into a thin line, and he did not look at all amused, but he said nothing, merely fixing his stern gaze upon the culprit until the silence became uncomfortable.

Colin had been staring at the floor, waiting for his uncle's wrath to descend upon him, but at last, he could tolerate it no longer and looked up with a sigh. "Are you going to punish me, Uncle Nick?"

"That remains to be seen," Nicholas replied gravely. "You owe Cousin Sarah an apology for putting her in such an uncomfortable position. I think that after you have made it, I shall accompany you to your bedchamber, where we shall have a little chat. That should help me decide whether or not further punishment is necessary." The boy looked as though he believed the conclusion to be foreordained, but Nicholas added softly, "I think you are truly sorry, Colin, and that is very important."

"Oh, yes sir, I am," Colin said stoutly. "I never meant . . ." He turned to Sarah. "Please believe I never meant to cause you embarrassment or discomfort. I never thought Lionel would . . . well, I'm very, *very* sorry. Must I apologize to Lionel as well, Uncle Nick?"

"No," replied his mentor shortly. He strode across the room to the door, waiting for the boy to pass through.

"Nicky?"

Nicholas paused, shutting the door behind Colin, and turned to Lady Packwood. Sarah was astonished to note amusement in his eyes. "Don't worry, ma'am. I've no intention of murdering him. But it is definitely time and past to discuss certain matters. I doubt he had any notion of the sort of mischief he might have caused."

"Nicky will handle that well, I think," commented Lady Packwood when he had gone. "Colin worships him, you know, so Nicky will be able to give him quite a lot of very sound advice."

Sarah nodded thoughtfully. She had not given the matter any consideration before, but she decided now that her ladyship was very likely right. At any rate, Nicholas would certainly not prose on and on. He was much too matter-of-fact.

She and Miss Penistone didn't wait for the tray to be brought in but returned to Dower House even before Nicholas came back to the library. Sarah was very sleepy and readily agreed to her companion's suggestion that they make an early night of it.

She awoke next morning fully refreshed. Betsy brought her her chocolate, and she sat up in bed sipping cautiously while Lizzie made several suggestions regarding possible attire for the day. Glancing out the window, Sarah was glad to see that the clouds of the day before had gone. It would not do for Sir Percival and Lionel to be delayed by a storm. But the day was clear, the sunlight brilliant, and it bade fair to be warm, so she agreed to Lizzie's suggestion of a simple cream muslin frock with a red silk sash and a rosebud-embroidered flounce. The tiny puffed sleeves had been gathered near the lower edge with red silk thread, and a narrow red ribbon was tied around Sarah's throat. Lizzie arranged her hair *à la Didon*, and she was ready to go downstairs, where she found Miss Penistone already in the dining room. Betsy was serving coddled eggs with ham and jellied muffins.

"You look charmingly this morning, my dear," Penny said calmly. "I am pleased to see you completely recovered from yesterday's unpleasantness."

Sarah grinned at her. Penny was also looking well. She no longer drew her hair back into the tight little bun at the nape of her neck but dressed it in a younger, far more becoming style. However, Sarah knew better than to comment on the change, so she merely replied that the incident could not have been all that bad. "After all, it has rid us of the loathsome Lionel, whilst allowing us to continue to enjoy her ladyship's company."

Since Miss Penistone had already gone so far as to express the opinion that Lionel Packwood was not quite nice in his ways, she could not, in good conscience, refute or rebuke, so she gently turned the conversation into more acceptable channels by asking Sarah what her plans were for the day. Sarah had no notion, but before she had a chance to say so, Betsy stepped in again to say that Master Colin was at the front door begging to have speech with her.

"Well, show him in," Sarah laughed, "and you'd better refill the muffin basket, for I daresay he'll want several." A moment later, Colin hurried in. He hesitated on the threshold, and Sarah grinned at him. "Come in, Colin, and sit down. Betsy is just bringing you some hot muffins."

"Thank you, ma'am," said the boy, slipping into a chair, "but I came to apologize again. I don't think I did it very well last evening, for I didn't perfectly understand the matter then, you know. But Uncle Nick explained things, and I do quite see now that I oughtn't to have said such stuff to Lionel."

Sarah smiled but held her tongue while Betsy plumped down a steaming, linen-covered basket and a cup of chocolate in front of him. He sniffed appreciatively and lifted the napkin to help himself to a muffin. Then, when Betsy had shut the door behind herself, he looked at Sarah expectantly.

"You made a fine apology last night, Colin," she said kindly, "and I hope your uncle was not dreadfully vexed with you, for I promise I am not. I might have been, of course, had you not owned up as you did, but after a night's reflection, I have come to the conclusion that none of it was truly your fault. Lionel should have known better than to take your word for my sentiments, and he should certainly *never* have behaved as he did under any circumstances!"

"No," the boy agreed after carefully swallowing the remains of his first muffin. "That's what Uncle Nick said." He reached for another. "These are first rate, ma'am. Do you think Betsy would show Cook how to make them?"

"You must ask her. I'm sure she will be flattered. What else did your uncle say?"

"Well, like you, he said it wasn't my fault that Lionel made such a cake of himself. They're gone, you know. Gram said to tell you they left at eight. Uncle Nick said that since Lionel is much older, he must bear all responsibility for what happened, but then he explained certain things to me." Colin's color rose noticeably, and he applied his attention to the buttering of his muffin. "He didn't really rake me down, but he said that I behaved in an ungentlemanly way, and now that I know better, he'll make me sorry I was born if I ever do it again." He looked her in the eye. "I won't though, you know, now I've seen what can happen. Uncle Nick told me exactly what that . . . what Lionel tried to do. I'm awful sorry!"

"We shall say no more about it," Sarah said firmly, remembering Lady Packwood's thoughts on the subject of prolonged discussion of one's sins. "The matter is over and done, and we are still good friends. Your uncle will very likely not refer to the matter again, so we shall not either. Agreed?"

The boy nodded, finishing off the third muffin. "That puts me in mind of something else," he added when he could speak. "Uncle Nick said to ask you if you'd like to ride over to Randolph's farm later—about ten, I think he said—to have a look at that sow's brood. I'm to go with him—Gram, too, I daresay—and he said to ask Miss Penny if she will come also," he added, smiling at that lady.

Miss Penistone declined politely, and Sarah, happily accepting the invitation on her own behalf, later confided to Colin that, despite that lady's unflagging serenity, she had a dreadful fear of horses and never rode. The boy soon took himself off, whistling, to inform his uncle and grandmother that Sarah would accompany them, and an hour later, he presented himself again to escort her to the stables.

Nicholas and Lady Packwood were already there. He was dressed simply, in buckskins and top boots with a dark leather jacket, while her ladyship sported a dashing habit that Sarah hadn't seen her wear before. It was severely cut of bright cherry velvet, and embellished with black embroidery at the sleeves and hem. The jacket fastened with black silk frogs, and the little red cap atop her smoothly coiffed head boasted a black ostrich plume that dipped down to the shoulder. As Nicholas tossed his mother into her saddle, Sarah caught a glimpse of neat kid half-boots topped with three-quarter-inch red fringe, and mentally changing the primary color to gold or russet, she decided then and there that the moment she could safely put off her mourning in public, she would order just such an outfit herself.

It was a cheerful group that turned onto the woods path, for Colin was excited at the prospect of seeing the piglets, and Nicholas exerted himself to be charming. They had been riding for some distance in pairs with Nicholas and her ladyship behind Colin and Sarah, when they came upon a widening of the trail that seemed to continue for about a quarter mile.

Suddenly, Lady Packwood urged her mount forward. "Colin! I'll wager five pounds to a groat you cannot reach that white-barked tree up ahead before I do!" And with barely a pause for the boy to collect his wits, she was off.

Laughing, Colin shouted that she would lose her money and kicked his horse to a gallop. Nicholas rode up alongside Sarah.

"Would you care to make a side bet on the outcome?" he asked, smiling at her in a way that made her insides feel a bit twittery.

"Well," Sarah replied seriously, "I think her ladyship could win if she had a mind to, for she had a headstart, after all, but I think she intends Colin to beat her."

"Maybe I should take you to Newmarket with me," he teased. "It seems that you have a knack for calling races."

Her smile was a shy one, and she made no reply to his sally. The racers reached the white-barked tree, and from Sarah's viewpoint, it looked to be a tie, but Colin was crowing that he had won.

"By a full head, Gram! You've lost your five pounds!"

Lady Packwood was laughing, trying to catch her breath. "You'll have to wait for it, my lad. I've not got a penny on me."

"Uncle Nick! I won, and now she won't pay!"

They drew in alongside the other two. Lady Packwood was still chuckling. "Don't look to me for it, brat," grinned his uncle. "The lady pays her own debts. But you'll get it, never fear. That's one who doesn't play and not pay." Lady Packwood reached out to ruffle her grandson's curls, but suddenly her face contorted in pain and she gave a sharp cry. Nicholas leaned quickly forward. "Mother! What is it?" Sarah, too, leaned anxiously toward her. Her ladyship had clapped a hand to her side but now managed a weak smile.

" 'Tis nothing, children, I assure you. Merely a stitch in my side. I daresay I allowed my woman to make the waistband of this habit a bit tight, that's all. I should know better than to ride neck or nothing when I've got it on."

"Would you like to dismount and sit for a spell?" Nicholas asked solicitously. "We can spread your blanket under a tree."

"That's an excellent notion," applauded his mother. "Then you may pick me up again when you return, or else I shall just go on home again when I feel better."

"Why, you mustn't stay here alone!" Sarah exclaimed, before Nicholas could speak. "I wouldn't hear of it. His lordship and Colin can go ahead, and I shall stay with you."

But his lordship objected to that scheme, saying that even the woods path was not necessarily safe for two lone females. "If it's only a stitch, it will pass quickly enough," he said. "We shall remain here until it does and then carry on as planned."

A frown of annoyance flitted across her ladyship's brow. "That sounds quite practical, dearest, but do you know I think I should do much better just to go back when I feel up to it, for I'm certain the pain will return if I attempt to go the distance. These things can be very unpleasant that way, you know. Now, before you say another word," she added firmly, "let me say that I shall not allow you to cancel your visit, because the excellent Randolph is simply dying to show off his sow to you, and you promised you would go. If you do not like to leave Sarah—and I quite understand that—then, Colin may look after me." Colin opened his mouth to protest, but a quelling look from under his grandmother's nicely arched brows caused him to shut it again. "He will take good care of me, I assure you, and perhaps you will allow him to ride over later with that groom of his—Jem, I think he's called—so he won't miss out on the piglets altogether."

"I cannot think you will be much safer with a boy for company than you would be with Sarah," commented her son with an odd, speculative gleam in his eye.

Colin looked indignant, but her ladyship only smiled again. "Nonsense, Nicky. Colin would be quite resourceful in a crisis. Besides," she added sweetly, with an air of one about to have the last word, "I have my pistol by me, so we shall be quite safe."

Nicholas chuckled, shaking his head at her, but he made no further objections. With nearly exaggerated care, he helped her to dismount and supported her to a nearby tree, while

Colin unsaddled her horse and brought the saddle blanket to spread upon the ground. "It's a shame you neglected to bring your vinaigrette, Mama," his lordship observed dryly.

Lady Packwood glared at him. "Yes, isn't it!" she replied. "Do go, Nicky dear."

Sarah frowned at Nicholas's seeming levity and watched worriedly until her ladyship seemed quite comfortable. She thought it sounded exactly like Lady Packwood to have her own pistol with her while, at the same time, to have neglected to bring anything so quackish as a vinaigrette, but she worried that the "stitch" might prove to be something more serious. Her ladyship still complained of pain, yet she did not seem pale, rather the contrary. Her color was excellent, even a little high. Could it be fever? But when she suggested this to Nicholas after he had remounted, and even added that perhaps both she and Colin ought to stay, he only chuckled.

"Your concern does you credit, Countess, but I beg you not to worry. It is my conviction that we have all been rather neatly outmaneuvered."

"I fear I don't understand your meaning, my lord."

"Piqued, repiqued, and capoted," he added cryptically. "The pistol was a very nice touch indeed."

Sarah opened her mouth to demand an explanation, but one suddenly presented itself to her, and she felt warmth suffuse her cheeks. Could Lady Packwood actually have been shamming the whole thing in order to throw her together with Nicholas? Glancing quickly at her companion, she was grateful to see that, although his eyes held a distinct twinkle, he was looking straight ahead. A few moments later, she had herself well in hand again, however, so that when he made a conversational gambit, she was able to reply appropriately.

Nicholas had clearly set himself to be pleasing, so the rest of their ride to the Randolph farm was very enjoyable. Mr. Randolph was delighted to see them both and expressed his sorrow at Lady Packwood's sudden indisposition. His plump wife, when the matter was explained to her, suggested several possible causes and cures, till Sarah was hard put to repress the laughter that kept threatening to bubble up. She dared not look at Nicholas and was very glad when Randolph finally escorted them out to the sty to view the sow, Judith, and her numerous offspring.

The piglets were darling, but Judith had whiskers all over

her long gray-pink snout, and Sarah found it difficult to understand why everyone was so pleased with her. The sow did nothing more than lie on her side expelling an occasional long-suffering grunt, while her progeny scrambled and squealed over one another in voracious attempts to attach themselves to any portion of her anatomy that seemed to offer itself. Judith, meanwhile, showed not the slightest interest in any of them. Sarah had expected her to treat them as a cat does its kittens or a bitch its puppies, but Nicholas chuckled when she mentioned this to him.

"Pigs are very unpredictable," he said. "I've seen a sow give birth and immediately roll over on top of the new piglet. I've also seen them, when the job was done, simply get up and leave with never another thought for their offspring. Believe me, Judith is doing very well indeed."

He was in excellent spirits on the return journey, and Sarah found that she was enjoying his company very much. He uttered not a single critical word but kept her laughing and chattering until they had returned to the white-barked tree, where he showed no surprise to discover that Lady Packwood and Colin had already gone. He merely noted that his mother must have recovered enough to ride back to the Park, and the fact was confirmed a short time later, when they encountered Colin and Jem.

"Gram said I may as well go along now," Colin explained. "She seems to be quite recovered, so I didn't think you would mind if I left her in Miss Penny's care," he added naively.

Nicholas grinned at him. "I'm sure you were a comfort to her, brat, and she couldn't be in better hands than Miss Penny's, so you go on and stay as long as Randolph will put up with you."

Sarah observed somewhat defiantly that she was much relieved to hear that Lady Packwood was recovered, but since her companion's only response was a mocking grin, she might have become a trifle flustered had he not had the presence of mind to call her attention to a spread of wildflowers on a grassy knoll some little way off and to ask her opinion as to the species. This method answered very well, and they were soon quite comfortable again.

They returned to the main house and went immediately to pay their respects to the erstwhile invalid, only to discover that she was enjoying the pleasure of a morning caller, a lady of uncertain years and hair of a dubious straw color that hung in clusters of side curls over her ears. Her three-quarter gown was puce, cut high to the neck and long to the wrist, and it fit rather snugly around her generous waistline. Lady Packwood introduced her as Mrs. Tibbetts.

"Shirley Tibbetts," amplified the visitor in a high-pitched voice, "not my mama-in-law, of course, who is old Mrs. Abigail Tibbetts, you know." She giggled slightly behind one gloved hand. "I'm sure you will remember her, my lord, though perhaps you will not remember me, for I don't believe we've had the pleasure." She batted her eyes at him. "Of meeting each other, that is. Until now, of course."

" 'Tis certain poor Moreland don't remember either you or your poor old mama-in-law, Mrs. Tibbetts, for he's got a shockingly bad memory, you know. You must tell him all about yourself; however," she added, twinkling at her son's expression of dismay, "I daresay he hasn't got time for it all right now, so perhaps you'd best get on with what you were saying before about your youngest. I am sure it must have been fascinating."

The sardonic tone was clearly lost on Mrs. Tibbetts, who promptly launched herself into a rather involved tale. It finally wound down to some sort of conclusion, and Lady Packwood made sympathetic noises, then rose and held out a hand to the visitor. "What a pity you must be going so soon," she said sweetly, "but I know you said you would not take up much of my time, so we must not keep you longer. Do call again, however, and if my butler tells you I am not at home, you must leave your calling card, you know. Say good day to dear Mrs. Tibbetts, my dears."

Mrs. Tibbetts had scrambled rather hastily to her feet, and Nicholas kindly offered to see her to the door. "Oh, no, my lord!" she protested, "though I am certainly flattered by such condescension from one in so elevated a position as yourself. But your butler will see me safely out, I'm sure." She giggled again behind her glove before dipping a farewell curtsy. "Delighted, my lady, Lady Moreland. Good day to you, my lord."

Lady Packwood had nearly ripped the bell cord from its moorings, so hearty a yank did she give it, and Dasher entered rather more hurriedly than usual.

"Ah, Dasher," said the earl smoothly, "Mrs. Tibbetts is leaving now. Please show her out."

"And if he ever shows that tedious woman *in* again," snapped Lady Packwood once the door was safely closed, "I shall quite cheerfully hand him his ears on a silver salver!"

She sat down again with an unladylike snort, whereupon Sarah chuckled and Nicholas crossed the room, bent over, and kissed his mother's cheek. " 'Tis known as just deserts, ma'am, is it not? We had a very nice visit with Randolph, by the by. He sends his respects."

"It wouldn't hurt you to show some respect yourself, young man!" retorted Lady Packwood with a withering glare. "Sarah, lamb," she went on in a milder tone, "do see if you can get Dasher back, and tell him I absolutely *require* a small glass of sherry before we have our luncheon."

The rest of the day passed without incident, and when the tea tray was brought in that evening, Lady Packwood announced that it was time and more to visit old Nanny Bates. Nicholas grinned at her, and to Sarah's surprise, she rounded on him indignantly.

"It is all very well and good for you to laugh, Mr. Impertinence, but I do not like the woman and never have. I should have gone at once to see her and got the business over with, but I didn't, so now I must. And you will go with me, sir!"

"I am at your service, my lady," he responded promptly, "but it really won't be such an ordeal, you know. She must be at least eighty, so she cannot possibly frighten you any longer."

"Much you know," scoffed her ladyship. "That woman was an absolute tyrant in the nursery. You can have no notion! Any suggestion I made was promptly labeled 'new-fangled nonsense,' and even your father sided with her. Said he had perfect confidence in her, since she had raised a good many more children than I had! Can you believe it? And it didn't stop when you went away to school either, because Darcy was still here, of course, and so I had to submit to being reminded to write a letter once a week—though I wrote nearly every day—and to being told not to send you this because it wouldn't be good for you or to send you that because it *would*. I tell you, if I hadn't been a rather strong-minded sort myself, that old witch would have driven me round the bend."

"But if you don't like her," Sarah protested, unable to imagine Lady Packwood afraid of anyone, "why must you visit her?"

"Because one must never be remiss in one's duties to one's

dependents, my dear," her ladyship replied simply. "She doesn't like me any more than I like her, but it would hurt her feelings if I should neglect to visit her, and that would be uncivil of me." She glanced fondly at her grinning son. "I may roast Nicky for his fusty notions, but there are certain civilities that must never be neglected by those of us in positions of privilege."

"We shall take Sarah with us," Nicholas announced. "Colin, too. It should be instructive for them to see you, my dear ma'am, wallowing in terror at the feet of a wiry, sharp-tongued old lady."

He expressed his disappointment as loudly as his mother expressed her relief the following day, for during the night the clouds rolled across the Common and morning was nearly as dark as midnight. Then, lightning began to flash and thunder to roll, and when the first torrent of rain descended, the expedition to East End village was of a necessity postponed.

The next three days continued the same, and the occupants of both the main house and Dower House passed their time in pursuits suitable to such weather. There was a good deal of cozy conversation and card playing, and the attics of Dower House provided an afternoonful of industry when the three ladies and Colin prepared a detailed inventory of the contents.

The fourth morning dawned sunny and clear, but Lady Packwood insisted that the rainy weather had made the road impassable. When her son shot her a derisive grin, she added that she was sure she had caught a chill as well.

"And mark my word, Nicholas, if I go to visit that woman today, I shall very likely pass my cold to her, and it will develop into inflamation of the lungs, and she will die, and I shall be blamed for it!"

Nicholas laughed at her but did not press the matter, and the late afternoon brought a diversion that provided further respite from the dreaded expedition. Sarah and Miss Penistone were sitting with Lady Packwood by the library fire, ostensibly keeping her company while she nursed her cold. Penny was mending, while Sarah read aloud from a thrilling gothic romance provided by her ladyship, who was knotting a fringe for a lacy shawl, when the hall door was unceremoniously thrust open and Sir Percival strode in, his boot tops spattered with mud, his riding cloak slung over his arm.

"Hello, my sweet," he said, bending over to kiss his wife's cheek. "I've brought company. Hope his lordship don't mind."

"Of course not, my love. How delightful! Who is it?"

"Fellow from my club," he replied. "Wife, too, though she ain't in the club, of course. Seems she's related to Lady Moreland." He beamed at Sarah and, with an air of producing an unexpected treat, confided, "The name is Hartley, my lady."

XV

Sarah had been sitting in the wing chair, the book in her lap, but she stared now at Sir Percival, and the color drained from her face. Hearing muffled voices, she looked around the back of the chair toward the open door. At first, she could see only Dasher's back, but then Lord Hartley came into view as the butler relieved him of his heavy cloak. He, too, was dressed for riding, and Sarah surmised that the two gentlemen must have ridden while Lady Hartley rode in the carriage. Her uncle turned toward her, and she knew he must have seen her, but he gave no sign of it, merely holding out a hand to someone behind him. A moment later, Sarah saw her aunt.

Lady Hartley, a tall woman of majestic proportions who carried herself with exaggerated hauture, was divested of her bonnet and silk-lined traveling cape. She was of an age with Lady Packwood, but the passing years had not been so kind to her; her dark brown hair was streaked with gray, and she had been described by uncharitable persons as "bracket-faced." Her mauve silk dress was stylish, but she had better sense than to follow fashions which would not suit her figure, so the pattern was a simple one.

Sir Percival stepped forward to see what was keeping his guests, and Sarah held her breath. A moment later, her aunt and uncle were being formally presented to Lady Packwood and Sarah was on her feet, clutching the book at her waist.

The amenities finished, Lady Hartley nodded briefly to Penny. "How do you do, Miss Penistone," she said in a tone of former mistress to lowly dependent. "I did not expect to see you here."

Penny dipped a curtsy. "I am very well, thank you, your ladyship." She made no reply to the second part of Lady Hartley's greeting, nor did one seem to be expected, and Lady

173

Hartley turned at last to Sarah. Unsuccessfully, Sarah tried to tell herself that her aunt no longer had any authority over her, that indeed, she outranked that lady and would take precedence over her at any dinner table. It did no good at all. Her knees quaked as that glacial hauture was turned her way.

"You look well enough, Lady Moreland." Sarah barely stopped herself making the sort of curtsy that had always been demanded of her as a child. Her aunt's tone and the use of the title made her feelings quite clear to one who had known her from childhood, though Sarah doubted that she sounded anything but chillingly polite to Lady Packwood or Sir Percival.

"Thank you, Aunt Aurelia," she replied carefully, and unable to think of anything further to say, she was deeply grateful to Sir Percival when he spoke up in his usual fashion.

"Hartley said they hadn't been here before, my sweet, so I thought why not, and Hartley said 'delighted' and was sure his lady would like it, though there were plans in the works for a bolt to Brighton, so I just brought 'em along. You look a bit peckish. Off your feed, are you?"

Lady Packwood smiled at him. "A mere chill from the damp weather, my love. I'm sure it will pass quickly enough. I feel right as a trivet now that you are here, and your surprise will no doubt liven things up a good deal."

"Daresay it will at that," he agreed. "Where's Moreland?"

"Off with Colin somewhere or other," she told him. "The boy has been storing away energy these past days, and Nicky thought it best to let some of it before Colin gets up to heaven knows what mischief." She glanced at the visitors. "Do take a seat, Lady Hartley, and you as well, my lord. We shall send Dasher for some refreshment, because I know you must be tired after your journey, though it was not such a long one, of course."

"Thank you," replied Lady Hartley loftily, "but I should prefer a cup of tea in my bedchamber, if you don't mind. I daresay you keep civilized hours here, but I should like to rest a bit and remove the evidence of travel before sitting down to dinner. You needn't send for a servant to show me the way, however," she added with a gimlet glance at her niece. "I'm quite certain Sarah will oblige."

"Of course, Aunt," Sarah said weakly. She glanced at Miss Penistone and received a sympathetic smile that was somehow not at all encouraging; then, taking a deep breath to settle her nerves, she led the way into the hall and up the stairs. With

Lady Hartley marching purposefully along behind her, Sarah thought she knew exactly how the aristocrats in France must have felt when they mounted the steps to face *Madame la Guillotine*. She had no idea what her aunt would say to her, but there could be no doubt that she was in for the trimming of her life.

The door to the blue guest bedchamber stood ajar, and Sarah caught a glimpse of her aunt's dresser moving to hang a russet silk gown in the wardrobe. They entered, and Lady Hartley promptly dismissed the woman and turned to face her niece.

"You deserve to be soundly whipped, Sarah."

Briefly, Sarah considered informing her that Nicholas would no doubt agree with that sentiment, but her aunt had no sense of humor, and Sarah did not trust her not to box her ears for impertinence, so she merely bowed her head meekly before the oncoming storm. However, that would not do for her ladyship.

"Have you nothing to say?"

"Only that I am sorry, Aunt Aurelia."

"Well, I should think there would be a good deal more than that. What in the world is that book you are clutching so tightly?"

Guiltily, Sarah realized she was still holding the gothic thriller, the exact sort of book she had been most strictly forbidden to read at home, but there seemed no recourse other than to relinquish it when Lady Hartley held out an imperious hand. "Just as I might have thought!" she condemned roundly after a brief glance at the title. "Trash! You should be ashamed of yourself, Sarah, but I daresay 'tis all of a piece. You have behaved altogether disgracefully, and the manner of your husband's untimely demise has not helped matters."

"I could not help the way he died, ma'am."

"Watch your tongue, my girl," Lady Hartley warned. "It may interest you to know that there have been bets laid in the London clubs as to whether or not you *could* have helped it."

Sarah stared at her. She had known there was scandal, but Nicholas had said nothing of any wagers. "Surely, Aunt Aurelia, no one truly believes I murdered my husband!"

Lady Hartley looked down at her, but there was no softening in the hard, gray eyes. "Gentlemen will make wagers over which raindrop will first reach the bottom of a window pane, Sarah," she pronounced caustically. "It was surely no great matter to find several who would bet on the possibility of your being a murderess. They certainly did not have to know you to do so. You might have thought of the potential scandal before you ever made plans to meet that deceitful fribble in Bond Street!"

Sarah saw no point in arguing that she could not have been expected to know beforehand that Darcy would be murdered, so she merely apologized again for her thoughtlessness. Lady Hartley was by no means finished with her, however, and said a good deal more that Sarah would have preferred not to hear, but by and large, it was not so bad as she had feared it might be. Although she felt a bit wrung out when she finally left her aunt and went back downstairs, she was also conscious of deep relief at having the dreaded encounter over and done with.

There was still her uncle to be faced, of course, but Lord Hartley, though he had rarely paid her any heed, was a kindly man who preferred a peaceful existence. Beyond making the observation that a sense of duty, spurred by Sir Percival's very kind invitation, had caused them to put off their visit to Brighton in order to see how she was getting on, he said very little about the matter. Sarah apologized for any embarrassment she might have caused him, but he merely replied that he was sure she would strive in future to be a good girl, and that was that.

It was soon time to dress for dinner, but Sarah returned to the main house alone, since Miss Penistone, for reasons of her own, elected to fend for herself. Nicholas and Colin had returned with barely enough time to change, so their first encounter with the visitors was at table, and once the introductions had been got through, Lady Hartley commented that it was surely unusual for a child as young as Colin to be permitted to dine in company.

"To be sure, my lady," returned Lady Packwood, "but we consider that it gives him experience in conversing with all manner of persons, you know, and a young man simply cannot have too much experience."

Lady Packwood's tone was nearly saccharin, and Lady Hartley gave her a rather sharp look, but the subject was dropped, to Colin's visible relief, and a new one introduced. On the whole, everyone seemed to be on his or her good behavior, so dinner was not the ordeal that some might have expected it to be. The only difficult moment occurred when Lady Packwood asked her husband cheerfully if he had overheard any interesting *on dits* while he was in London. Lady Hartley interjected with studied calm that, since her niece seemed to be providing the most interesting ones of late, she rather thought they might speak of something else, if it was all the same to the others.

Nicholas had moved into the breach with experienced ease, but Sarah had no idea later what it was that he had said exactly. She was still appalled by the information that her name was being bandied freely in the London clubs. It had been bad enough to think that she would be cut by her old friends, should she return to the city. But this was far worse. Something had to be done and as quickly as possible. The murderer must be found!

Feeling a need to have a moment to herself after dinner, she left her aunt and Lady Packwood conversing amicably enough in the library and went out onto the terrace for a breath of fresh air. She walked to the end of the terrace furthest from the library and, hoping the flagstones had been washed clean by the rain, sat down on the edge to have a good think. But even the quiet night under a heaven aglow with stars was not sufficient to induce logical thought, and Sarah's mind seemed a bumblebath of disconnected fragments. She was at the point of wondering whether it would be worth the inevitable scolds just to take herself off to bed without even saying good night, when a rustle in the shrubbery preceded the appearance of Colin with Erebus at his heels.

Sarah greeted them cheerfully enough, not really surprised to see Colin and thinking that perhaps a chat with him was exactly what she needed. He sat down beside her, and the big dog plumped down at their feet.

"I'm glad *that* dinner is over," the boy declared, sotto voice.

She chuckled. "Aunt Aurelia is a rather formidable woman. I told you."

"Yes, but so is Gram. I kept expecting fireworks."

"So did I," Sarah agreed, "but I think they each recognized in the other an opponent who would give as good as she got. Perhaps they decided to spare the rest of us."

Colin nodded. "What did her ladyship mean about you providing food for gossip in London?"

Sarah sighed, but she could think of no reason that would be acceptable to him for not explaining. He listened carefully, and when she had finished, he seemed disturbed.

"But that's dreadful. We must find the answer to this mystery."

"Yes, indeed," she agreed. "Else I shall very likely be ruined forever. As it is, I dare not show my face in Town. The only good thing is that I doubt Aunt Aurelia would take me back now, even if your uncle decided to send me, as he once threatened to do."

But Colin was still thinking and did not reply. After a few moments' silence, he looked up at her again. "You know, we haven't really done any more about Mr. Oakes. I think we must make a push to discover exactly what that fellow is about."

"But we can do very little with so many people about. I confess I've scarcely given him a thought since Sir Percival and Lady Packwood arrived," Sarah said. "How can we go about any sort of investigation with my aunt and uncle here as well? Not to mention that it would do neither of us any good to put your Uncle Nicholas out of temper."

Colin grinned at her. "I believe you are as afraid of Uncle Nick as you are of Lady Hartley."

Sarah laughed, shaking her head at him. At that moment, Erebus lifted his head at the unmistakable sound of the library door opening, and Colin melted immediately into the shrubbery. Sarah turned to see who was coming, though her instinct told her before she saw him.

"Hiding out, Countess?" Nicholas spoke in a low tone. "I told them I would just be certain that you were all right."

"Surely, I'm perfectly safe here, my lord." But she smiled at him. After that dinner, Nicholas by himself did not seem in the least awesome.

He chuckled, taking a seat beside her. "To tell the truth, I believe you are far safer out here than in the library. Your uncle and Sir Percival made good their escape by going straight to the billiards room with a second bottle of port, but my mother and your aunt are busily taking each other's measure, much like a pair of fighting cocks. At the moment they seem to have found a mutual target in my late nephew, but there may be feathers flying at any moment, and I confess I had no wish to be caught between them."

"I do not think my aunt would appreciate being likened to a fighting cock, sir," Sarah said demurely.

"Then I must beg you won't repeat it to her," he replied with mock seriousness, "or to my mother either. I'd not wish my head given to either of them for washing, if you don't mind."

"Your mother would call you 'Mr. Impertinence' again, I daresay."

"At the very least." He paused, then asked gently, "Was Lady Hartley very severe with you, Countess?"

The moon was beginning to show its face above the stable-yard, and Sarah fastened her gaze to it. "She said a great deal, of course. That was only to be expected, but it was not so bad as I had feared. I daresay I had exaggerated her temper in my imagination. There was one thing. . . ." Her voice trailed off.

"Dare I ask you to confide in me?" Nicholas asked. He spoke quietly, still in that gentle tone, a little as though he thought her mood a fragile one.

"She said there are bets being laid in the London clubs as to whether or not I killed Darcy," Sarah muttered tightly. Then she turned to him, her gaze an accusing one. "Why didn't you tell me?"

"I didn't know," he replied simply. "Reading through the betting books is not one of my favorite pastimes, and whether you choose to believe it or not, my last visit to London was not spent in the clubs at all. I think I had dinner at White's one night, but that was all, and it was not a social evening. I was in Town only briefly, after all, and my time was consumed with your affairs, my own, and Darcy's."

"I see." He was watching her carefully, and Sarah knew it was important to him that she believe what he was telling her. "Would you have told me had you heard of it, my lord?"

With a rueful smile, he shook his head. "Very likely not, and I was afraid you would ask. Truthfully, had I given the matter much thought, I think I might have deduced that such things would be happening. Gentlemen will bet on whatever strikes their fancy, you know, no matter how ridiculous. I should not have told you, because the information would have done you no good, would only have hurt you. One reason for keeping you here, Countess, was to protect you from the cruel things that thoughtless people are capable of saying. Your aunt clearly has no such protective feelings."

"She feels that such scandal reflects upon her, my lord."

"Well, of course she does," he agreed sharply. "She is a woman to whom appearance is everything, I believe."

"She prefers propriety to scandal, sir, as do you yourself. I should have expected you to defend her, but you seem to condemn instead."

"Of course, I do," Nicholas retorted. "Lady Hartley is a perfectly selfish woman. No one of sensibility can fail to discern it!"

Sarah hid a smile. This was surely a new Nicholas! But her aunt had a rare talent for putting up other people's backs, so it shouldn't be surprising that she had managed to set Nicholas against her. A few moments later, Dasher emerged from the library to inform his master that Lady Packwood had requested his immediate presence.

"It seems I shall have to present myself, Countess, but I refuse to deal with them alone. You must lend me your support." He held out a hand to her, and she let him help her to her feet. Having done so much, she could scarcely object when he tucked her hand in the crook of his arm and led her inside.

The following evening, Nicholas informed Miss Penistone in no uncertain terms that she was to present herself at dinner, that one evening of scratching for sustenance at Dower House was sufficient. She merely smiled at him and said that, of course, she would do as he requested, that she had only stayed away thinking it would be more comfortable for everyone else. It was Sarah who discovered that, rather than starving at Dower House, Penny had had an excellent meal in the housekeeper's room with Cook and Dasher and Betsy. Had anyone asked what she thought about that, Sarah would have replied that no doubt Betsy had invited her, and Penny had merely taken the sensible course.

The Hartleys stayed only two more days, much to everyone's relief. Lady Hartley said she would have liked to stay longer, but having already canceled several engagements and postponed their visit to Brighton, she felt it necessary now to return.

Once her aunt and uncle were safely away, Sarah immediately put her mind to the problem she found most pressing. Colin had said they would have to search out the mysterious Mr. Oakes, and she agreed with him but thought it would be a trifle dangerous, since Nicholas would undoubtedly disapprove of such doings. On the other hand, she remembered another suggestion of Colin's, made some time ago and disparaged. Now, in view of her aunt's information, any course seemed worth pursuing. She sent for Dasher.

"Dasher, I want to open the cellars," she told him bluntly when he responded to her summons.

"Of course, my lady. I shall attend to it at once." He turned on his heel, evidently thinking that was the end of it, but turned back when Sarah cleared her throat a little hesitantly. "Was there something more, my lady?"

"No, Dasher, that is all," she replied, watching him closely. "I just . . . well, I rather expected you to ask why, or to say we must ask his lordship, or some such thing."

"As to that, my lady, his lordship has already said that I am to regard your orders as his own, and I should never think to question his. If he were to ask me if I am arranging to open the Dower House cellars, I should have to tell him, of course. But I daresay it won't occur to him to ask," he added comfortably.

There was nothing in his expression to indicate curiosity, but then he had never shown any particular curiosity that Sarah could remember. Dasher merely went about his business, unflappably and efficiently. By mid-afternoon there were two workmen in the passageway of the Dower House kitchens, methodically and carefully chipping away at a wall of brick.

The following morning dawned cheerfully sunny, and the expedition to visit Nanny Bates could no longer be put off. Lady Packwood remarked caustically that she really ought to be packing her trunks to leave for the Continent, since poor Sir Percival had been kicking his heels quite long enough. Her loving spouse replied amiably that he had rather enjoyed Lord Hartley's company and had not felt guilty about leaving her to her own devices, since she had the company of dear Sarah and Lady Hartley as well. She had nearly answered him with a snort before Nicholas laughingly bore her off to the forecourt, where a comfortable chaise was awaiting their pleasure. John Coachman was driving with Nicholas's Timmy up as guard, and Nicholas had elected to ride in the coach with the others. He and Colin took the forward seats, leaving the more comfortable rear seat for the ladies.

It was a jolly enough drive, despite the deplorable state of the track across the Common and the not much better state of the London road. What with all the bouncing and jouncing and the difficulty of conversation, there was still much laughter and joking, until the carriage approached East End, when there was a noticeable change in Lady Packwood's mood. She became quieter and more reserved, until finally she refrained from speaking altogether. Nicholas teased her, but to no avail, and Sarah was certain her ladyship's color had faded away entirely by the time John Coachman drew his horses to a halt in front of a tiny thatch-roofed cottage on the western edge of the village.

There was a neat picket fence around an equally neat and colorful garden, and the gate neither squeaked nor creaked when Colin pushed it open for the ladies to pass through. Nicholas preceded them to the dark red front door and pounded upon it loudly enough to wake the dead, Sarah thought. Nevertheless, it was several moments before it opened.

A tiny gray-haired lady with sparkling blue eyes stood there, staring up at him in delight. "Master Nicky! How perfectly wonderful to see you again so soon!" Then her gaze shot past him and encountered the rest of his party, flickering quickly over Colin and Sarah and coming to rest upon Lady Packwood. "And your ladyship," she added with an unmistakable, but indecipherable, gleam in her eye.

"Yes, indeed," Nicholas said heartily. "I have brought Mama to pay you a call and the new Lady Moreland, Master Darcy's widow, you know. And young Colin, of course. I daresay it's been donkey's years since you've laid eyes upon him, but he's been at Harrow, and Lady Honoria and Bessling are on the Continent. Are we to come in, Nanny, or do you mean us to conduct this visit on the stoop?"

She stood aside. "Impertinent. Always was; always will be, I suppose. A shame, too, but I daresay it's too late to do anything about it now."

"Entirely too late," Nicholas agreed as he ushered her to a comfortable chair near the crackling fire. A basket of knitting reposed on the floor beside it, and Nanny immediately picked up her work and carried on with it while she talked. It was a huge thing, knitted in all manner of gay colors, and Sarah finally decided it was meant to be a bedcover of some sort. Nanny never once glanced at the stuff in her lap, but her needles clicked away merrily, and she never seemed to drop a stitch or lose her place in the conversation.

They stayed quite half an hour, and by the end of that time, Nanny had discovered all there was worth knowing about Colin's schooling, Darcy's murder, and Lady Packwood's marriage. Surprisingly, she seemed to approve of the latter. "I will say this for you, my lady. You choose your men well. That

Packwood is very well thought of, they say. Plump in the pockets. Not that you need the money, of course, since I know my lord Moreland left you more than an independence. Still it shows good sense. You were a pea-goose in the old days. No saying but what you still are, but about some things you showed sense even then. Daresay you've matured a bit, too."

Lady Packwood seemed nearly undone by such rare praise, and Sarah almost laughed aloud. Colin grinned but wiped it off his face immediately at a sign from his equally afflicted uncle. Sarah herself was let off lightly. Nanny saw nothing amiss in her having married Darcy, thus showing that she was either unaware of his more exasperating qualities or had chosen to ignore them. She merely assumed that Sarah was in distress at his untimely demise and, with what must have been rare tact, left her alone.

Everyone expressed relief once they were back in the coach, and Nicholas told John Coachman to whip them up. The return journey was whiled away by reminiscences of Nanny at Ash Park. The pace was necessarily slow, of course, and became slower yet once they had turned onto the rutted track. Sarah remembered the first time she had come this way, and an exchanged glance with Nicholas showed that he knew just what she was thinking. The coach had rumbled up a low, tree-topped hill and begun the downward journey, when suddenly there was an explosion, the unmistakable sound of additional hoofbeats, and the coach came to a rocking halt.

"Stand and deliver!" The voice that called out was a harsh one, but no more harsh than the eyes of the villain who rode up to the coach door and swung down from his horse.

At the first sharp sound, Nicholas had reached for the leather holster in the door of the chaise, but when he saw his mother reach at the same moment for her reticule, he paused. "Leave it, ma'am," he ordered, returning his own hand to his lap.

The door was yanked unceremoniously open. "Keep yer dabs where I kin see 'em, coves, 'n ever' one'll come outa this wiv a whole skin."

XVI

There were two highwaymen. Both were masked and wore rough clothing, though the one who remained on his horse, his pistols leveled at John Coachman and Timmy, seemed to have a rather nattier appearance than his cohort.

The fellow who had pulled open the coach door now kicked the steps down and ordered them out into the road. His jaw rigid with anger, Nicholas descended first, then turned to assist his mother.

"Hold it there, me lord," growled the villain. "Yer blockin' me view. And raise yer fambles, if ye please."

Nicholas obeyed, and Sarah and Lady Packwood, the former nervously and the latter indignantly clutching her reticule, alit from the coach. Colin followed, glancing uncertainly at his uncle.

"Got a barker, me lord? Wouldn't want no trouble, ye know. Ladies present 'n all."

"Inside," Nicholas replied smoothly. "Leather holster in the side panel." He smiled encouragingly at Colin.

"I'll just have a look-see." The rogue started to move toward the coach but stopped at a sharp whistle from his partner. He looked up inquiringly.

"Tie 'em first." The words were muffled, the voice gruff, and Sarah looked up at him for the first time. He seemed to be taller than the other and not so broad across the shoulders. The shape of his face showed long and thin beneath the mask that covered it from the bridge of his nose to below his chin where it was tucked into a neatly tied neckcloth. On the other hand, his partner's face was round and full, the jut of his nose not nearly so long and that of his chin not so square or so prominent as the horseman's. The mask, in his case, was tucked into the collar of his dark jersey. Both men wore heavy duffel jackets and slouch hats pulled low over their foreheads.

As Sarah looked up at the horseman, she encountered a brief, chilly gaze from narrowed gray eyes before he turned his attention back to the men on the box. His partner tossed some leather thongs to Nicholas.

"You do the honors, me lord. The nipperkin first."

Nicholas moved to tie Colin's hands, and when the bandit's gaze followed him, Lady Packwood took the opportunity to slip a step or two behind Sarah. Sarah watched the horseman, but he kept his eyes focused on John Coachman and Timmy.

"Maman! Rien à faire!" Nicholas kept his voice controlled, but the urgency in his tone was unmistakable. Sarah glanced quickly around at her ladyship, who was looking annoyed.

" 'Ere, what's this then! Ain't the King's English good enough? What did you say to her?"

"I merely told her not to worry," Nicholas returned, his eye still warily upon Lady Packwood.

The bandit gave a derisive snort and altered his position so that he had a better view of her ladyship. "What did 'e say, me lady?"

Lady Packwood's shrug was accompanied by a grimace of disgust. "He said to do nothing," she replied tartly, holding out her reticule to him. "I daresay you will want this."

"Yer right about that." He took it, blinking in surprise as he hefted its weight and using his teeth and his free hand to open it. Turning it upside down, he gave a chuckle when a small, silver-mounted pistol fell out. "A popgun. Looky here, boss. Flash mort's goin' t' pertect 'erself!" He shook out the rest of the contents, but there was nothing else to interest him, so keeping his gaze mistrustfully upon her ladyship and Nicholas, he bent over, picked up the pistol, and dropped it into his pocket. "Hustle it up there, me lord. Ladies next."

Sarah watched Nicholas appraisingly as he moved to fasten her hands behind her back. He had himself under tight rein, but his touch was gentle, and he gave her hand a little comforting squeeze before he bound her wrists together and moved on to do the same for his mother. Then, the bandit tied Nicholas and searched his pockets, removing his ring, his watch, and his fobs, as well as his purse. Next went Sarah's two rings, the only pieces she wore with her mourning, and Lady Packwood's jewelry and watch. Colin had nothing to interest the men, and the coach, though carefully searched, revealed nothing but the holstered weapon, which they took. The spokesman seemed disappointed but resigned to the meager haul, noting aloud that the jewels at least would bring something. Before he remounted, he scooped up the shotgun that Timmy had dropped when ordered to do so, and the two highwaymen soon disappeared into the trees again.

Timmy jumped down from the box and ran to Nicholas. "Sorry, your lordship!" he said hastily as he untied the thong. "Caught us unawares. My fault, I expect." He eyed Nicholas uneasily, clearly expecting at least a tongue-lashing, if not more severe punishment for dereliction of duty. But Nicholas smiled briefly and squeezed his shoulder.

"You kept your head, lad. Nothing else you could have done with the pair of them so well-armed. See to Master Colin, if you please."

Sarah caught Timmy's look of gratitude and realized suddenly that he, like Dasher and, for that matter, the tenants and most of the other servants, had a very high regard for his master. Despite the outrageously dictatorial manner he took with *some* people, Nicholas seemed to have a knack for acquiring the respect and admiration of those who served him. She smiled at him.

"Are you all right, Countess?"

"Oh yes, my lord," she replied, wanting him to believe that she was at least as calm as he was. She thought of all the warnings he had given her and shuddered a little to think that, by defying him, she had risked such a confrontation by herself. "I . . ." She swallowed, then spoke more firmly, "I'm glad it's over."

"I, too," he muttered. She was free, and he moved to perform the same service for his mother, who had remained strangely silent. She eyed him now accusingly.

"I shall box your ears, Nicholas."

Dropping his hands from her wrists, he leaned over her shoulder to kiss her cheek. "What's that you say, madam? I seem to have developed a devilish weakness in my fingers. Hope you don't mind riding back as you are."

"Odious boy! Unfasten me at once!"

He chuckled. "You have reared no cloth-head, my lady. I've had my ears boxed by you upon other occasions, and I assure you most earnestly that I've no desire to repeat the experience."

She glared at him. "A little resolution, Nicholas, and I

should still have my sapphires, Sarah would still have her rings, and you would still have your self-respect!"

He straightened up, moving to face her, and Sarah caught her breath at his expression of mingled pain and anger. "You might even have remained alive long enough to enjoy those baubles, ma'am," he said roughly, "but I was not willing to risk the alternative. At the very least, had you drawn your little weapon, either Timmy or John Coachman would have been killed, for the most you might have accomplished would have been to wound one of the ruffians before the other let fire. Now, turn around!"

But her ladyship's temper had evaporated. "You are quite right," she said slowly. "I might have got us all killed." Pausing, she gave him a rueful look. "I should not have said what I did, Nicky, in any case. It was temper talking, not your mother." She smiled contritely. "Perhaps, 'tis my ears that require attention, sir."

He chucked her under the chin, his good humor restored. "Not from me, madam. 'Twould be more than my life is worth. If you did not retaliate in kind by sheer reflex, I should still have to face Sir Percival."

"Dear me," she laughed, "do you think Percy would fly to my defense?"

"I think," replied her undutiful son, straight-faced, "that he would even leave his dinner to do so . . . if necessary."

"No!" breathed her ladyship in mock awe. Sarah and Colin burst into laughter, and even Timmy and the coachman could be heard to chuckle. Nicholas sternly ordered his incorrigible mother to turn around so that he might loose her bonds, and they were soon comfortably on their way again.

"I didn't even know you still remembered your French, Nicky," commented Lady Packwood, once they were well underway.

He shrugged. "I've kept my hand in the last few years."

"With Wellington's forces, I collect."

He nodded, and Colin spoke up. "We must report this, must we not, Uncle Nick?"

"To be sure, brat. I think I shall visit Sir William Miles as soon as we return. Would you like to ride along with me?"

But surprisingly, Colin declined the offer, and not until after Nicholas had departed again did Sarah discover the reason for it, when the boy presented himself at Dower House and requested private speech with her. "We've got to make a plan," he said earnestly, once they were alone in the drawing room. "After today, Uncle Nick will very likely be stricter than ever about our riding outside the Park. If we are going to discover what our friend Mr. Oakes is up to, we'd better move fast."

There was something nagging at the back of her mind, tickling her memory. It was the sort of feeling she got when something was wrong or perhaps only when she had forgotten to do something she ought to have done. Although she couldn't imagine what caused it or think when it had started, it created a certain unease. Nevertheless, she could only agree, for Colin was right. Mr. Oakes was their only lead to Darcy's killer, and if they were to achieve anything, they must find him before Nicholas cracked down on their riding altogether. If only the Bow Street horse patrols or the Army would move back into the neighborhood. Once the problem of the highwaymen became past history, as it had always done before under such vigilance, they might be able to concentrate properly upon the problem of capturing a murderer!

At Colin's urging, she changed into her riding habit, pausing only long enough to inspect the progress of the workmen in the kitchen passage. It was obviously going slowly, but the wall of brick was a good deal smaller than it had been before and looked, indeed, as though the job would be finished by dinnertime. Sarah decided that it would probably be better to wait until the following day to tell Colin what she had done. Since the door would swing into the passage, it couldn't be opened until the last row of bricks was gone, and she was certain the boy would make a nuisance of himself if she told him about it before that. Tomorrow would be soon enough, after the workmen had declared the place safe.

Sarah had a fleeting vision of Nicholas's probable reaction to their exploration of the Dower House cellars. To do him justice, she was convinced that he believed them unsafe, for she had long since ceased to think of him as, even remotely, having anything to do with Darcy's death; nevertheless, she was certain he would oppose opening the cellars. She repressed the thought. Compared to the necessity for putting a period to the London gossip, his wishes and anxieties were unimportant.

She rejoined Colin, and they spent the afternoon visiting one tenant farm after another, accompanied by Jem, who followed so carefully upon their heels that Sarah knew he was afraid to lose sight of them for even a moment. Nicholas, she thought with a touch of bitterness, must have torn a proper strip off the poor lad. She had apologized to Jem long since, of course, but he had never told her what had passed between himself and his master after that fateful ride, and she had never dared to ask Nicholas.

They discovered nothing beyond the fact that the farms were all occupied now and were coming into good trim. Several of the farmers had met Mr. Oakes, to be sure, but few showed much, if any, interest in the man, and none had seen him within the last day or so. It was a discouraged pair that Jem escorted back to the Park.

Dusk was fast descending as they neared the huge entry gates. Sarah and Colin were discussing their lack of success and projecting plans for future investigations, when Jem said suddenly, "Company ahead, young master."

They peered into the gloom and discerned three horsemen riding toward them. It was Colin who recognized them first. "It's Uncle Nick on the left," he said then. "But the other two . . ." He squinted, then his jaw dropped. "By Jove, ma'am, that's Oakes!"

The others had seen them and reined in some distance ahead, but Sarah could see that Colin was right. Jeremy Oakes and Nicholas spoke briefly to one another; then, Oakes and the other man, whom Sarah did not recognize, rode off toward the common, and Nicholas urged his mount forward. They met him at the gates. Jem conscientiously dropped back a little.

"And where have you two been?"

Sarah and Colin glanced at each other. "Went for a ride, sir," the boy replied airily. "Needed exercise after all that sitting in the coach, you know."

"Yet, you turned down a chance to ride with me, did you not?" Nicholas's tone was gentle, but there lurked an unmistakable note of danger.

Colin, hearing it, looked again at Sarah, then sighed with resignation. "Yes, sir."

Nicholas frowned but said nothing further until they reached the courtyard. Then, he drew rein. "Jem will take the horses round to the stables," he said briefly. "I want to see you in the library. Both of you," he added with a sharp look at the silent Sarah. He swung down and lifted her from her saddle, then stood aside politely to allow them to precede him.

Sarah could tell from Colin's expression that he was busily

racking his brain for an acceptable tale to tell his uncle. Her own mind was occupied, too, as she wondered what his lordship had been doing in such company, but she feared the boy would only succeed in making more trouble for both of them if he concocted some Banbury tale or other for Nicholas's edification.

Nicholas walked toward the desk where, dropping his riding whip, he proceeded to take off his gloves. "Have you come up with a better reason for your ride, brat?" He dropped the gloves atop the whip and, turning a stern eye upon his nephew, leaned back against the desk, crossing his feet and folding his arms against his broad chest. "Well, Colin? I am waiting."

"Please, my lord . . ." But Sarah was waved to silence. She looked helplessly at Colin. He didn't appear to be particularly distressed; instead, he seemed to be weighing various alternatives. Sarah shook her head meaningly, and he raised a quizzical eyebrow.

"Cut line, brat."

"Tell him, Colin."

Both commands came at once, but it was to Sarah that the boy looked. "The truth?" He sounded surprised. She nodded while, at the same time, his lordship blandly expressed the opinion that, in his consideration, the truth was unquestionably their wisest option. "Very well," said Colin with a dubious shrug. Briefly, he outlined their suspicions regarding Mr. Oakes and their conviction that Nicholas would not allow them to pursue their investigations after the morning's unfortunate incident. "It is absolutely obligatory that we clear Cousin Sarah's name," he added fiercely, "so please, Uncle Nick, don't say we must stop!"

Nicholas had heard him out in silence, and if a brief glint or two of amusement lit his eye during the discourse, they were restrained enough that neither Sarah nor Colin noticed. "I collect that this has been going on for some time, has it not?" There was a pregnant silence. "Since Darcy's funeral?" he pursued. "I seem to recall, for example, a horse that needed to be reshod. If my memory serves me accurately, Mr. Oakes had been nosing about not long before that."

"Exactly!" Colin exclaimed. "Don't you see, Uncle Nick? He's been behaving suspiciously all along! You must see that he's the link. If we can get him to open the budget, I daresay we'll have the killer!"

"What I see," replied his uncle in measured accents, "is a

young gentleman who has been interfering in matters that are none of his concern, who has told falsehoods and practiced deceit to gain his own ends. That sort of shenanigan is going to end right now, sir, or you and I are going to have a confrontation that will make the aftermath of your ghost walk seem like a country dance. Do you follow me, or shall I make matters clearer?"

Paling, Colin nodded. Then, since more of an answer seemed to be required, he lifted his chin and said, "I understand, sir. It won't happen again."

"It will be as well for you if it does not," Nicholas retorted sternly, adding, "I believe we can do without your company for the present. I suggest you retire to your bedchamber, where you might pass the time quite profitably until breakfast by meditating upon your various sins."

"Yes, sir," Colin muttered. A moment later, the door had shut behind him, and Sarah turned on Nicholas.

"That was unfair!" she said angrily. "It was not well done of you, my lord, to scold him with me standing right here! He did what he did and said what he said only to protect me!"

"Perhaps he did, Countess,' Nicholas replied evenly, "but his methods were of a nature that I will not tolerate."

"They were improper, I suppose!" she stormed, hardly knowing what she was saying, only knowing that, for whatever reason, she was furious with him.

"Indeed they were, as you know very well," he returned. "Which brings me to the fact that I have a word or two for you as well, madam."

"Do you, my lord?" Her eyes flashed dangerously. "Do you perhaps intend to send me to bed without supper, too?"

"If you continue to behave this way, my lady, I am far more likely to put you across my knee."

"You wouldn't dare!"

"Don't put me to the test, Countess," he warned. "Sit down and behave yourself. I want to talk to you."

"I have no wish to sit in your company, sir," she retorted rudely. "I tire of your endless scolds and lectures. 'Tis *my* name that is being discussed in London. *I* am the one everyone thinks killed Darcy. I want his killer laid by the heels, and no one else is lifting a finger except Colin!"

"Don't be melodramatic!" he snapped. "I abhor Cheltenham farce. It may interest you to know, besides, that my name is very probably in all those same betting books. It would be odd indeed if it were not. So I also have a stake in finding Darcy's killer. However, there are ways and ways of doing things, and you and Colin are more likely to upset carefully laid plans than to catch the killer. I utterly forbid either of you to engage in any further activities of that nature." He paused, but before she could protest, a new thought occurred to him. "I have not precisely rescinded my orders regarding your riding, by the way, and I shall remind the stable personnel of that fact. Who was it who saddled your horse today? Jem?" She was silent, and he moved toward her, frowning. "Tell me, Sarah." She shook her head stubbornly, whereupon he put his hands to her shoulders and gave her a little shake. Angrily, she twisted away, lifting an indignant hand, but he caught it easily. "Not today, Countess. Let us try to retain our composure."

"Well, I shan't tell you, and you have no right to force me!" Jerking her hand away, Sarah suddenly realized that she was close to tears and resorted to fury to cover them up. "You are impossible, sir! Despicable! So puffed up in notions of propriety and . . . and *tyranny* that you have no compassion, no understanding of others weaker than yourself!"

"Sarah!"

"No, don't say any more! I don't wish to hear any more! And you won't be troubled by my presence at dinner either, my lord! I should *prefer* to remain in my bedchamber!" Yanking open the French doors, Sarah turned a deaf ear to his shouts and, raging inwardly, fairly flew across the terrace and down the dark path to Dower House. His lordship was quite obviously incapable of understanding how important it was to her to discover Darcy's murderer and would far rather spend his time reprimanding Colin or the poor stableboys. In short, he was altogether abominable, and it was a relief to have told him so! But when she reached the candlelit haven of her bedchamber, she flung herself onto the bed and let the tears come in wracking sobs until she could sob no more.

It was nearly half an hour later that Miss Penistone entered. "You must dress for dinner now, Miss Sarah," she said matter-of-factly. "I shall ring for Lizzie."

"That won't be necessary, Penny," Sarah said, sitting up on the bed and attempting to sound dignified, but looking more like a woebegone child. "I shall not be going to dinner tonight."

Miss Penistone seemed not to notice the tearstains or the damp wisps of hair sticking to Sarah's face. "Of course you must go to dinner," she said briskly, moving to the washstand

and pouring cool water into the porcelain basin. "Come and wash your face, whilst I ring." She moved to pull the bell.

"No! Penny, do not ring," Sarah insisted. "I am staying right here."

Miss Penistone turned back, her hand hesitating near the bell tassel. There was amusement and something else in her eyes, but her tone was much as ever. "I should advise you to leave off your sulks, my lady, and make the best of things. I had hoped you might have come to your senses by now, but since you have not, perhaps I should tell you that his lordship has said he will come to fetch you himself if you are late."

"He wouldn't!" But she knew he would if he had said so. And carry her to dinner over his shoulder, no doubt, like a sack of corn, if she wouldn't go peaceably. Penny merely gave a knowing little smile and pulled the cord. "And I am not sulking," Sarah declared as she got up and went to splash water on her face. "He was utterly hateful!"

"No doubt he was, my dear," Penny agreed, "though it is not my place to say so, of course. He seemed not to understand, however, exactly what it was that he had done."

"He said that much to you!" Sarah was astonished.

"No, no, but he seemed confused, not quite himself. Except, of course, when he issued his ultimatum. He said then that he didn't care to have her ladyship ring a peal over him for keeping you from your dinner."

"He is keeping Colin from his," Sarah pointed out. When Penny said nothing, she hunched a shoulder. "Oh, very well. I suppose it *is* different. To tell the truth, Penny, I do not know what made me fly into such a pelter with him. It just happened." But she did remember that he had brought her near to tears. Even so, why had she become so angry? It was as though he sparked something off inside her whenever they were together. As though there was always conflict between them. It had been so from the beginning, of course. She had been antagonized the first time they met, when he criticized where others had praised. But why should she let it bother her so? Unquestionably, it was time to take control of herself and the situation as well.

Sarah straightened, tilted her chin, and even managed a nearly normal smile when Lizzie answered Penny's summons. "My gold silk, Lizzie," she ordered. "And hurry. I don't wish to be late." She began pulling pins from her hair and allowed Penny to help her from her riding habit. She would show him!

Sulks indeed! The trick was simply to let him see that his moods could not affect her, that she was a grand lady supremely indifferent to his criticisms or his accolades, should he choose to deliver either. She would hold herself aloof from all that. After all, she would have to put up with him for quite some time yet. It might as well be as painless as possible.

In record time, she was ready. Her dress no longer showed the slightest trace of a bloodstain. Indeed, the gold silk shimmered as she moved, while emeralds at her throat and ears sparkled green fire. Lizzie brushed her hair till it glistened, then parted it in the middle, and swept the two wings into a knot of curls banded by a narrow braid at the top of her head. Sarah surveyed the results in her mirror.

"Perfect. Shall we go, Penny?"

Shaking out the skirt of her lavender silk dinner gown, Miss Penistone agreed that it was more than time. Sarah realized that, despite the rush, they were indeed a few minutes late, so it was no great surprise to her to discover, when they reached the top of the stairs, that Nicholas was on the point of entering the hall.

"Good evening, my lord," she greeted him, imitating Lady Hartley's chilly hauture. "How kind of you to give us your escort."

XVII

Nicholas's eyes held a touch of mockery, but he made no comment upon her appearance, merely greeting both ladies amicably and holding the door open for them to pass through. They could not manage the pathway three abreast, so he stood politely aside, and Sarah passed him with her nose in the air. Miss Penistone shot her a look of reproach, but it was ignored, and if that lady wondered how long his lordship would tolerate such Turkish treatment, she kept the thought to herself.

The pathway was dark and Sarah stumbled once, but she had to catch herself, for Nicholas made no move to come to her assistance, only stepping forward when they reached the flagstone terrace to open the doors. Lady Packwood and Sir Percival looked up as they entered.

"My, how grand you look tonight, my dear," Lady Packwood commented cheerfully. "Complete to a shade!"

"Fine as fivepence," agreed Sir Percival, flicking snuff from his sleeve. "Looks like a golden statue, don't she, my sweet?"

Sarah blushed, as Sir Percival's words unleashed a spate of memories, and wished that she had worn something else. She glanced at Nicholas quickly enough to catch a sharp look before he turned away to the wine tray.

"Anyone else?" he inquired smoothly.

The others declining, he helped himself to a small glass of mountain, tossing it down rather quickly when Dasher entered to ask if they were now ready to dine.

If anyone had asked Sarah three days later, or even the following morning, to repeat the gist of the table talk that evening, she would have been hard pressed to comply. She might have remembered making a lot of airy gestures, tossing out light, cheerful comments by the peck, or maintaining a chilly politeness whenever called upon to notice his lordship's presence, and she would have been vaguely aware that Sir Percival had disapproved of their having fallen victim to a pair of nasty highwaymen, but she would never remember a single other topic or a specific phrase.

Telling herself that she was delighted when Sir Percival suggested to Nicholas after dinner that the two of them take their port to the billiards room, she followed Lady Packwood back to the library, thinking they could enjoy a comfortable coze, uninterrupted by any of his lordship's usual, fusty comments. However, less than a half hour later, Sarah stifled a yawn. She could not understand it, but the evening seemed to have turned sadly flat. Surely, Lady Packwood's conversation was as amusing as ever, and Penny's knitting needles clicked away with comforting familiarity, but she herself was having much difficulty sustaining her part of things. She half expected her ladyship to demand to know what was wrong with her and did not know whether to be grateful or indignant when she did not. A few moments and several yawns later, she could stand it no longer.

"I don't know how it is," she said, not realizing she had interrupted Lady Packwood's anecdote midsentence, "but I seem to be exceedingly fatigued this evening. I beg you will forgive me, ma'am, if I excuse myself."

"Of course, my dear," replied her ladyship agreeably, while Penny obligingly bestowed her knitting. "I expect you are still recovering from this morning's shocking incident. A good night's rest will put you right again." Since Sarah thought it would not be quite tactful to admit that she had not really thought once all evening about the highwaymen, she accepted the excuse and gratefully made her escape without noticing when Lady Packwood, exchanging a glance with Penny, shook her head in tolerant amusement.

It was still only half past ten when Lizzie snuffed out the candles and bade Sarah a fond good night, and suddenly she was no longer sleepy at all. Try as she would to erase her mind of thought, the vision of a gentleman with fair curls and blue eyes that crinkled when he laughed kept intruding. How ridiculous to dwell upon that face, she scolded herself. Particularly when the laughter was so rare. He nearly always frowned, did he not? Was nearly always vexed or disapproving. Besides, she was a widow with most of her year's mourning still ahead of her. Not that that made a difference where he was concerned, of course, except that it meant he would continue to carp and censure and make himself generally irritating. A whole year! No parties, no pleasures, no fun! It was too much. Entirely too much! Had she not made up her mind to ignore his moods and his notions of propriety as well? Why on earth could she not put his lordship out of her head entirely!

Sarah punched her pillow into a more comfortable shape and plopped her head down again, determined to capture sleep. But it continued to elude her. It seemed that she no sooner found a comfortable position for her head than her back began to ache. But when she turned over, the back of her knee began to itch. She scratched it with a toenail and decided that the problem was actually that the bedclothes had become disarranged.

Sitting up, Sarah yanked and straightened until she had pulled the patchwork coverlet loose from the foot of the bed. With a sigh, she threw off the covers and got up. First, she straightened the bed properly, but as she was about to climb in again, she decided against it. Admit it, she thought, you just are not ready to sleep.

Perhaps, she could go downstairs and find something to read. There was, if she was not mistaken, a new issue of the *Ladies' Monthly Museum* in the drawing room. She slipped her feet into a pair of soft slippers and found a silk dressing gown on a hook in her wardrobe. But as she wrapped it around herself, she changed her mind again. What she really needed was a hot posset or at least some warm milk. Either one ought to send her right off. Maybe someone was still up. But when she opened her door, only darkness greeted her. Darkness and silence.

Sarah sighed and shut the door again. She really didn't want to go downstairs by herself just to fix warm milk. She wasn't even sure where Betsy kept the items necessary to prepare it. A hot posset was out of the question. And she didn't really want to read either. Restlessly, she walked to the front window to adjust it, although no adjustment was necessary.

It was a glorious night. A slender crescent moon hung over the dark shapes of the trees, and the stars were out in riotous profusion, dancing like silver glitter against the black, black sky. As she watched, a shooting star arched over the trees hiding the main house from view. She looked more closely. Not even a flicker of light shone through the thick foliage from the library window, so it was later than she had thought, and they had all gone to bed.

Well, not all. As she formed the thought, a flash of light caught her attention amidst the trees below. Sarah chuckled. That boy! Up to his tricks again. Clearly, he had not learned his lesson the first time. But still, considering her present mood, he might at least provide diversion, so long as his lordship didn't catch him at his nonsense again.

Just then, she heard a tentative woof. Erebus! On the thought, she hurried to the door, down the dark stairs, and out onto the front veranda. The dog must not disturb Nicholas, or Colin would be in for it again. There was a second bark, louder, less tentative. She hurried toward the sound, not wanting to call out, wanting only to stifle the noise. She reached the path and stopped. It was very dark and very quiet.

A third bark, then two more in quick succession. They came from her right, the thickest part of the wood. Her eyes had adjusted to the darkness, but it was still difficult to find her way through the shrubbery, particularly with twigs and branches snatching at her dressing gown. Suddenly she came into a small clearing and saw the dog on the other side near a large boulder. He heard her and woofed a greeting, galumphing toward her, then turning back almost immediately to the rock. Looking back, he woofed again, then pawed at something on the ground that produced a distinctly wooden sound.

"Hush, Erebus." Sarah went closer, and he moved aside, inviting her to inspect his discovery. "Merciful heavens!" she exclaimed. The dog had been pawing at a pair of wooden doors set at an angle into the ground behind the boulder. "Move over, dog." She pushed him out of the way and, finding a metal handle on one of the doors, managed to pull it open. Yawning blackness met her gaze. Without a light it was impossible to tell how deep it was, but Sarah was certain she had found a secret entrance to the Dower House cellars.

"That devil," she breathed. Then she chuckled. Swift calculation told her that she was between fifty and seventy-five feet from the house, and she doubted that Colin, even with the aid of his light, would cover that distance through an unfamiliar tunnel very quickly. "Stay, Erebus," she ordered sharply. "Guard!" The big dog plumped down with a long-suffering sigh that clearly expressed his opinion of human vagaries, but Sarah, her eyes alight with mischief, was already hastening back toward the house.

She found candlestick and flint just inside the front door

where they were always kept, and once the candle was lit, lost no time hurrying to the kitchen passage. Just as she had hoped, the bricks were gone, the doorway completely accessible. She would give Colin the shock of his young life!

The door opened easily, showing that the workmen had even soaped the hinges, and a flight of stone steps presented itself. She had feared she might have to contend with a rickety, wooden staircase, but unless the stones were damp—and they did not seem so—she would be perfectly safe.

She had half-expected to see the glow of a lantern or another candle, but the lower portion of the cellar was in total darkness. Delighted to have beaten him but rather hoping he would arrive soon, she slowly descended the stairs, ears pricked for any sound, half-fearing to hear the rustle and scuttle of rats. But there was only silence. She continued down the steps until she reached the bottom. Then, holding her candle high, she looked around, but the cellar seemed totally barren. She could see no sign of dampness and, though she wasn't perfectly certain what it was, no sign of dry rot either.

Frowning, she moved forward across the stone floor. Where was Colin? Surely, she hadn't been wrong about the tunnel. Surely, it led straight to this cellar. A shadow of something solid caught her eye, when the candlelight reflected off a low, solid shape near the opposite wall. Sarah moved closer. It seemed to be some sort of trunk or chest. A chill shot up her spine, and she was aware of sudden gooseflesh as she remembered Colin's suspicions of buried treasure. Could it truly be a treasure chest?

She hurried forward, holding the candle ahead so that its light would give the answer as quickly as possible. There were two trunks! But they were not rounded, nor banded in shining brass, as one might properly expect a treasure chest to be. They were not even locked! Probably nothing more than forgotten storage chests, she told herself firmly.

Kneeling beside the nearer of the two, Sarah brushed away a twig that had attached itself to her dressing gown and, with a shiver, noticed the chill in the cellar for the first time. Well, she would just peep inside the chest and then go back upstairs. If Erebus still waited by the entry she would know Colin had not returned, that something had happened to him. And, if she couldn't find him herself, she would—God forbid—just have to fetch his lordship. It occurred to her that she had noticed no door that might be the cellar entrance to the tunnel. Maybe it, too, had been bricked up. At any rate, she hoped Colin was all right. She would rather not have another uncomfortable midnight scene, since, besides chastising Colin, Nicholas would most likely disapprove loudly and at length of her own visit to the cellar. But she tossed her head in defiance at the thought and reached to open the trunk.

The heavy lid stuck, and she could not manage it one-handed, so she set her candlestick down carefully, then bent to her task with a will. There was a satisfying creak, and the lid came up. She couldn't see the contents properly until she had retrieved her candle, but then she let her breath out in a long sigh of amazement. She had indeed discovered treasure!

Diamonds reflected fire from the candle. Rubies glistened, emeralds sparkled; indeed, there seemed to be jewels of every color and hue! There were likewise two small strongboxes minus their locks, and both contained gold and silver coins as well as paper money. Sarah simply stared. The Ashton family treasure! But then, she looked more closely at one of the notes, and George III stared back at her. Family treasure or not, it had certainly not been resting here or anywhere else since Cromwell's day!

So intent was she upon her discovery that she didn't hear the whispering hush of sound as a section of the wall on her left slid open. But a draft caught her candle, causing it to flicker. The brief, resulting dimness was offset by a stronger light penetrating the cellar, and it was this plus the draft that warned her. She turned with a cheerful grin.

"I thought you'd never . . . good God! Beck!"

"My lady." Darcy's erstwhile valet nodded with icy poise, his chilly gray eyes colder than ever. "May I ask how you come to be here?" Stepping into the cellar, he slid the panel nearly but not quite shut behind him and held his lantern high.

"We've been refurbishing," Sarah said quickly, watching him closely. "I ordered the cellars opened again."

"I see." He glanced around as though to make sure she was unaccompanied, then hung the lantern from a jutting nail. Sarah stifled another shiver, this time caused by the chill of fear. "Is it not a trifle late to be exploring?" he asked.

"Don't be ridiculous," she retorted. "Of course it is, but I saw you from my window and thought you were Lord Moreland's nephew, Colin."

"That is unfortunate." Beck stepped forward into the full light of the lantern, and his long, thin face and prominent, square jaw were thrown into strong relief. Sarah gasped, gazing with dismay now at the neatly tied neckcloth and paradoxical duffel coat.

"It was you!"

Beck sighed. "I was afraid of that. I had no notion, you see, until Jerry had already stopped the coach. Wouldn't have done it otherwise. Surprised his bloody lordship didn't recognize me, for that matter, but sure you would, my lady. 'Tis a pity, still and all."

Sarah caught her breath again at the look in his eye. "What do you mean?"

"You or me," he replied simply. "Got to be one or the other. Surely, you can see my side of it. Much rather it be you."

"I don't understand you! You talk gibberish!"

"They would hang me."

She stared at him, swallowing with difficulty. "It might only be transportation, unless you've robbed the Mail, of course."

Beck shrugged. "All the same, no sense in taking the risk, my lady, when it's such a simple thing to avoid it. Shame to waste such a delicious bit o' skirt though," he added, reverting to the dialect of his associates. "His lordship always showed excellent taste." He moved slowly toward her.

Sarah backed away, still holding her candle. "Why, Beck? You could have made an excellent wage as a gentleman's valet."

"No wage can equal them boxes, my pretty one." He leered. "What a body you've got! To think he never had the proper use of it. Told me himself. Said he was going to make up for it though, that you had gone too far at last. Shouldn't have knocked him down, my lady. Made him mad as fire." He continued steadily toward her, purpose strong in his eye.

Sarah gasped. "You were in London! How could you possibly know about that?"

Beck allowed himself a sardonic smile. "Now you understand why there would be no question of transportation. I've nothing to lose, my lady, and all to gain. It will do you no good to keep backing away, you know. The wall is but two feet behind you."

"You killed him," Sarah whispered. "Why?"

Beck gestured toward the trunks. "That's why. Whole business was my notion from start to finish. Not that he didn't go along willingly enough at the beginning, mind you. But then, he got cold feet. He was of a mind to turn respectable, thanks to your damned fortune, but I wasn't to get any of that. He wanted out, and when I suggested that I could make trouble for him, he threatened to turn *me* in if I didn't keep a still tongue in my head. Said the busies would be more like to listen to him than to me. Right about that, I expect."

Sarah grasped his meaning with difficulty. "Then Darcy . . . he was . . . and you said 'Jerry' . . . that would be Jeremy Oakes, I expect. But you and Darcy must have tried to double-cross him, for he doesn't seem to have known where you hid the booty." Evidently her surmises were correct, for he did not deny them. Indeed, he seemed only amused, laughing softly as he closed the distance between them.

"Enough of this. Think of me as a romantic knight of the road. Everyone knows what great lovers highwaymen are, how daring we are. Think of yourself as the heroine of a romantic tale with but a few moments of life yet to cherish. You nearly drove me mad when I lived in the same house with you, wench. Now it can't make any difference. Come here." Smiling wickedly, he reached toward her.

"No!" And with a lunge, Sarah threw her candle full in his face and darted past him toward the stone steps, screaming, hoping Penny or someone might hear her. But Beck was too quick. Dodging the flying candle easily, he stretched out his hand and grabbed her by the arm, whirling her around, pulling her to him. Desperately, Sarah tried to wrench away from him and kicked angrily at his shin, but her slippers were little protection, and she only bruised her toes. Meanwhile, her struggles resulted in very little advantage to herself. If anything, they aided Beck as he attempted to tear her dressing gown from her body.

Despite her initial lack of success, Sarah continued to struggle madly, but she managed to keep sheer panic at bay, and somehow a small part of her mind managed to take in the fact that they had turned so that Beck now had his back to the treasure trunks. She had been trying desperately to pull away from him, so that when she suddenly propelled herself forward with all her might, she caught him completely off guard and off balance. Catching his heel on one of the trunks, he went crashing backward, his hands involuntarily releasing Sarah as he made a futile attempt to save himself.

She had lost her dressing gown, but without giving it a thought, she snatched up the skirts of her nightdress in order to keep from tripping over them, and scrambled away toward the stone steps. However, despite his thunderous fall, Beck's desperation to stop her seemed to overcome any of the pain he must have felt. He got to his feet somehow and, snarling, lunged after her.

The lantern light barely pierced the gloom ahead, and Sarah moved more by instinct than anything else. She could hear him coming, but she had to feel for the steps, fearing to stumble lest he catch her again. She knew there would be no mercy. He would no doubt kill her at once, and though she realized that she had very likely succeeded in defending her virtue, it would be of little use to her dead.

Her foot kicked against the lowest step, but at the same moment, Beck reached out and grabbed the back of her night-dress. Sarah struggled, crying out, and heard the gown rip, just as she was roughly shoved aside by a dark shape hurtling down the steps. After a resounding and, under the circumstances, quite satisfactory crack of bone against bone, Beck collapsed, and the lantern cast its faint glow across the familiar features of her rescuer.

"Nicholas! Oh, Nicholas!" And, bursting into tears, she cast herself into his arms. It seemed perfectly natural that those strong arms should gather her close to that broad chest, holding her tightly, keeping her safe.

Nicholas let her sob for a moment or two, doing nothing more than stroking her hair and muttering such intelligent stuff as "There, there," and "It's all right, Countess," and so forth. But finally, her sobs began to diminish, and she became aware of her state of near-undress. Her first thought was that she ought to cover herself, but she was oddly reluctant to remove herself from the safety of his embrace.

"How is she, my lord?" Sarah stiffened at the unfamiliar voice coming from behind her.

"Well enough, considering everything." Nicholas spoke grimly, but he must have felt her reaction, for there were definite overtones of amusement. Hesitantly, she looked over her shoulder. Mr. Jeremy Oakes stood there gazing at her with undisguised admiration. Two other men, both wearing dark blue jackets, red waistcoats, and black hats moved from the tunnel entrance, through the circle of lantern light, toward the unconscious Beck.

"Lady Moreland," Nicholas pronounced in formal tones, "I should like to present Mr. Jeremy Oakes of Bow Street. Mr.

Oakes, would you be so kind as to pass Lady Moreland that dressing gown at your feet?"

Bow Street! And considering the very thin material of her nightdress, she might just as well be standing there naked! Sarah felt heat rush to her face, then a curious lightheadedness. But that was all she felt before she fainted dead away in his lordship's arms.

XVIII

Late the following morning Sarah awoke with vague memories of being carried up the stairs, of a grim and dangerous look in his lordship's eye before she had resolutely shut hers again, and of Miss Penistone's calm voice and gentle hands tucking her into her own bed. There was a moment or two of disorientation before she remembered everything, but then her first thought was of Jeremy Oakes. Who would ever have suspected him to be a Bow Street Runner? Just wait until Colin heard about that! And Nicholas must have known all along.

But just thinking of Nicholas unleashed a flood of tumbled thoughts. How safe she had felt in his arms! How glad she had been to see him! And, how angry he must be with her now. This last thought was a bit daunting. Looking back with the usual clarity afforded by hindsight, she could see how imprudent she had been. And it wasn't as though he hadn't warned her, because he'd done so in no uncertain terms the night of Colin's ghostwalk.

Sighing, Sarah snuggled deeper under her covers, hoping no one would come to see how she did. The longer they thought her asleep, the longer it would be before she must face him. She wondered what he would do, remembering that he had threatened to return her to her aunt's protection if she didn't behave. But that had been a matter of her safety, and surely she was safe enough now that Mr. Oakes and his patrol had taken Beck into custody.

Besides, she didn't want to return to London, and she realized suddenly that the notion even had a different flavor to it. Before, it had been frightening because of the scandal. Now, she would resist going anywhere. She had come to love Ash Park. Turning that thought over in her mind, she realized it had a flattish, incomplete ring to it. It wasn't precisely Ash

Park she loved, though it was a very nice place now, of course. It was the master of Ash Park.

The new thought was a bit of a shock, but it explained a good many things, right back to her pique when Nicholas had not ripped up at Darcy over the abduction. It also explained why his moods had such power to affect hers, why she had wanted his approval, why she reacted so unpredictably to his scolds, and certainly it explained why she had flung herself into his arms the previous night and not minded at all that she was scantily clad. She loved him. There, she had put the matter into words. So, what now? He surely didn't love her. To hear him talk, she was naught but a millstone round his neck, a spoiled, poorly-behaved, feckless wench who flouted his commands and upset his plans. He would tear a strip off her for last night's business and no doubt thoroughly enjoy doing it.

And even if he didn't dislike her, what could possibly come of it? As Darcy's widow, she faced months of mourning. And with his lordship's fine sense of propriety, she would certainly never dare to let him guess her feelings toward him. Surely, his every sensibility would be outraged. She would have to be stoical, and as the good Lord knew, she was not stoical by nature. But, one thing was certain. She would do her best to avoid displeasing him in future. That brought her thoughts racing back to the present, for he was doubtless much displeased with her now.

With sudden determination, she flung back the covers and rang for Lizzie. Her newly acknowledged feelings, or perhaps merely the memory of his arms around her, caused a delicious tingling sensation in the pit of her stomach at the thought of seeing him, though she did not doubt the meeting would be of a decidedly disagreeable nature. As well to get over the heavy ground as lightly as possible, her sporting friends would say.

Lizzie came quickly, armed with the information that Master Colin was waiting below about as patiently as a cat on hot bricks. Sarah laughed, but a few moments later she stood shifting from foot to foot as Lizzie did up the tiny pearl buttons on the back of a charming apricot morning frock.

"Miss Sarah! How d'ye expect me to do these buttons if ye don't stand still? And there's the sash yet, too!"

Obligingly, Sarah ceased her fidgeting. But when Lizzie would have had her sit to have her hair done properly, she rebelled. "Just put it in a snood, Lizzie. The lace one will do." Having made up her mind to have the ordeal with his lordship over and done, she would brook no further delays. Besides, Colin might be able to tell her what sort of mood Nicholas was in.

But this he could not do. "He's not here," the boy said simply, when she put the question to him. "Wasn't here when I got up and Dasher won't say where he went, but I expect there were some sort of formalities to be got through after that business last night." He tried very hard to be nonchalant, but when Sarah invited him to keep her company while she broke her fast, he accepted with alacrity. Miss Penistone joined them soon after Betsy had placed a lovely light omelet, muffins, jam, and a pot of chocolate on the table before Sarah. It quickly became clear that she was as curious as Colin about the events of the preceding night. But where the boy expressed great disgust at having slept through the entire adventure, Penny could only be grateful that she had nearly done likewise.

She had indeed helped put the semiconscious Sarah back to bed, but that had been only because his lordship, not knowing where to lay his hands upon a fresh nightdress, had come pounding at her door. Sarah blushed when this was recounted to her, but Penny assured her that, though he had indeed carried her to bed, it had been Penny who had replaced the ruined gown with the new one.

"Well, yes, that's all very well," Colin observed, clearly having no interest in nightdresses, "but how could Mr. Oakes be a Runner? I thought they all wore red waistcoats. They are known as 'robin redbreasts,' are they not?"

Sarah had thought so, too, but Miss Penistone explained that only the members of the Horse Patrols wore such a uniform, that the Runners themselves, who were, after all, the *crème de la crème* of Bow Street, always wore ordinary clothes.

"For you know, my dears, it quite goes against the English grain to support a uniformed police force. 'Twould smack too much of the military sort one finds on the Continent, and that would never do. Besides, the Runners are primarily employed as detectives, and how could they possibly do their job properly, if they were so easily recognizable? Why, every man jack around here would have shut up like an oyster had Mr. Oakes been known for a Runner!"

They could not deny it, but Colin was still greatly chagrined to think that, while he thought himself to be chasing a villain, he had actually been chasing a Bow Street Runner. "And to think it was Beck all the time. A valet!"

"Much more than a valet," Sarah put in grimly, but she added in consolation, "At least you were right about the hidden entrance to the cellars, Colin, *and* about the treasure."

He chuckled at that. "I'd like to have seen it. You don't suppose it's still there, do you?"

It wasn't. Sarah took him down to the cellars when she had finished her meal, only to discover that the place was now completely empty. She couldn't find a means of opening the sliding door from inside, so at his insistence, she showed him the boulder entrance, and after much trial and error, they finally contrived to open the panel. Sarah decided that the difficulty of the mechanism must have been responsible for the slowness of Beck's arrival the previous night. No doubt, Darcy had been the one to operate it in the past.

Colin was fascinated by the tunnel and the secret panel, but she finally convinced him that they ought to be available when his uncle returned, whereupon he went quite cheerfully on his way. Then, certain that the explorations had undone her appearance, she retired immediately to her bedchamber and rang for Lizzie to repair the damages. Lizzie clucked and scolded, insisting that her charge seemed to have developed a penchant for turning herself into a perfect shag-rag, but Sarah only chuckled at her. The front window was open, and Lizzie had no sooner twitched the skirt of the moss-green silk frock into place than Sarah was certain she heard a carriage approaching. A few moments later, she and Penny entered the library to find Lady Packwood disappointingly in sole possession.

"Good afternoon, my dear," she greeted, adding a cheerful nod to Penny. "Sit down and tell me all about last night. I trust you've recovered, for all I've heard is what Colin managed to worm out of the servants. I've been waiting impatiently for him to return from his visit to you, but now Dasher informs me he's gone off to the stables. Boys! Men, too, for that matter. Here Nicky's gone off heaven knows where, and Percy says it don't concern us. I ask you, how much can one be expected to endure!"

Laughing, Sarah obliged her with an outline of the night's events, sketching her own role lightly and without dwelling upon Beck's assault. She merely said she had managed to elude him and had started up the stairs when his lordship arrived.

"And dubbed him chancery suit upon the nob!" announced Colin proudly from the doorway.

"Dubbed him what?" demanded his grandmother.

"Tipped him a settler," explained the boy sweetly.

"Go in or get out, brat," ordered his uncle behind him, "and speak the King's English to her ladyship, if you please."

Grinning impudently, Colin moved to stand by the fireplace. "Very well, sir. In plain English then, ma'am, Uncle Nick planted him a facer that knocked him into horsenails."

Lady Packwood laughed. "So pleased to have the matter properly explained. I collect that you knocked the villain down, Nicky, and if I read between the lines of Sarah's tale, very likely saved her life."

Sarah flushed, avoiding Nicholas's eye. His voice was carefully even. "I daresay, ma'am, but the villain is now safely locked in Newgate. I saw him sentenced myself."

"Will they hang him?" Colin demanded.

"Of course," Nicholas replied, watching Sarah.

"You knew about Mr. Oakes, didn't you?"

"To be sure, Countess. I hired him."

"You hired him!" Sarah's indignation lent a spark to her eye and an edge to her voice.

"Indeed. Although to be perfectly truthful, he was already engaged upon the matter, in a manner of speaking. I tried to tell you yesterday, but you weren't in a precisely attentive mood at the time." He cast her a speaking look, then continued. "When I went up to Town after the murder, I went directly to Bow Street and spoke privately with Sir Nathaniel Conant, the Chief Magistrate there. It was he who informed me that Mr. Oakes was already searching for certain highwaymen in this vicinity. I simply hired him to investigate the murder as well, though we'd no notion then, of course, that the two matters were connected. Sir Nathaniel promised to provide a full Patrol once we had a definite lead."

Lady Packwood shook her head. "Gone are the days when a victim could send a special message to Mr. John Fielding, when he was Chief Magistrate, and be paid for his trouble. Mr. Fielding promised to dispatch a patrol in pursuit on a quarter-hour's notice. I can remember my papa showing me an advertisement to that effect."

Nicholas smiled at her. "Nevertheless, ma'am, we can scarcely complain of shabby treatment. Sir Nathaniel informed me that a murder or any atrocious crime would always be investigated free of charge, but I knew that most Runners ask for a fee—country cases usually require a guinea plus fourteen shillings for living expenses per day—so I told Sir Nathaniel to tote it up to me. In addition, I offered Mr. Oakes a generous reward if he proved successful."

"But why didn't you tell us?"

"Because, brat, Mr. Oakes asked me to keep mum. If word of a Runner's presence had got out, the villains would most likely have gone to ground. He wanted their confidence bolstered, if anything, so they would come into the open."

"Well, it seems to me Cousin Sarah ought to get the reward," Colin said brightly. "After all, she's the one who discovered Beck and recognized him for the highwayman."

"Don't worry, brat," Nicholas said with meaning. "Cousin Sarah will get exactly what she deserves."

"I collect that the murder was the result of a falling out among thieves," put in Lady Packwood quickly. "How lowering to think one is related, no matter how haphazardly, to a highwayman. At least, however, he seems to have been a successful one."

"Very," Nicholas agreed shortly. "But, at least we need not suffer the indignity of knowing an Ashton has been hanged."

"Nonsense, Nicky. One was hanged just last year, a John Ashton, though I daresay you missed it, being with the Duke and all. But I heard quite a lot about it from friends who wished to know if he was related to old Moreland."

"I did miss it," his lordship agreed. "It must have been a bit trying."

"Well, it was, for what must the stupid man do, but run up the steps of the Newgate gallows as fast as he could to dance and kick and shout to the crowd, 'Look at me! I am Lord Wellington!' "

"Good heavens!"

"Exactly so. It was necessary for two men to hold him. When the signal was given, Ashton actually rebounded from the rope to the platform, apparently unhurt, and cried out loudly, 'What do ye think of me? Am I not Lord Wellington now?' At length the executioner was compelled to get upon the scaffold himself to push him off!"

"Seems stubborn enough to have been related after all," Nicholas teased, relaxing again.

"Exactly what Percy said," pronounced her ladyship with an indignant sniff. "Still and all, I'm grateful to Beck for saving us such an indignity. Really, it seems almost a shame that the man must die after performing such a signal service."

Sarah tried without success to repress a chuckle, and Colin didn't even try to suppress his amusement, but Nicholas frowned heavily. "Believe it when I say the scoundrel deserves his fate," he said grimly. "And now, if the rest of you will excuse us, I should like to have a private word with Lady Moreland."

Sarah stiffened, watching in some dismay as Lady Packwood, Penny, and Colin obediently left her to her fate. She had stood automatically when they did and thought the room must have turned chilly, for she shivered when the door closed, leaving her shut in alone with his lordship.

Nicholas moved to stand near the desk, and as the silence in the room lengthened, Sarah turned to face him. Her hands seemed to have a will of their own, clutching at each other just below her breasts when she would have liked them to rest relaxed at her side.

"Please, my lord," she began, bravely enough, "I know I behaved badly last night, that I should have heeded your warnings. I . . . I believed it was Colin again and sought to surprise him. It never occurred to me. . . ." She broke off, but he remained silent, waiting politely for her to continue. She swallowed with difficulty. Truly, he was looking very severe. "It *should* have occurred to me. I know that now, and you must have much that you wish to say upon that subject, sir, but I beg you will not be too harsh."

"You deserve that I should scold you, do you not?" He spoke quietly, and Sarah nodded, her hands clutched more tightly than ever, her face pale. "In fact, Countess, you deserve to be punished severely for such foolhardiness." Sarah was silent, her eyes downcast. "You might have been killed, you know. You damned well nearly were, for that matter. Had it not been that Mr. Oakes was hot on Beck's trail, had in fact laid a trap for him——"

Sarah's head came up sharply. "A trap!"

"To be sure. I did recognize him, you see. I had a bit more information than you had by then, of course, so it is not entirely wonderful that I knew him. Oakes was already suspicious of Darcy and had been searching for their cache for some time. We thought Beck might lead us to it but lost sight of him briefly in the woods—it was only Oakes and me, for we feared too many would spook him. At any rate, we saw you and Erebus and found the tunnel entrance." He shook his head. "I must say, that entrance must have been better hidden when we were children, else I cannot imagine how we missed discovering it years ago. At any rate, I was about to make our presence known to you, when you turned back toward the house, so I thought you safe. I had no idea you had opened the stair door." He glared at her accusingly, and Sarah bit her lower lip but did not take her eyes from his. "Oakes took a moment or two to send Timmy for his Patrol," he went on, "and then we waited, thinking that Beck would just come out again. But he didn't, so we went in and soon heard your voice. Perhaps you can imagine my astonishment." Guiltily, Sarah dropped her eyes again. "I raced across the garden and through Dower House to cut off his escape by that route. We couldn't burst in from the passage, you know, not having a notion how well-armed the man was. Besides, he might have escaped up the stairs."

An uncomfortable silence followed his words, but Sarah finally forced herself to speak. "What will you do now, my lord?" It took nearly all her courage to ask. Maybe he *would* send her away, and she didn't think she could bear it if he did.

"I have given the matter much thought," Nicholas said gravely, leaning against the desk, "and I've come to the conclusion, my lady, that you simply cannot be trusted to look after yourself sensibly, that it would be dangerous to let you continue as you have before."

"But surely, the danger is past!" Sarah protested. From the sound of things, he was either going to return her to Hartley House or shut her up in a convent forever.

"There is always danger of one sort or another," he insisted. "Highwaymen or footpads or mischief of your own brewing. You cannot be trusted to toe the line, Countess. Not without someone to keep a strict eye out for you."

"But I have Penny!" Sarah cried, "and I will be good, my lord. Please don't send me away!"

"You would not wish to go?" She shook her head vehemently, tears welling up in her eyes. "Why not, Countess?" he asked gently.

But this she couldn't tell him. He would only despise her for making such a mockery of her state of mourning. She loved him with all her heart, but he would never accept such flouting of propriety. She remained silent, dropping her gaze.

"You seem much affected, madam. I pray you, do not fear to confide in me." His voice was very low, the tone nearly caressing. Why was he doing this to her!

"For the love of heaven, Nicky! Stop torturing the poor girl and get on with it!" The admonition started even before her ladyship actually opened the door, and she entered glaring.

"You were eavesdropping!" he accused.

"Well, of course I was. But I did send Colin away," she added virtuously. "Now, do get to the point, Nicky. Miss Penny and I have been on tenterhooks."

"And what do you suppose the point to be, madam?" her son inquired softly.

"Marriage," replied her ladyship flatly. "Hers to you, of course. Don't be nonsensical."

Sarah's gaze flew to Nicholas and encountered a rueful grin. Her heart seemed to be trying to get out of her chest, and she scarcely dared to breathe. "My lord?"

"She is a curse I bear," he said, "but it happens she is right. I didn't know how to ask when it came to the point. Will you have me, Countess? I rather thought at one point last night that my suit might not be refused outright."

Sarah blushed at the reference. "But what of the proprieties, my lord?"

"Hang the proprieties," he returned, not taking his eyes from hers. "I got a special license whilst I was in Town. We'll have that preacher fellow from East End—the one that married you to Darcy. Daresay he'll do the thing if you don't dislike the idea too much."

"But the scandal, sir! My aunt and uncle!"

"Hang the scandal, too," he replied bluntly. "We shall take a leaf from young Lionel's book and go to France. Italy, too, and wherever else the fancy takes us. Colin can visit friends or go with us to his parents till school starts again, and by the time we get back, no one will care a straw how or when we tied the knot. Daresay your Miss Penistone won't mind looking after things here—along with a suitable steward, of course."

"As to that, your lordship," spoke up Penny from behind

Lady Packwood, "it must depend upon whether Mr. Dasher will be accompanying your lordship. He has, you see, done me the very great honor of asking me to be his wife."

"I'll be damned!" chuckled his lordship, while Sarah turned on her companion in astonishment. "He's a lucky man, Miss Peniston, and I trust he's aware of the fact. But I think he'd make an excellent steward. I daresay I can find another valet."

"*And* another butler!" added her ladyship tartly. "I shan't inquire about how you managed a special license, Nicky, but does this mean that you intend to travel with us?"

"For a time, perhaps, if you will allow it," Nicholas replied, still watching his intended. "But Sarah hasn't answered me."

"What's this, then, my sweet? Don't tell me there's been more ructions, for I don't hold with 'em."

"Oh, my love!" exclaimed Lady Packwood, turning with delight to her spouse. "Nicholas has asked Sarah to marry him."

"High time for it, too," retorted Sir Percival. "Prodigious improper for 'em to be livin' under the same roof without it!"

"Very true," agreed Sarah, relaxing with a smile and turning a twinkling eye toward Nicholas while Lady Packwood tried to remind her spouse of the existence of Dower House and Miss Peniston. "When it's put like that, my lord," Sarah continued, tongue very firmly in cheek, "how can I refuse? The proprieties *must* be observed."

"Exactly what I thought myself," agreed his lordship, ringing for his butler. "Dasher, show Mr. Stanley in."

"Nicholas!"

He chuckled. "Well, I didn't want to give you time to change your mind. First page from Lionel's book, second from Sir Percy's."

The little minister entered a few moments later. When he saw Sarah, he very politely asked if he might just have a moment to scan the license once more. The opportunity was granted and a moment later, just as politely, he agreed to proceed. Colin was called to bear witness, and even Erebus was allowed to plop himself down upon the hearthstones to observe the ceremony during which Sarah ceased to be a dowager and became, once again, Countess of Moreland.

Little Mr. Stanley happily agreed to stay to dinner, but despite the happy occasion, the gentlemen did not linger over their port, and he was speedily sent on his way. Lady Packwood pointedly announced, when Sir Percival and Nicholas entered the library, that it had been a very long day, and before Sarah could think 'pig's whisper,' she was alone with her new husband in his bedchamber. She moved quite naturally into his arms.

"Happy, sweetheart?"

"Very, my lord." He guided her toward the large, velvet-draped bed, but at the bedside, involuntarily, Sarah hesitated. "I think you should know, sir, that despite my previous marriage . . ."

"I know, little Countess, and I shall be gentle. I expected that, after your previous experiences, you might be a bit frightened at first." He drew her closer then began with practiced fingers to remove her dress.

"I . . . I'm not afraid, sir," Sarah muttered. "Not with you." The sensations caused by his fingers touching her bare skin made her tremble. Her dress was soon off, and she stood before him in her lacy shift. Nicholas removed his coat and began to undo his shirt. "How . . . how did you manage the license, my lord?" It seemed a silly question, but the other matter was even more difficult than she had thought it might be, and she had to speak. One couldn't just stand there and watch him undress.

"It required the devil of a lot of fast talking," he said, amused. "I had to see the archbishop himself, but I convinced him that, while grounds for annulment existed, it would be a good deal less complicated and less time-consuming all round to allow the license."

"Annulment!"

"Your marriage to Darcy was never consummated, sweetheart. By law, that is grounds for annulment."

"But how did you know?"

"I suspected the night he was murdered. You were so positive you were not pregnant, and there was something in your expression that led me to think it was not for the usual reason. Then, that day in the woods when I kissed you, I was sure. Your reaction was too much that of outraged virginity."

Sarah stared at his bare chest. " 'Tis true enough, my lord, and I know not what is expected of me."

"I'll teach you, sweetheart. And my name is Nicholas. I've heard you use it twice, and I've a strong desire to hear it again." She blushed delightfully. "Come, my lady. You have promised obedience, have you not?"

"Yes, m . . . Nicholas," she replied shyly.

"Very good. Now get into bed, where I shall be pleased to commence your lessons."

Again, she obeyed him, finding that it was becoming easier all the time. Her shift soon came off as he slowly but confidently began to introduce her to delights she had never before imagined. Her senses seemed to reach greater heights with each new caress. She had never dreamed her body held such secrets. But Nicholas, with gentle skill, guided her to a release of passion so intense that it amazed them both. And when they had reached the peak and descended once again, he held her gently in his arms.

"You are so beautiful, little Countess, and I love you so very much. I suppose I have done since the moment I first laid eyes upon you, surrounded by all those drooling young sycophants."

"But you were always so critical!"

"Didn't want you getting a big head and spoiling all that perfection." Sarah wrinkled her nose at him. "All right, I suppose it began as a way to make you notice me amongst the crowd."

"I did. I thought you perfectly odious."

"No doubt. But imagine my consternation when I left Town for a mere fortnight and returned to find you had eloped with the deplorable Darcy!"

"But I didn't!"

Nicholas hugged her. "I know, but it made me mad as fire nonetheless, and then, after the murder you seemed more unattainable than ever. The damned proprieties! I'd been preaching them at you so long that I'd come to let them rule the roost. I nearly went mad." She chuckled, and he lifted himself onto an elbow to look down at her, grinning. "Do you know, Countess, I don't believe you've said yet that you love me. I'm quite certain—have been since last night—that you do, but I should like to hear the words upon your lips."

Sarah looked up at him, her whole face glowing. "Oh, Nicholas, of course I love you." Then her eyes sparkled mischief, and she added, "I don't know how I should get on without you, *my love.*"

His own eyes danced. " 'Tis far better that I teach you more about how to get on *with* me, my sweet."

Outside, on the landing, the big black dog, forgotten for once by everyone, thumped his tail in approval of the sudden burst of laughter issuing from the bridal chamber. He would ask no awkward questions, however, and hopefully anyone else chancing to overhear such merriment would be tactful enough not to mention it.

About the Author

A fourth-generation Californian, Amanda Scott was
born and raised in Salinas and graduated with a degree in history from Mills College in Oakland. She did
graduate work at the University of North Carolina at
Chapel Hill, specializing in British history, before
obtaining her MA from San Jose State University.
She lives with her husband and young son in Sacra-
mento. Her hobbies include camping, backpacking,
and gourmet cooking. Her previous Regency, *The
Fugitive Heiress*, is also available in a Signet edition.